PIRATES

PIRATES

Greg Cummings

Cutting
Edge
Press

A Cutting Edge Press Paperback Original

Published in 2014 by Cutting Edge Press

www.cuttingedgepress.co.uk

Printed and bound in Great Britain by Biddles

ISBN: 978-1-908122-62-9
E-PUB ISBN: 978-1-908122-56-8

To my parents, Monica and Ian Cummings
for showing me the world

ACKNOWLEDGMENTS

Sandra 'Kigongo' Richardson and Jody Baker for invaluable contributions to plot and character, Susan Opie and Maggie Phillips for helping me make it a better book, Ian and Monica Cummings (dad and mom) for putting me up at their home in Mexico for four months while I wrote it, Robin Klein and Martin Hay for so much support, Paul Swallow, Saffeya Shebli and Shara Zaval for driving me towards bestsellerdom, Volkan Kaynak, Andrea and Dara OhUiginn, and David Cummings for their kindness, Sally Hay, AJ Catoline, Darren Dooley, Xavier Gilbert, Olivier de Pontbriand, Matt Bailey, and Monica Foster for places to kip on my way back to Uganda, Doug Galbraith, Peter Sol Rogers, Alex Clerek, James Black, John Caruthers, Bob Evans, Fraser Richie, Patrice Basha, Jonny Gibbings, J'nean and Greg Carr, Peter Guber, Richard Bangs, Andrew Cavell, Rick Bate, Harris Glaser and Geoffrey Carr for tips, facts and encouragement along the way, Fatuma Abdul Rahman for taking care of everything around me, Joshua. Lulu, Kamu, Alfred, Gordon, Hassan, Bruce, Brown, Sam, Dade, Betty and Sniper for good times at the Corner House Bar, Juliet Nanzala for her patience, Bozaka for his many boda journeys, and last but not least Bobby Williamson, Don Thompson, and the rest of the crowd at JKs for taking the piss.

"Every kid wants to be a pirate. Look at any map of any coast in the world, and I guarantee you'll find places named 'Pirate's Cove' or 'Smuggler's Bay.' There's a romance about it. It's a fantasy, and I got to live it." – Mickey Munday

PROLOGUE

Fathoms below the Gulf of Aden the five divers work in the indigo gloom, their zinc and copper helmets faintly shimmering in the lightless depths of an unnamed abyss. Progress is slow for the aquanauts as they struggle to salvage a cable buried beneath the seabed: the Red Sea Telegraph Cable, abandoned by the British in 1861.

Trudging through a cloud of grey silt, churned up by their advance across the ocean floor, they haul up metre after metre of their salvage, like an endless jungle vine. Suddenly, after freeing its tail end from the seabed, the lead diver falls backward. He quickly regains his balance and examines what looks like a curious fruit tree. The cable is frayed and corroded, and the gutta-percha has disintegrated, but the seven copper strands and the eighteen iron armouring wires remain, thickly covered in myriad aqua-fauna and splayed out in every direction like branches. From his belt he removes another antique piece of equipment, a key and sounder, used for telegraph line testing, attaches it to one of the seven strands, and then taps out a message in Morse code: "Allahu Akbar!"

In the Yemeni port of Aden, at the other end of the Red Sea Telegraph Cable is the commander of the operation, who's been waiting for a signal that will let him know the divers have located the limit of the submarine line. His sounder suddenly pips into life, with a series of dots and dashes that he quickly translates from code.

Strangely, the first message is, "...Her Majesty's possessions in Aden are secure..." only followed seconds later by, "Allahu Akbar!" Nevertheless, it's enough for him to know the mission has been a success.

With their work in the abyss complete, the divers signal to their tenders on the surface to begin the slow ascent from the ocean floor. After several decompression stops, all five eventually surface beside a small fishing trawler which hoists them aboard with a crane. The telegraph cable is already secured astern, and the boat begins to navigate slowly southward towards the coast of Somalia.

It's mid-morning and there's not a cloud in the sky. The divers, now draped in white robes and AK-47s, pace the deck. It takes the trawler the rest of the day to drag the line across the remaining three hundred kilometres to the coast of Africa. Eventually they reach a secluded cove in Puntland, where they're met by a small group of jihadists. The cable is dragged ashore and spliced to another already land-side. The team have established a dedicated communications link between the Arabian peninsula and the Horn of Africa, which cannot be tapped.

CHAPTER ONE

Brandishing a baseball bat like an exclamation mark, Mehemet Abdul Rahman eased open the large brass-studded Zanzibari door to his house and stepped out into the dead of night. Against this stretch of the Somali coastline the Indian Ocean was windless and hushed, gently beating the shore beyond the perimeter of his compound. Apart from his wife, children and servants asleep indoors, usually there was not another soul for miles in either direction. Nothing stirred, though he was certain he'd heard something. A trespasser, someone who was presently hiding in the mottled shadows of twisted juniper, palm and aloes draped across his garden.

He held his baseball bat with both hands, as though expecting a sudden curve ball from an unseen pitcher, all the while knowing it was of little use against an assassin armed with an AK-47. There was a loaded .38 snub-nose tucked into the back of his pyjamas, but he believed he stood a better chance if he appeared unarmed to the intruder. He would duck and roll out of the line of fire the instant he heard a charging handle being released.

Although in his mid-fifties Mehemet was in good physical shape, well-built, of medium height, and with a full head of dark hair. As he crept through the shadows, his distinct Roman nose caught the gleam of his garden lights, though it was his sense of hearing he was most relying on. A twig snapped. He dropped the bat, reached around, grabbed his pistol and aimed it at the shadows. "Who is it? Who goes there?"

"Mehemet," came a frightened voice, "it is I, Abdu Takar." An elderly, lanky, bearded man with his hands raised above his turban stepped into the light. Mehemet recognised him at once as one of the Majeerteen elders to whom his wife deferred during clan disputes.

"Abdu?" cried Mehemet, replacing his gun into the back of his pyjamas. "What the hell are you doing creeping around outside my house in the middle of the night?"

"I've come to warn you, my friend. You are in very grave danger. Assassins are on their way from the Yemen to kill you. You must leave Puntland this very night."

"Whose assassins?"

"Al-Qaeda's."

"Who told you this?"

"That's not important. We know it to be reliable information. Al-Qaeda fighters are on their way here now by boat from the Arabian Peninsula, with the intention of killing you."

As an expatriate American who had lived for the past decade and a half in Puntland, Somalia's semi-autonomous state, no one was more aware than Mehemet Abdul Rahman of the radical elements on both sides of the Gulf of Aden that had begun infiltrating the region. He was the infidel in their midst, an obstacle to their unscrupulous designs. Mehemet turned back towards the house, but Abdu caught him by the shoulder. "You cannot fight them, my friend. You must leave."

"I must protect my wife and children!"

"It is you they want. We will see to it Khadija and the children are protected."

Mehemet pulled himself away from Abdu and went straight back into his house to where his wife lay sleeping in their bed.

"Khadija," he whispered, gently stroking her auburn hair that was spread out across her pillow like a splash. "Khadija. Wake up." She stirred, turning slowly to gaze at her husband with a smile. Mehemet turned on the bedside lamp and Khadija squinted in the sudden burst of light.

"What is it, my love?" she croaked.

"You've got to go, Khadija," he said.

Her Somali features were elfin – full lips, doe eyes, petite nose – but as she became aware of what he was saying, they quickly formed into a frown. "Go where?" she asked.

"It's not safe here," said Mehemet, opening the cupboard where he kept his M-60 assault rifle. He hesitated upon seeing the weapon but grabbed an already packed black duffel bag instead, into which he stuffed his pistol.

She sat bolt upright. "I don't understand..."

"You and the children must get away from Bender Siyaada tonight," he said, quickly changing into a black sweater and black jeans. "Abdu Takar is here to take you to safety."

"Abdu? Here?" asked Khadija, leaping from her bed and frantically searching for her own clothes. "Tell me who, Mehemet? Who is after us?"

"Abdu will explain everything to you," he said, heading for the living room. "C'mon, there's no time to waste." A few minutes later, a confused Khadija and her four children, still rubbing the sleep from their eyes, were fully clothed and gathered at the front door. Mehemet turned off all the lights while Abdu and the servants began ushering them outside into the humid blackness. Mehemet clutched the shoulders of his eldest boy and said, "You are in charge now, Nadif."

"What about you?" asked Khadija, turning in desperation to her husband. "Aren't you coming with us?"

"I have to make my own way," said Mehemet solemnly, "without you."

"But Mehemet..." she cried.

"Forgive me, my love, but it has to be this way. I must leave Somalia tonight, alone."

The tears began to roll from her beautiful eyes. "When will I see you again?"

Mehemet pulled her into a passionate embrace, and whispered in her ear, "We live in a strange world, Khadija. But no matter what happens, I love you. I will always love you. Have faith in us." With that he released her, dashed over the garden wall and disappeared.

"Quickly," shouted Abdu, bundling the distraught Khadija and her children through the compound gate. First light was breaking on the horizon, though it was still too dark to see the coast. Khadija looked south, knowing Mehemet would be heading in that direction. Then she heard the sound of an approaching speedboat; they immediately began running across the sand to where a Land Cruiser was waiting by the road, with its engine idling but its headlamps turned off. As soon as they reached the car and opened the doors, the interior light came on, alerting the approaching speedboat to their flight. Bullets began flying all around them. The family quickly leapt inside the car and sped away.

The attacking speedboat hit the beach with a loud scrape and a whine, and a band of fighters scrambled ashore, firing their weapons. They tried to pursue the fleeing vehicle on foot but were too late. The fighters then turned and headed for the solitary house on the beach, searching the entire compound for anyone left behind, while their commander stood guard outside the gate. They found nothing, except Mehemet's M-60 assault rifle.

"Omar, we found this," said a mujahideen fighter, handing the American weapon and a bandolier of a hundred rounds to his commander, who unravelled his headscarf to get a better look, as did the others. It was clear from their appearances that these were not Yemeni assassins after all, as Abdu Takar had said they would be, but Somalian.

"The infidel was expecting us," said Omar, releasing the safety on the American machine gun and aiming it at the iron gate. He then opened fire and did not stop shooting until he'd expended the entire bandolier. When the smoke finally cleared it became apparent from the pattern of bullet holes in the gate that he'd written "*al-Shabaab*" in Arab script. "The lads."

CHAPTER TWO

"What do you want here?" demanded the old askari on one side of the large iron gate.

"You know very well," protested the equally elderly woman on the other side.

"*Hapana!*" yelled the *askari*, "No! You cannot enter! *Afendi* does not know you, and you will not pass through this gate." He was a tall, dark Acholi, from the same northern Ugandan tribe as Idi Amin, dressed in colonial-style khakis – short-sleeved shirt and shorts. He stooped over the peephole in the gate, and wagged a bony finger at the woman on the other side, who stood back from the smell of his breath but refused to leave.

"Who's at the gate, Aturu?" asked Derek Strangely, shuffling out of his bungalow into the blazing equatorial sun. He wore only a purple *kanga*, and was followed by his dog, Rafiki, a mongrel of mixed origin, like Derek. It was mid-morning.

"She must not enter, *afendi*," replied Aturu, standing to attention.

"Is it Agnes?" asked Derek, approaching the gate.

"I don't know this woman," the guard said, slamming shut the peephole.

"C'mon, Aturu, let Agnes in."

"*Hapana!* I cannot!"

"Jesus, Aturu, she's my maid." A pair of white-bellied go-away birds flew in to roost atop the tall olyusambia tree growing in the property opposite, and started cackling.

"I'm not opening for this woman, *afendi*. Even if you beat me."

"Fine. Then stand aside! *I'll* let her in." Derek pushed past his askari and tried to unbolt the doorway that led through the gate, but Aturu had padlocked it. "The key, Aturu..." The askari smiled broadly; he was missing most of his teeth. Rafiki barked at him, but he stood his ground. Then Derek stepped up closer to him and sniffed. "Have you been drinking?"

"No, sah!" said Aturu, still grinning through a misshapen rift across his wrinkled face.

"Well then, give me the key." Reluctantly the old northerner reached into his khaki shorts and produced his greatest possession: the key to the padlock that opened the gate to Mr Derek's house in Kampala. With it he wielded great power.

Derek opened the gate, and Agnes barged through and rounded on Aturu. "*What's wrong with your problem?*" He tried to dodge her blows, protesting loudly in his defence, but she continued her assault. Rafiki circled the squabbling Ugandans, barking incessantly. Derek simply turned and walked back to his bungalow; he was used to the routine by now.

He had recently made some adjustments in his life. One of them was taking on full-time domestic staff to help him feel more secure at home. But his *askari* was proving a handful. There was such a thing as too much security. He sat down on his sagging sofa and examined his dilapidated living room. A clean patch of wall, as big as a window, marked the spot where a map of Congo used to hang.

On his driveway was another empty space where his black-on-black Land Rover Discovery III had once been parked. Without Pedro to drive it, or to stop him, Derek had sold "the Blackback" to the first Big Man who came along. He no longer had any need for a safari vehicle. After all the negative publicity that followed his ordeal in the Congo, no one wanted to hire him, not even to guide their day trip to Lake Mburo. The money from the Blackback had been barely enough to support him since.

The cacophony at the gate had died down and Rafiki was curled up at his feet. The only sound was birdlife, an overabundance of it coming from every power line and treetop. "At least the power lines have some use," thought Derek, pointlessly aiming his remote at an inert television on the other side of the room. Avian life was about the only entertainment he could rely on these days. With over a thousand species ranging through the country, it was hard to avoid an interest in ornithology in Uganda. There was one particular bird, a common bulbul, that perched outside his window every morning before the sun was up and began singing, *"Get straight to it, Strangely! Get straight to it Strangely!"* like an insistent nanny. He made a point of never rising before hearing it.

"How the hell can I get straight to it, when there's no goddamn electricity?" was his usual response. Uganda's relentless power outages were the main bone of contention for anyone living there. Derek found them especially hard to endure in the morning, as he was never fully awake until he'd drunk a mug of black coffee. Brewing it over a coal fire was just too complicated and time-consuming. And neither Agnes nor Aturu ever grasped the concept of a good cup of Joe.

Power cuts in the evening, however, were much more bearable. He would simply hang a paraffin lamp in the starflower tree next to his veranda, sit down on the grass with a cold Club, and watch a billion stars twinkle. "They don't call it the Dark Continent for nothing," he'd smile to himself.

Derek's phone rang. It was not a number he recognised. "Derek Strangely."

"Yo, Gorilla Man! How's it hanging?"

"Who's this?" asked Derek, stroking his black and silver beard.

"Johnny Oceans."

"No fucking way! I thought you were dead."

"If that's true, then Kampala's hell. Meet me at Fat Boyz in twenty minutes."

"I'm on my way." Derek quickly dressed in a pair of jeans, T-shirt, and flipflops, and headed out of the door, tying his greying hair back in a ponytail while issuing instructions to Aturu to feed Rafiki and get some more charcoal.

"But, *afendi*, it is my job to guard the gate. You can send Agnes for charcoal."

"Not now, Aturu," barked Derek, closing the gate behind him to howls of protest from Rafiki. After taking a few short steps he was accosted by a boda boda, one of Kampala's omnipresent motorcycle taxis. "*Jjebale'ko sebo,*" said Derek, greeting the driver in accordance with the Bugandan custom of exchanging niceties before proceeding with anything. Accordingly, the boda driver returned the greeting.

"Take me to Kisementi," instructed Derek, donning his Ray-Ban Wayfarer sunglasses.

"Kisementi, Kamwokya?" asked the driver.

"Eh-heh!" replied Derek, jumping on the back. The ride was a far cry from the luxury of the Blackback but he didn't care much. *Boda bodas* were the poor man's helicopter in these parts. When they reached the end of his street, the driver arced into Kira Road and sped down the hill, cutting around vehicles and pedestrians like a sun-addled bat.

He narrowly missed a traffic cop, a stout woman dressed in khaki, black beret and boots standing at the side of the road, who did not even blink. Despite the fact few Ugandan motorists demonstrated any grasp of the Highway Code, this traffic cop wasn't interested in trying to enforce the law. Like so many in her profession, extortion was her racket. She was looking out for drivers in expensive cars talking on their mobile phones. Before long, she had pulled one over, a big man in an Audi. "Another Ugandan Driving Imbecile," quipped Derek, looking back over his shoulder, as she cheerily sidled up to the unfortunate motorist's window.

"Where are you from?" asked Derek's *boda* driver as they sped away.

"Canada," replied Derek, "but I've lived my whole life in Africa."

"Then you're an African," laughed the driver. "My name is Boda Tiger. And your name?"

"Mr Derek."

Ducking into the vortex behind Tiger's back long enough to keep his flame lit, Derek sparked up a joint. He took a long, thick toke, held it in for a few seconds then blasted the smoke back out again in a fit of coughing. He was careful to keep the blunt cupped in his hand, lest one of the many traffic cops along the road spotted its distinctive trumpet shape. Not that any of them would bother chasing him. In all likelihood they lacked the air-time on their cell phones even to call it in. Nevertheless, there was no mistaking the aroma emanating from the back of Derek's *boda*.

Through pie-eyes and Wayfarers he surveyed his surroundings. In the vivid light of a clear morning, the city looked like an old master's painting to which children had been allowed to add daubs of their own brightly coloured paint. He marvelled at the panorama, as three of Kampala's seven hills came into view, each one crowned with a communications mast rising above some minister's gimcrack folly, looming over a clutter of orange rooftops that increased in density towards the valley, as though the literal consequence of an economic landslide. Brilliant sunshine and stark shadows gave everything a vividness that was almost too intense to bear.

He thought about Pedro, his erstwhile driver and rastafarian partner-in-crime, at this moment in time riding his softail and growing his dreadlocks on the Mexican coast, after vowing never again to return to Africa. Things just weren't the same in KLA without him.

He spotted a large billboard featuring one of his former girlfriends, gazing back at him with those familiar bedroom eyes while sucking salaciously on a sweating bottle of lager. Consequently, he did not notice the police officer coming up behind him on the back of another *boda*, and was startled by the hand that suddenly gripped his right shoulder, causing him to jerk to the left, free of its hold, then send his *boda boda* fishtailing. "Stop!" cried the officer, who was wearing the blue camouflage of the regular police – the busting kind – and about to attempt another lunge. "You're under arrest!"

"It's the Po Po!" shouted Derek, flinging his burning spliff into a gutter. *"Tu wende!"* Tiger rapidly accelerated out of reach, then began to weave through the traffic at high speed. The cop remained in hot pursuit. "Listen, *sebo*," said Derek, clasping the motorcycle's rear metal rack with both hands, "do whatever you have to do, but I will pay you twenty thousand shillings if you outrun this fool." Without looking back, or even in *any* direction, Tiger responded by making a sharp right, clear across a busy thoroughfare, narrowly escaping a collision with an oncoming mini-bus taxi, then swerving to the left into Old Kira Road. With no hesitation. the pursuing *boda* made the same erratic move, and sped after them down the hill.

"Turn right here," barked Derek, and Tiger veered hard through a narrow gap between a wooden phone kiosk and a ramshackle scrapyard, then down a bumpy road that led into the mud-clogged, lunar landscape of Kamwokya, a clamorous shanty town wedged between Kololo hill and the swamps below. Driver and passenger swayed savagely from side to side, as they zigzagged through the slalom run of potholes, people and livestock. Dodging a work detail of boys filling in the rifts in the road with rocks and soil, they narrowly missed another *boda* driver who was involved in a melee between two shop owners, then swerved to avoid an infant who'd wandered into the road crying.

The backstreets were crowded with more animal life than human: half a dozen cows, a goat on a rope that ran directly across their path and throttled himself, a gaggle of geese that chased after them until dispersed by the blue *afendi* still hot on their trail. Even kaloles took flight, those ungainly, lappet-faced storks that rummage around Kampala's dumps like ugly spies, but are among the most graceful flyers in the African sky. Tiger burst through a line of laundry, then sped back out on to the main road, immediately hitting a speed bump that sent them skyward after the storks.

In the brash equatorial sunlight Kamwokya was a riot to the senses: the sight of village belles in drab clothing sashaying between yellow Mobile Money cubicles and hair saloons, the odour of roasting goat fat and open sewers, the flavour of exhaust from the taxi ahead, the din of car horns clashing with DVD stalls, and the bump to the ass of potholes within potholes.

Their *boda* barely missed a *matoke* seller sitting straight-legged by the road, beside half a dozen sizable bunches of dark green bananas, then sped past hardware stores, iron gate makers, butcheries (the preferred local spelling), a pork joint where a dozen young men were huddled around two pool tables, the Pleasure Hotel, the Valey Inn, and a stall displaying piles of mattresses and plastic containers that tumbled in their slipstream, scattering rainbow-coloured wares all across the road. It was all a haze to Derek, even as they passed a group of pretty young women shouting, "*Muzungu! Muzungu!*", as he remained insensible to everything but the pursuing afendi on the boda behind, now caught up in a mess of mattresses and containers.

Tiger was careful to avoid the shit-mottled, viscoelastic waste water flowing in and out of people's shops and homes, and decelerated as they approached a five-metre-wide stretch of it where the road dipped below the surface. Barely clearing their feet, they proceeded cautiously through the slough, swerving at the last moment to avoid a well-known, car-sized pothole concealed beneath it.

The pursuing officer was not so careful, and drove straight through the middle, hitting the hidden pothole with an impact that caused him to be soaked from head to toe in sewage, and brought the chase to an abrupt end. Derek and Tiger stopped to high-five each other on the other side of the puddle, then drove off through the throng of market-goers. "At least it's Friday," said Derek, relaxing his posture. Friday was market day in Kamwokya, and he knew the police officer and his driver would easily find a change of clothes. Still, he dreaded the next time he ran into him.

As they approached their destination his thoughts turned to the phone call he'd received thirty minutes earlier from the American. After fourteen years everyone had given up on ever finding Johnny Oceans, dead or alive. Now, suddenly, he was back. But from where? Derek was keen to find out and, as Tiger pulled into the Kisementi car park, he searched for his old friend through the dazzling reflected glare of countless automobile surfaces surrounding its drinking establishments. "There he is," he cried, spotting a man seated on the front terrace of Fat Boyz Bar & Grill, which boasted "Warm Beer – Lousy Food". There was no mistaking that Roman nose.

Derek paid Tiger, then dashed up the steps to give his long-lost friend a heartfelt hug. Johnny Oceans had a full head of black hair, a puka-shell choker around his neck, and a large, rugged black watch around his left wrist. He was well-tanned, physically fit, and dressed in a turquoise Hawaiian shirt and jeans. Except for an expression of inner contentment, he looked much the same as he had a decade and half ago. "Wherever you've been hiding, it's obviously done you the world of good, *rafiki*," said Derek, grabbing a seat. A waiter arrived to take their order. Oceans asked for a Coca-Cola, and although it was still not yet midday Derek ordered a cold Club beer.

"The last time I saw you was 1998," said Derek. "We were out scuba-diving on the Malindi-Watamu bank, about twelve kilometres off the Kenyan coast, totally baked, I seem to recall. You signalled you were going to surface." Derek laughed, thrust his thumb upward a few times, then shook his head in disbelief. "I continued on my solo dive for another ten minutes, *ten goddamn minutes*, but when I got back to the boat you had fucking vanished. No clue, no note; *nothing!*"

"I thought you'd be OK," smiled Oceans.

"Drifting on the open sea with no fuel, *hapana*, I was not OK. I was in fucking peril. Luckily, Azziza Nshuti came along in her speedboat."

"Who?"

"Madame Nshuti, the Congolese smuggler. *Jesus, where have you been?*"

"Is that why you didn't report me missing for a week?"

"Listen, man, there was no way I wanted to get caught up in that ordeal. Johnny Oceans, member of the notorious DeVini family, Meyer Lansky's gaming connection in the 1950s, disappears and I'm the last person on earth to see him alive. Uh-uh! No thank you. And besides, I thought you'd show up sooner or later. I just didn't expect it to be fourteen years later."

A cloud eclipsed the equatorial sun, followed by a refreshing breeze that transformed their shirts into fluttering flags and took the heat out of the day for an instant. Then the sunshine returned, plastering the walls, awnings and car park with a blinding light that soaked up the midday shadows like a sponge.

"Did those gorillas give you a hard time?"

"You have no fucking idea! It was like 'The Godfather' meets 'Lord of War'. The day they arrived on the Kenyan coast is still fresh in my memory like it was yesterday. I remember Azziza was about to catch her flight back to Kinshasa and the two of us were just chilling in the sand. I spotted them through the heat haze, a hundred metres away, tramping up the beach towards us, side by side: the three Wise Guys. Only a gumba from New York shows up at a beach resort in a rayon tracksuit."

"What did they say to you?" asked Oceans, chuckling.

"Oh, you wouldn't believe the charm offensive. The fat guy, sweating profusely and dabbing his jowls with a hanky, asks in a high-pitched voice, 'Are you Derek Strangely?' I say, 'Yeah.' Then he asks, 'Who's the *mulli*?'" Oceans could not contain himself after that, and doubled over with laughter, extending his hand all the while to indicate Derek should hang on before continuing his story. "Not a good move," continued Derek after his friend had regained some composure. "Madame Nshuti was no *mulli*."

"What did *she say*?" asked Oceans, wiping the tears from his eyes.

"Let me see if I can remember her exact words. She stood up – she was an imposing woman, with stunning good looks – and she said, 'It's clearly a joke that you men are called wise guys. But if you want to last a day in Africa, you'll be wise to show the locals more respect.'" "Then she left for the airport, without even kissing *me* goodbye."

"I'm so sorry, dawg…he he…You got to remember, those paisans had never before left the Tri-state area. To them Africa was somewhere east of Bronx Zoo."

"Yes, well, as the last person to see you alive, I ended spending a lot of time with your paisans. Bobby, Jimmy, Petey, Tony ... Do you have *any* relatives with names that don't end in 'y'?"

"Sure, Sal, Luca, Rocko ..."

"Well, your gumbas took over the Blue Marlin Bar for a whole fucking week, and ran up a huge tab which they never paid. They complained about everything – the lack of sausage and peppers mostly – and did whatever they fucking pleased. The *matatus* flipped them out; they wanted to whack the drivers of those damn bus taxis. And the bugs; they fucking hated the bugs. One time Petey got up in the middle of the night and started shooting at the goddamn geckoes on the walls of his room. I told him geckoes keep the bugs away, but he was having none of it."

"Oh man, I wish I'd been there to see that."

"I fucking wished you'd been there. I tried my best to entertain them, being a safari guide and all. But those wise guys had no interest whatsoever in going on safari, not fishing, diving, seeing any of the sites. All they did was drink alcohol all day long, that is when they weren't trying to muscle in on the local forex racket. That didn't go down too well. Swahili Muslims don't take too kindly to being called pigs. Your boys even asked me if I wanted to be their coke mule."

Oceans stopped laughing, shook his head with incredulity then said, "That's my family, Derek, not me..."

"So?" asked Derek, taking a slow swig of his beer during which he eyed his long-lost friend inquisitively. "I'm curious to know what had happened to *you*. Did you go back to the old country, lie low in your ancestral village while things blew over, or what?" But Oceans steered clear of the subject, glancing around at the other people on the terrace to see if anyone was listening in on their conversation.

"Let me tell you something," he said, moving in closer. "When my Uncle Dino started out in the business in 1920s he was just a kid, working as a craps casino dealer at Rex's Cigar Store, in Steubenville, Ohio. Before long he was the youngest 'bust out' man in Steubenville."

"What's a 'bust out' man?"

"He's the guy whose job it is to switch crooked dice in and out of the craps games, the sort of Baboo the gangsters who ran the rackets hated, that is until they hired him to ward off undesirables, hustle the *spacones* with lots of money to burn, and break lucky winning streaks."

"Sounds like a worthwhile talent to have in the gaming business."

"Yeah, but it could be used to devastating effect. I remember one night when only a handful of hard-core gamblers remained in the casino, including two brothers from New York. One was playing with high stakes in a closed game at the blackjack table, and losing excessively; his brother had already lost a shitload of money. Before long they both came up and asked Uncle Bobby for credit. 'You're OK,' he snapped at one of them, 'but not him', jabbing his finger at the other, who walked away in humiliation. Later that night the brother he snubbed hung himself, and Uncle Bobby ordered one of the casino workers to plant ten thousand dollars on his body before informing the other brother, to make it look as though his gambling losses were not a factor in his suicide, that he had other motives for taking his own life. When the surviving brother failed to pay *his* debt after he returned to New York City, who dunned him for the payment? Who else? The mob!" Oceans drank back the last of his soda, and burped. "I had to get the fuck out!"

"So? Where did you go?"

"You really wanna know?"

"Damn straight!"

Oceans stood up and surveyed the bar, beat his chest a few times nonchalantly, the smiled back down at Derek. "I'll tell you everything, but not here. C'mon, we're going on safari."

CHAPTER THREE

Derek and Johnny were seated beside an excellent fire at the base of a small granite kopje overlooking Kidepo Valley National Park, in northeastern Uganda. They'd flown up on a private single-engine that Johnny Oceans had chartered, which landed them in Kidepo Airfield, where they were met by park staff who chauffeured them to a camping site at the foot of a kopje.

"I've been to some spectacular places in my lifetime," sighed Johnny, "but this is the shit!" Derek just nodded. Words could not express the way he felt about this particular East African wilderness. The sun was setting and the fiery light of dusk had transformed the valley into a *son et lumière*, recalling the time millions of years ago when it was a cataclysmic inferno, venting the planet's burning mantle through a cluster of volcanoes.

"Except in the far reaches of the imagination," said Derek, "no one would ever believe this place existed. It's as if those volcanoes got up and danced around until they all keeled over with exhaustion. And this is how they were found: burnt out and contorted on the Mesozoic dance floor." He poured himself a double shot of Wild Turkey into a cut-glass tumbler filled with ice, and then said, "Right, Johnny Oceans. You owe me an epic, and it better be a good one."

"Yeah, I guess you've earned it, Gorilla Man," said Johnny, sitting up. "OK, where to start...No, I didn't go back to the old country. What happened fourteen years ago on the Malindi-Watamu bank, after I gave you that signal, was quite incredible. I surfaced, and had just started removing my scuba gear in the boat, when out of nowhere comes this dhow. I didn't even hear them approaching, but they came up alongside and snatched me from my dingy, hauled me on to their dhow and held me at gunpoint until they'd sailed away."

"Jesus, who were these guys?" gasped Derek, choking on wisps of woodsmoke that found his face no matter how much he tried to dodge them.

"Somali pirates."

"No shit, pirates? Back then? No one had even heard of Somali pirates in 1998."

"There's no question they were novices," replied Johnny, sipping his mug of ginger tea, "simple fisherman more than anything. At least we had that in common."

"Did they harm you?"

"No, not at all," smiled Johnny. "They were totally cool. Eventually we reached Puntland in northern Somalia, where they took me ashore. They weren't sure what to do with me at first. Shit, I was their hostage but all we did was fish tuna and marlin all day. In time—" He stopped abruptly and spun around. "*What was that? Sounded like a high-pitched guffaw in the distance?*"

"Just hyenas," said Derek. "Carry on..."

Johnny hesitated, scrutinising the darkness. There was a chance predators would try to come near, but Derek had taken the precaution of erecting a fence of thorns around their campsite to keep animals at bay. Johnny turned back, and continued. "In time, they told me I was free to go, but I chose to stay, not least for the incredible tuna fishing. I'm telling you, Derek, it was yellow-fin genocide all day long!"

"You sure do love your tuna, Johnny Oceans," laughed Derek, as he stoked the fire, causing sparks to erupt from the embers. "So, you're telling me that all this time you were in Somalia? Damn, you must have really wanted to get away from Uncle Bobby."

"Somalia's incredible, man; I love it. It's nothing like people think it is." Johnny glanced around their surroundings but, except for the fire and his and Derek's glowing faces, there was nothing but blackness. "A bit like this place…"

"Even so, it would have taken a brave wise guy to venture in there after you."

"*Forgedaboutid!* It took a while to detox from the casino racket, that's for sure, but Puntland had everything I needed. Man, they've got black-finned marlin the size of Cadillacs. Five hundred kilos or more – I shit you not. And the diving, oh, you wouldn't believe the diving. It's like an underwater basilica down there."

"You make the place sound like heaven, but this is Somalia we're talking about…"

"Puntland. It ain't like the south. It's a semi-autonomous state. Sure, the people are Muslims, but they're not Islamists. The Land of Punt is its own land, with its own people – mostly from the Majeerteen clan."

"Did they make you feel at home, these Majeerteen?"

"Not to begin with, not until I earned their confidence. The Majeerteen are notoriously xenophobic. It takes a long time to earn their trust. I think at that time I was the only American in Puntland, but that didn't matter. For the first time in my life I got a sense of my own identity, you know, my place in the scheme of things." Johnny gazed thoughtfully at the fire, as he recalled the profound transformation he had experienced in the Horn of Africa. "After a while I immersed myself in their culture, converted to Islam, changed my name to Abdul Rahman, and married a Somali woman." He paused and dropped his head, overwhelmed by the thought of his wife.

"Is she beautiful?" asked Derek, reclining back in his chair.

"Khadija? Uh, like no other woman."

"Really?" Derek clasped his hands behind his head and gazed up at the stars. "Tell me, how beautiful?"

"Think of Iman, David Bowie's wife, only twenty years younger."

"Wow! Where is she now?"

"I had to leave her behind. It was the most difficult thing I've ever done in my entire life. But after years of living in peace in Puntland, our lives were in danger. I had to leave, and in a hurry, in order to free her of the threat."

"Who was after you?"

"Al-Qaeda."

"Jesus Christ..."

Derek's blasphemy hung for an interminable spell in the still night air, and neither of them said a word. Not that they felt threatened. Even though they knew they were being watched by unseen creatures, the tranquillity of their setting was unsurpassed and they felt invulnerable in the Kidepo Valley. Except for a flat, horizontal gap to the east, about forty degrees wide, that opened the way to South Sudan, they were surrounded by towering summits, starkly silhouetted against the starry firmament, encircling them like the cupped hand of a benevolent giant.

"The threat of jihad in the north of Somalia has never been greater," continued Johnny, "and it's now coming from both sides of the Gulf of Aden. Al-Qaeda on the Arabian Peninsula has joined forces with al-Shabaab in Somalia, in order to infiltrate the north, which has remained out of Islamist control until now. The only hope for Puntland lies in the hands of a Majeerteen clan elder, who's currently residing in the Kakuma Refugee Camp, in northern Kenya." He sat back, and let his words sink in.

Derek was lost in the constellations, dancing a quadrille with a menagerie of mythological creatures in the sky. Then it hit him, like a meteor to his head, and he sat up. "You know, Kakuma's the Swahili word for 'nowhere' but, as the crow flies, that refugee camp can't be a hundred kilometres from here, in the Rift Valley."

"You're a safari guide," said Johnny, downing the rest of his tea. "Can you take me there? I'll pay you good money."

Derek raised an eyebrow, looked over at his friend, then took a swig of his whiskey and swallowed hard. "Well, we'd have to drive some distance before we reached any legitimate border, but I guess I could give it a go..."

"Derek," said Johnny, with a cold, calculated stare, "I'm not looking for a legitimate border crossing."

Lieutenant Simon Hay had just flown in from Afghanistan, where he was stationed with British Special Forces, and was in the conference room of Nairobi's Fairview Hotel leading a safety briefing for three dozen aid workers, every one of whom was involved in missions to provide humanitarian relief to the Somalis. "All right, ladies," he bellowed with an enduring smirk on his face, despite the fact he was addressing an evenly gendered audience, "what's the first rule of security?" He was clean-shaven, built like a brick shithouse and as he paced the floor every footfall resounded across the room. "Anyone?"

"A well-adjusted childhood?" asked a young woman seated in the second row.

"Erm. Can I ask anyone who speaks up to first state their name, nationality and the organisation they work for," said Simon.

"Maddy Jones," she replied, pushing her hair back and straightening her posture, whereby she innocently thrust her notable cleavage forward. She was in her late twenties and dressed in a bleached white, short-sleeved linen blouse that contrasted appealingly with her tan. Her eyes were green, wide apart, and her hair fell in long, strawberry-blonde waves around her neck and arms. "Australian, and I'm with the World Food Programme. I'll be working Kakuma Refugee Camp in western Kenya."

"Are you a nurse?" asked Simon.

"No, I'm a food distribution manager."

"Crikey! At Kakuma? How'd you get that then...*Only joking!* No, the first rule of security is knowing who is responsible for your security. For instance, do any of you know who manages security at this hotel?"

"You?" asked a cocky Frenchman in the front row.

"Hardly. We're across the street from the Israeli Embassy, staying in a hotel full of infidels, which is owned by a naturalised Polish Jew – which puts this location high on the list of terror targets. What if I told you it was the Kenyan Police managing security here? Yeah, just felt all the little hairs on the back of your neck stand on end, didn't you? Well you needn't worry, my lovelies, because actually it's Mossad. Now, what are the chances of a terror attack slipping through Israeli intelligence's security net? Exactly! The point is, know who is responsible for your security."

He went up to a whiteboard and with a red felt-tip wrote, "1. Who? 2. U," then turned back to his audience. "Which brings me to the second rule of security. You are responsible for your security. It is essential, no matter who's looking after your protection, be it Kenyan police or AMISOM – African Union Mission in Somalia – soldiers, *that you take full responsibility yourself.* Your actions may endanger not only yourself, but you could end up jeopardising the security of the very people you've come here to help. Is that clear?"

Like the others Maddy smiled and nodded, though she had already endured a number of similar training sessions both in Brisbane and at the World Food Programme headquarters in Rome. Simon smiled back at her. He sensed a chemistry between them.

"I'm going to hand out a sheet on the importance of cultural awareness," he continued, ambling his way between his audience. "Read this carefully, Maddy," he said, winking as he handed her a copy, "because I'll ask you questions later."

After concluding the briefing, Simon ate his dinner alone, and then made his way to the Fairview's pool-side bar, hoping he might find Maddy Jones. Various groups of people were conversing at tables and across the leafy grounds that were lit up with coloured spotlights. There she was, off in a corner, seated by herself with her back to him; there was no mistaking that hair. She was nursing a Tusker beer while working on her laptop. "My kind of bird," he thought, approaching her casually as he ran a few faithful chat-up lines through his head.

"No, I'm not your bloody pet," she snapped, when he was just a few steps away, which caught him off guard.

"Sorry?" replied Simon, but she ignored him. It was then that he noticed she was wearing earbuds and talking to her computer. He decided to seat himself at the next table and wait for her to finish her conversation.

"Look, Bill, you know how much this job means to me," she continued, taking a gulp of her Tusker and roughly returning it to the table. "Why can't you take an interest? What?...Oh, must you be a boofhead all your life? Kenya is nowhere *near* Pakistan...And those are Sikhs you're talking about...Google it...I dunno...Maybe you can surf down in Malindi or Mombasa. I'm going in the opposite direction. You could use a little direction yourself, you know. You can't be a waxxy all your life, smoking weed all day long and sunbaking on the Gold Coast...Look, I'm not going to go on chatting all night, I'm up at dawn. I'll call you the minute I get settled. Kooroo." She removed her earbuds, closed the lid of her laptop, and downed the rest of her Tusker. She was about to get up and leave when she noticed Simon seated at the next table. "Oh, hello. How long have you been there?"

"Only just arrived, love," he said. "I was wondering if you might join me for a drink."

"Sorry," she said, with a big, heartfelt smile, "Gotta get some sleep, mate."

With the equatorial sun in their eyes, Derek and Johnny headed east up a gradual incline towards a gap in the elevation of the Rift Valley escarpment. They both carried large packs on their backs and small ones on their chests, which contained all their camping gear and supplies. Behind them followed Robert, a tall Karamajong warrior, who was wearing nothing but a traditional cloth slung over his left shoulder and carrying only a spear. His skin was pockmarked with dozens of small circular scars, arranged in neat parallel rows across his chest, giving it the appearance of ostrich leather. Each scar represented one of his victims; Robert bore the marks of a veteran cattle raider.

"Dude, we can't take this man with us into Kenya," Derek whispered to Johnny. "These people are the sworn enemies of the Turkana."

"*Forgedaboutid,*" laughed Johnny, "we'll be fine. Besides, who better to get us out of Karamoja than a Karamajong?"

"But we're headed straight into Turkanaland. Taking this man with us would be insane."

"I said *forgedaboutid*," replied Johnny, pushing aside his shirt to reveal a holstered pistol. "Extraordinary people do remarkable things in tough circumstances."

Derek dropped the subject. "*After ten metres, take a heading of sixty-four degrees for one kilometre,*" said a digitised female voice emanating from a small speaker strapped to his belt, "*then one-hundred-four degrees for point nine-six kilometres.*" It was a handheld global positioning unit-cum-satellite navigation device for hikers, which he'd modified to vocalise directions along the way.

"Why don't we just follow this dried-up riverbed?" asked Johnny.

"Because it's too meandering; we'd end up trekking twice as far. Like I told you, I worked out the path of least resistance."

"He's right," said Robert. "This is the way I would go."

"You're a genius," said Johnny.

Derek had established the best course on his iPad using Google Earth. First he drew a straight line, as the crow flies, from their camp to Kakuma. But that took them through extreme ups and downs, so he adjusted their path away from those obstructions, weaving along riverbeds and over saddles, while trying not to add too much distance to the journey. In this way he was able to determine the most direct route with the least demanding elevation profile. The hundred-and-ten-kilometre journey would take them at least two days to complete.

Their packs contained only essential gear: tents, sleeping bags, navigation equipment, and a Primus Eta PackLite stove, which was a small, collapsible cooking set that could boil water in two minutes and comprised all their culinary needs, including a good-sized pot and a lid that could also be used as a colander.

They had stocked up on supplies in a village shortly after setting out. Even the most remote Karamajong settlements had at least one Somali trader running a supply store in it. Goods arrived through a network that connected remotest Uganda and Kenya to the coast, via the refugee camps, and much of it was stolen from relief-aid supplies. Derek concentrated on high-value, lightweight foodstuffs: maize, dried tilapia, finger millet, cooking oil, sugar and salt. And, although ten litres of water was as much as they could manage, Robert assured them they would find more along the way.

The plan was to cover as much distance as possible on the first day, before camping for the night somewhere in the Kenyan wilderness, and then hike the final stretch to Kakuma the following day. They would pass from Karamoja to Turkanaland, via the Ilemi Triangle, the most dangerous region in Kenya.

Derek stumbled on a trench, ten metres wide and ten metres deep with steep slopes, and said, "Damn, I didn't see *this* on Google Earth."

"There are many more just like it," laughed Robert, his coal-black complexion reflecting the sun with a forceful radiance.

"What's the matter with you?" asked Johnny, putting his hand on Derek's shoulder. "I thought you'd be fitter after all those gorilla treks."

"Fuck you. I take little old ladies on gentle walks in the park. You guys are like early man. Slow down!"

"We've got a timetable to keep." Johnny's timetable contradicted the one preferred by Derek, who believed they should have waited one more day and set off before dawn, like any seasoned hiker would have been inclined to do. Johnny explained that by leaving when they did, they would reach the Kenyan border at around two in the afternoon, when no one, not even wild animals, would be out. Consequently they were trekking in a scorching, mid-morning heat that made grappling with deep trenches all the more tiring.

"*Take a heading of seventy-four degrees, down five hundred metres, for six kilometres, at which point you will reach...*"

"Will you shut that damn thing up," yelled Johnny. "I think we can figure out our way from here, don't you?"

Derek unplugged the speaker from his GPS unit and stuffed it in the pack on his chest. His pride was hurt though he did his best to hide the fact. The roll of one-hundred-dollar bills tucked into the front pocket of his backpack helped. Oceans had offered him ten thousand in cash to guide him to Kakuma – five up front and five on arrival. Ten grand wouldn't go far back in Kampala, but times were tough and he had mounting debts.

He wondered if he should have stuck it out for more money. How much do you charge someone to guide them through the gates of hell? Johnny was certainly not short of a dime. When Derek last saw him he was managing his uncle's casino in Malindi and operating his own fishing charter, but how he managed to make a living in Somalia was anyone's guess.

"Behold the Great Rift Valley," said Derek, drawing a deep, satisfied breath, as they reached the top of the escarpment. They were standing fourteen hundred and eighty metres above sea level, and the ground fell away abruptly beneath them. Without a parallel escarpment on the other side, the valley simply went on forever, a vast region of arid scrubland extending far into northwestern Kenya.

"Sure is some view," said Johnny. "I guess it's all downhill from here."

"Not exactly," said Derek, "but we'll cross that ridge when we come to it."

Johnny looked up, blocking the sun with his left arm. Half a dozen vultures circled overhead. "Aren't they being a bit hasty?"

"Why, do you think you have the mark of death on your head?" laughed Derek. "Don't worry, they're just lappet-faced vultures riding the thermals, like hang gliders."

They stood for a moment, watching the predators spiralling clockwise and counterclockwise above their heads, like a morbid mobile in a giant's playroom.

"We could do with some hang gliders right about now," muttered Johnny.

"No shit, but we would sure as hell alert the Kenyan border patrol to our arrival if we suddenly came swooping down off this ridge in broad daylight like giant birds. I'd say we're much better off on foot."

"Please," said Robert, starting down the slope, "we must continue." Johnny followed and held out his hand to help Derek down the first steep ledge.

"That's quite a watch you got there," said Derek.

"Yeah, it's a Kobold Phantom Tactical. My brother-in-law, Maxamid Malik, gave it to me as a wedding gift."

"Looks expensive. What does your brother-in-law do for a living?"

"He's a pirate."

Around fifty light aircraft were arranged in rows outside half a dozen hangars lining the runway at Wilson Airport, testament to Kenya's booming safari trade as much as the poor condition of its roads. The sun broke briefly through a gap in Nairobi's perennially overcast sky, bathing the airport in brilliance, as the six passengers made their way across the tarmac towards a waiting Cessna Golden Eagle that would take them to Kakuma Refugee Camp. Maddy Jones was among them, looking demure in a navy silk scarf and a baggy blue linen trouser suit, which she'd carefully selected to conceal her figure.

"G'day," she said, the last to clamber aboard. "There's not much room in the back of one of these twin engines, is there?" No sooner had she boarded than the door was closed behind her and the engines began to whine. A middle-aged man from Denmark stood up and offered her his seat on the left-hand side of the cabin, which had the most legroom. It was as though he'd been saving it for her. "Thank you," she said, with a killer smile. He took the seat behind her.

"Everyone buckled in?" asked the pilot, a sun-tanned man with thick sandy hair and a clipped "White Highlander" Kenyan accent. "We'll be taking off in a southeastern direction above Nairobi National Park, before banking steeply to the left over the city, then bearing northwest towards the Rift Valley and on to Turkanaland. Our flying time to Kakuma will be roughly three hours. Enjoy the flight."

After a short taxi down the runway, the plane took off over the park, scattering a herd of hartebeest across the savannah beneath them. *A glimpse of the world through God's eyes...*" thought Maddy, gazing out of the window and imagining she was Meryl Streep in "Out of Africa", one of her all-time favourite movies. But the illusion soon shattered as they flew over a four-lane highway jammed with morning traffic, and the urban sprawl spread out beyond it.

"That's Eastleigh," said the Dane behind her, pointing to a grid of low-rise buildings hemmed in by a mantle of rusted tin roofs, "the biggest Somalian community outside Somalia."

"They're the lucky ones," said Maddy. "They made it this far." When she first heard about the famine in the Horn of Africa, the worst the world had seen in half a century, she knew she had to get involved, and wanted to go where help was most needed: Somalia. But few other countries in the world discourage visitors more successfully; the number of aid workers who'd been abducted or murdered there was unconscionable. So she chose the next best thing: a Somalian refugee camp in Kenya.

On the right-hand side of the plane the slopes of an immense mountain rose up from the fertile highlands like an enormous tree, though the summit remained obscured by a blanket of cloud. "It looks like the old man is hiding his face this morning," said the pilot. Their flight path took them across a patchwork of green fields divided by a dense forest that widened and flowed like a broad green river over a waterfall. "I should warn you that when we cross the escarpment the ride will become much bumpier. This is due to clear air turbulence in the Rift Valley, and it's nothing to worry about."

As if on cue, the twin-engine Cessna began rocking violently from side to side, then jolted upward and plummeted back down again. Everyone gripped their arm rests in horror, as below them the steep and jagged escarpment swung in and out of view. The aircraft continued lurching up and down like a string puppet. Panelling creaked and chairs rattled. Maddy knocked her head against the cabin window. Then, as quickly as it had all started it stopped, and the plane flew on smoothly over the valley. "Like I said, nothing to worry about," said the pilot.

It was midday, and the temperature was well above forty degrees Celsius. Derek was starting to flag but Robert and Johnny had seemingly inexhaustible reserves of energy and insisted on continuing headlong to Kakuma. They were in the middle of the Ilemi Triangle, disputed territory between Kenya and Sudan – the result of a 19th-century colonial farce which had remained unresolved – yet they saw no signs of the lawlessness for which it was renowned.

Mercifully they found themselves on mostly flat terrain. The path ahead of them melted into a haze that looked like a lake. They weren't fooled by the mirage, and besides they had plenty of water. During their descent of the escarpment they had been able to replenish their supply from a trickling brook, which Robert informed them was the Naputiro River. So far they had encountered no other living soul during their trek.

"How far to the border?" asked Johnny, looking around for any sign of it.

Derek stopped, unzipped his front pack and checked his GPS. He then bashed it a few times with his hand. "Looks like my GPS unit is dead." A nearby troop of baboons watched with fearful curiosity.

"Check on your iPad."

"Can't. It's out of juice."

"Great. That's just great, Mr Safari Guide," said Johnny.

"Why don't you ask the swinging dick," snapped Derek, "he should be able to tell us where we are."

"The Karamajong know no borders," said Robert, 'just Karamoja and Turkanaland."

"I'd say we're *already* in Kenya," said Johnny.

"Which means we still have at least seventy-five kilometres more to travel," groaned Derek. He was about to re-shoulder his backpack and resume the hike when he heard one of the baboons utter an alarm call. He glanced up and saw that they were all looking in one direction. There was something crossing the savannah in the distance, so he grabbed his binoculars.

"What is it?" asked Johnny.

"Lion! Eleven o'clock," said Derek, "headed right this way. Check him out on my bins." He handed his binoculars to Johnny, and then noticed that Robert had suddenly become quite agitated.

"Holy shit!" said Johnny. "He can't be more than a hundred

metres away. What the hell do we do if he charges? There's not a goddamn tree in sight!"

"Don't worry, there's very little chance he'll attack in the middle of the day."

"What chance?" asked Robert, who had begun frantically looking in every direction, as though trying to determine an escape plan. "We must run!" he cried.

"Are you out of your mind?" said Derek. "That's the worst thing you could do. He'll think you're scared; that's a sure sign of worthy prey. No, we must casually but confidently get out of his path. C'mon, let's head over this way. Stick together and don't turn your back on him. Slowly...confidently...Oh shit! He's adjusting his bearing."

"Johnny, your pistol," exclaimed Robert, but Johnny already had it in his hand.

"Don't even think about shooting him!" barked Derek. "Just stay calm. Shit, I've never met a Karamajong who doesn't know what to do with fucking a lion..."

The lion was getting nearer. "He doesn't look happy," gasped Johnny.

"Don't look in his eyes; look off to the side. If you can't take your eyes off him, then stare at his tail."

"I can't see his tail!" barked Johnny.

Derek turned to the other two. Their eyes were as wide as saucers. "Don't panic, guys. Just follow my lead. Now, on my say-so, Johnny, you fire a few shots in the air, and Robert, you start shouting, loudly and assertively, but wait until my say-so." The lion began to charge. "Don't move, stand your ground. *No one move.* Ready...*easy now...easy now...*" The lion was barely ten metres away. "OK, *fire!*" Johnny started firing madly in the air, and they all began making loud, deranged noises. The lion skidded to a halt, turned on his heels and bolted. The shooting and bellowing continued unabated for another few seconds until he was out of sight.

"Phew! That was close," said Derek, wiping his brow.

"You did good, Gorilla Man. That's some fucking nerve you got there."

Meanwhile Robert was visibly shaken and had to sit down. "There are no lions in Moroto, where I was raised," he said. "This is the first time in my life I have ever met one."

CHAPTER FOUR

Ali al-Rubaysh's third-storey apartment was bathed in the lustre of late-afternoon sunshine. Located four streets up from the waterfront in al-Mukalla, an ancient port on the Hadramaut Coast of Yemen, he had a commanding view of the Gulf of Aden. *"The sun doesn't rise upon a land that does not contain a man from Hadramaut,"* said Rubaysh, gazing through his picture window at the sea, which sparkled with a thousand pinpoints of shimmering light, as though a silvery leviathan had surfaced from its depths.

As a Hadrami Sayyid, directly descended from Mohammed, Rubaysh could trace his ancestry back millennia to a time when the Arabs from the Hadramaut Coast ruled the entire Indian Ocean. He was also a seasoned terrorist, one-time leader of the Aden-Abyan Islamic Army, former inmate of Guantanamo Bay, and now a military commander in Al-Qaeda Arabian Peninsula, commonly known as AQAP. Consequently, he tried to disguise his high-born features with tussocky facial hair and heavy spectacles, though he usually dressed nobly at home, in a white cotton dish-dash that swayed from side to side as he went about his business.

Watching him from an armchair was Omar Abu Hamza, a twenty-three-year-old al-Shabaab commander from Somalia. He was long and slender, with a complexion like blued steel, and sported a similar beard to Rubaysh's: clean-shaven on his chin, upper lip and cheeks, but bushy around the jowls. He was wearing a grey polyester jacket two sizes too large, and mismatched socks that shot out of his slacks like gun barrels. Their meeting had been kept secret even from their own superiors.

Rubaysh emerged from the kitchen, smiling and carrying a silver tray laden with a mint tea service and a bundle of *khat* he'd bought in the market that afternoon. "So the American got away," he said, placing the tray in the centre of his coffee table. He spoke with an accent that reflected his English public-school education, though often, as now, he purposely tried to sound more Arab, in order to make his guests feel more at home. "And his wife?" Omar shook his head. "At least if you'd captured that *sharmouta*, we could have flushed him out."

He poured the tea into two glass cups, and was about to divide the *khat* into two equal halves but Omar gestured that he would not partake. Unlike the Shabaab mujahideen, Rubaysh and others in AQAP were not averse to chewing *khat*. He sat down opposite his Somali visitor and immediately began plucking the leaves from his half of the bundle, placing them in his mouth, and munching until all the juice had been consumed.

"He knew we were coming," said Omar. "We arrived just minutes too late. If the American is still on the Horn, my men will find him."

"These days you'll find many Americans on the Horn," said Rubaysh, using his tongue to shift the pulp into the corner of his mouth, "mostly in the ranks of your militia, al-Shabaab. We even have blond-haired, blue-eyed jihadists in al-Qaeda! Still, there was only one I was interested in, and that was Mehemet Abdul Rahman...*Inshe Allah*, you have some *good* news for me."

"I could have told you this news by telegraph," snapped Omar. "Why did you insist I come here in person? I had to leave in the middle of the night, at great risk to my own life, and cross the Gulf in high winds and choppy seas. What could be so important to warrant such a visit?"

Rubaysh removed his glasses, pressed his left palm against his chin, swivelled it back and forth a couple of times, then twisted his head sharply clockwise, making a loud cracking sound at the back of his neck. "What I am about to tell you is extremely sensitive, and I did not wish for our messages to fall into the wrong hands. *Masha Allah*, you were able to reach here safely as quickly as you did."

"Thanks to the almighty Allah who sustains all the mujahideen."

"It has not gone unnoticed by al-Qaeda that these days al-Shabaab is fighting the Kafir on many fronts in Somalia, more aggressively than ever before. Now Kenya has invaded, AMISOM has pushed you out of Mogadishu and Kismayo, away from your lucrative port taxes, and the US keep sending those fucking drones. Correct?"

Omar took a few contemplative sips of his tea then said, "We need more money and recruits."

"Is that why Shabaab sold those two Spanish hostages you took in Dadaab? You should have beheaded them. You need to do more terrorising. We have taken you under our wing and now we must fly together. *Allahu Akbar*. The problem is Shabaab militants are all concentrated in the south, fighting a conventional war. The north is rich pickings for jihad."

"That is why we have established a base in Galaga, in the Karkaar Mountains, but the Majeerteen are racists who despise outsiders, unlike al-Shabaab who welcomes all mujahideen who wish to defend Islam."

"So, you teach the racists a lesson," proclaimed Rubaysh, putting down his tea. "And it must be done now, because the Majeerteen are becoming too rich from this piracy business, and soon they will be powerful. Strike a blow at the heart of Puntland," he said, beating his fist into the palm of his hand, "as you did in 2008, and then another, and another." They glared at each other for a second. Both pairs of eyes were unemotional, as though they no longer drew blood from their hearts. They were cold-blooded killers.

Rubaysh sat back and breathed deeply. "Look at me. The Americans gave me a badge of honour when they sent me to that Cuban pig pen of theirs. They tried to break me with torture, but instead they turned me into a better warrior."

"This is why we have aligned ourselves with al-Qaeda," said Omar. "Al-Shabaab also want to fight the Kafir. But they are cowards, and they hide. A mujahideen will bravely martyr himself in an American aeroplane, but they refuse to even put pilots in the ones they send in retaliation."

Rubaysh leaned forward and put his hand on Omar's shoulder. "They have failed to see the bridge that connects us, my friend. South Yemenis have always been closer to Somalians than we are with the rest of the Arab world. *This* is our true identity."

Omar nodded sagely. Rubaysh pulled him closer and rasped, "We'll part the sea as Musa did." His words hung there for a moment, like gold-embroidered Arabic on a black velvet wall hanging. Then he stood up and moved towards the window. The light had faded from the apartment, and the sun was sinking fast. "The Gulf of Aden…How many million barrels of oil do you suppose pass through it every day?"

"I don't know," said Omar.

"Ten per cent of the world's oil trade. That's millions of barrels a day, worth billions of dollars…Al-Qaeda has grown stronger during the Arab Spring, especially in Yemen. Our forces are better-trained and more sophisticated now."

A muezzin's call reminded them of their religious duty. "Come," said Rubaysh, "let us go to the mosque and pray to Allah. We have much to thank him for."

"You still haven't told me why you called me here."

"Ah, yes," said Rubaysh, smiling. He reached into a briefcase beside his chair, retrieved a sheet of paper and handed to Omar. "Look at this diagram." It showed two drums side by side tethered to the seabed beneath the surface over which sailed a ship.

Omar pointed to the symbol H_2S written across the drums, and asked, "What does that stand for?"

"Hydrogen sulphide," smiled Rubaysh. "It kills instantly." Omar nodded profoundly and rubbed his chin. "The drums can be made to any size. Triggered remotely they quickly rise to the surface. Once in contact with air, they explode with a cloud of deadly noxious gas."

"Ingenious," laughed Omar.

"You see how we have adapted, my Somali friend...I promise you, when we're through with them, the Kafir will have shed enough tears to turn the deserts into oceans."

CHAPTER FIVE

Khadija Abdul Rahman and Abdu Takar stood on the beach outside her compound in Bender Siyaada under the midday sun – two elegant blemishes on an otherwise flawless canvas of azure, turquoise and beige. Abdu was dressed in a blue *macawiis*, a traditional sarong, and a plain white shirt, and Khadija was wearing a long white rippling *direh*. It was only three days after the attack, but she refused to hide any longer; her American husband Mehemet may have been forced to flee Puntland, but she would not be a prisoner in her own land.

Workmen were dismantling her gate. The Arabic words written across it in bullet holes made her stomach turn, but she refused to be a victim of terror. Her compound was as she had left it: an oasis of shady palms. The cupola-capped, white-stone building had been built by her grandfather, and was her home when she was a young child. Later, it formed part of her dowry, though her first husband never stayed for very long. Only after she got married the second time, to Mehemet, did she feel secure enough to move back in to Bender Siyaada.

She hesitated before entering, fearing what she might find beyond the large wooden Zanzibari door. Abdu stepped in front of her and gently pushed it open. She gasped. The place had been ransacked. Lamps were overturned, cushions ripped open, glassware and crockery in pieces everywhere. It was difficult to know where to start. "*Inshe Allah*, I will not let this defeat me," she whispered. "I am determined to put back everything as it was."

Stepping through the detritus strewn across her living-room floor, she carefully collected various fragments of broken possessions, and tried to piece them back together: heirlooms handed down through generations. She spotted a portrait of her late father, lying smashed into a million pieces on the floor. She picked it up and held it to her breast, sat down heavily on her couch with her shoulders gently heaving, and then dropped her head into her hand. "Please don't cry," said Abdu, touching her shoulder.

Khadija's childhood had been painful. She was born just eight months after Major General Mohamed Siad Barre took power in Somalia. Her fondest memories were of her father. He was a poet and a musician, but also an outspoken critic of "Comrade Siad", who had him imprisoned in 1974, when Khadija was just four years old. That was also the year Puntland experienced the *Abaartii Dabadheer*, "the Lingering Drought", and the Majeerteen faced starvation if they remained in the north. Her mother was five months pregnant when she joined the exodus heading south, with little Khadija in tow. After travelling fifteen hundred kilometres across the desert, on a succession of buses, cars, beasts of burden and foot, they eventually reached a refugee camp in Kismayo. The day they arrived they learned that Khadija's father had been killed in prison. It was the saddest day of her life. Her brother, who was born in the camp, never knew his father, but Khadija remembered him fondly and adored him.

"Where's my brother?" she asked, wiping the tears from her eyes, but Abdu pretended he had not heard her. "I asked you, where is Maxamid Malik?"

"He's in jail," said Abdu.

"Again?" she shouted.

"The Puntland Coast Guard brought him in yesterday."

"*How!* Those fools never do their jobs."

"It was a clan dispute. You know how those things happen. Maxamid's just too hotheaded."

"Well, get him out of there, Abdu. I need him by my side."

"I'm afraid there's more bad news," said Abdu, stepping backward. "It's about your son, Nadif."

Khadija leapt to her feet. "What about him?"

"Al-Shabaab has been trying to recruit him at his madrasa."

"*Bastards!* How dare they? Where is he?"

"He's at your mother's in Bosaso."

Khadija began to move decisively around her house. She had to reach Bosaso, twenty kilometres away, before the muezzins' call to prayer. Nadif would naturally want to go to the mosque. Abdu offered to drive but she insisted on going alone. "I want a meeting with the clan elders," she said, as she jumped into the driver's seat of her Land Cruiser, "*tonight*, in Bender Siyaada!" She then sped out of her compound and headed east in the direction of the Puntland capital.

"*Badaadintu badah*", Somali for "survivors of the sea", was carved across the wall above the heads of the scores of prisoners confined in a five-by-five-metre lockup in Bosaso Prison, next to the port. Their cell had no beds, no toilets, and just one small ocean-facing window, too high to reach on another man's shoulders. The only other exit was a solid iron door, riddled with corrosion but nevertheless impermeable. On the rare occasions it was opened, the cross-breeze provided momentary relief from the stench of excrement, rot and sweat.

Eighteen pirates had just been brought in, all captured by the Combined Task Force 150 in the Gulf of Aden. The new arrivals were greeted with high-fives, hugs and the knocking of fists: a fraternity of *badaadintu badah*. Whatever gangs they belonged to they had one thing in common: they were all Majeerteen fishermen. They did not fight among themselves, as they had common vested interests and a great sense of clan pride. It was against their code to behave as thugs when on shore. Every one of them could recite the litany of injustices that forced them to trade in their fishing nets for weapons, and hijack whatever foreign ships they found in Somali waters.

Maxamid Malik stood in the middle of a row of men with his back against a wall that abutted the ocean, where a light spray sometimes rained down on their heads. It was an exclusive spot. He led his own gang of pirates from a base on the Hafun Peninsula, two hundred and fifty kilometres away, on the other side of the Horn. He glared at the other prisoners with a fearsome expression, manifest in feral eyes, bony cheeks and thin grey lips. At nearly two metres tall he could scare the hell out of a ship's crew even before he boarded. "How long can there be honour among thieves," he asked, scratching his hennaed goatee, "when even the sea complains of starvation?"

"Maxamid," shouted one of the new arrivals, striding forward to knock fists with the lanky pirate, "we missed you in the Gulf." It was Faraad, one of many who had set out from Hafun in a multi-gang flotilla a few days before, intent on launching a surge of attacks in the Gulf of Aden. He was short, with a stocky build, and had a receding hairline.

"We were unlucky," said Maxamid. "We sailed too close to the wind, and got nabbed near Abdul al Kuri. Who caught you?"

"American Navy," growled Faraad, "near Aden."

"We were arrested by Puntland Coast Guard," said Ibrahim, another pirate from Maxamid's ranks who was standing next to him, "and they confiscated our skiff."

"What?" cried Faraad. "Those bastards never do their jobs."

"They did not stop any other boats in the flotilla," said Maxamid, "yet no amount of bribes could persuade them to change their minds about escorting us to Bosaso." He paused to listen to the sound of hull and engines skimming across the port. "We were set up. And I have a pretty good idea who was behind it. As soon as I am released from here, I will rectify the situation."

"God forbid, they will destroy our livelihoods, and we will die hungry in the desert."

The entire cell was suddenly silenced by a thunderous clang followed by a piercing creaking sound, as the iron door was unbolted and swung open. Then came an uproarious cheer. "What is it?" asked Faraad, who was too short to see the cause of the commotion.

"Time for *khat*," snapped Maxamid.

Khadija's mind was not on her driving. The coastal route to Bosaso was less a road than a series of tracks over a broad swathe of semi-desert plain, where she rarely encountered another vehicle. The sun was low in a cloudless azure sky that stretched from the sea to the Karkaar mountains, their shadows tumbling into each other like colossal dominoes. That's where al-Shabaab militants had their base. The authorities knew where they were, and regularly sent soldiers to raid their hideout in Galaga. Yet somehow they kept their foothold in Puntland. "They will not take my son," she cried, gripping the steering wheel of her Land Cruiser.

Was anybody listening to the voices of Somali women? Like Khadija, most of them had endured intolerable tragedy in the name of jihad, orphans and widows who'd lost parents, siblings, husbands and children. The restrictions on women, derived from archaic tradition, demanded that they somehow endure it all in silence. Any Somali woman who stood up to her man was seen as wild and deviant.

But things were changing now. She was surprised to find a consensus among her "old girls" from Eastleigh Academy when she caught up with them on Twitter and Facebook. None was afraid to speak out any more.

"Somali women have been disturbingly silent for too long," posted one. "It's time to stop the unbridled atrocities being perpetrated by our brothers in the name of Islam."

"If you are brave, and love Somalia," another tweeted, "form a united front against al-Shabaab, which is bent on destroying our culture and faith."

"I don't know of a single Somali woman undeserving of praise, nor one who doesn't think she had a strong mother."

"Somali women must be strong, in order to stay sane when our faraxs have gone insane."

Khadija truly believed the common-sense attitude she found among Somali women could somehow be channelled towards genuine change in her country. Solidarity through social networks was a proven force in the world today, as ordinary people had clearly demonstrated during the Arab Spring. But Somalia lacked a recognisable government to demonstrate against, let alone a square in which to gather in protest. Change would have to come despite of that.

She checked her iPhone to see if there were any new messages, then her Twitter account – @QueenArawello – which had so far attracted a thousand followers. She slowed down. A familiar obstruction lay ahead, a lagoon about eighty metres wide, which flowed across the road. It appeared shallow enough, but during the rainy season it was impassable, and motorists were forced to take a bumpy detour that added a half hour to the journey. She could ill afford any delays now, so she accelerated and drove straight through it, sending a plume of saline water upward like giant green butterfly wings.

With the flat, empty landscape before her stretching from horizon to horizon, she put her pedal to the metal, and accelerated to a hundred and twenty kilometres per hour. Her rear-view mirror was vibrating so dramatically, it obscured her view and at first she didn't notice the beat-up white pickup truck approaching from behind. She didn't expect to find anyone else on the road. Soon it was tailgating her, swerving erratically from side to side, and blasting its horn. She tried to make out the driver but there was too much dust and grime on her trail. This had all the hallmarks of a terrorist kidnapping. She veered to the right to allow him to overtake, but he followed her, so she signalled for him to pass, but he remained on her tail. She could not shake him.

Suddenly the pickup truck accelerated and swerved around her, and Khadija saw half a dozen armed men seated in the back, wearing military fatigues with red checkered keffiyeh wrapped around their heads. She immediately screeched to a halt, tossing a plume of sand into the air that completely enveloped her Land Cruiser. Bosaso was at least five kilometres away. With no one else in sight, she had no means of escape.

When the dust had settled she saw her car was surrounded by armed men with their faces hidden by their *keffiyeh*. "Get out of the vehicle!" commanded one militant, rapping on her window with the butt of his AK-47. Khadija popped the handle of her door and, using both hands, slowly eased it open, forcing the men to back away. Then she stepped out and stood beside her car, next to the "No Weapons" sticker on her door. "Where are you going?" barked the militant.

"I have urgent business in Bosaso to attend to," said Khadija, trying to remain calm.

"Why aren't you wearing your burka?" he shouted.

"There is no fatwa in Puntland that requires it," said Khadija.

"Women should wear the burka at all times when in public!"

"Wearing the burka is not a religious practice, and, as far as I'm concerned, it is the face of jihad. I am not a soldier in your holy war."

"You conduct yourself like a *Kafir*! Since when does a woman drive a car? *Sharmouta!*" The militant spat on the ground and then stepped closer to Khadija. "Islam forbids a woman to drive a car."

"No, it does not," she said, easing back. "I have been driving a car for twenty years."

"You should stay in your house, wear the *hijab* and abstain from showing off your adornments to non-*mahrams*, with fear of Allah."

"I don't need you to teach me my faith."

"Where is your husband?" he barked.

"Where is your wife?" she snapped. The militant raised his weapon and aimed it at her chest. Then a voice from the pickup truck ordered him to cease. The men retreated and climbed back into their vehicle. Khadija slumped against her car and clutched her forehead. The fear she had dared not display now ran across her like a clutch of spiders.

In a deep gorge tucked away in the foothills of the Karkaar mountains, the militants clambered out of their white pickup truck and started up a trail. One of them moved more purposefully than the others, striding ahead through the sandstone passes, draped in metres of ammunition. "Stay close behind," he said. After a short distance they heard a whistle like the peal of a hawk, and the lead man stopped.

"What is it?" asked the man behind him.

"A signal," he replied, and whistled back three times. There was no response, which meant they could proceed. They walked a dozen more metres, passing through the shadows of a narrow ravine and around sheer walls of sandstone, before coming upon the remains of a house that had been built into the rocks. A large black flag with "global jihad" written across it in white Arabic was fluttering above the heads of five heavily armed men who stood guard at the entrance to the house with their keffiyeh wrapped around their faces. Mehmet Abdul Rahman's M-60 machine gun was propped up beside the door.

"Are these the bomb makers from Kismayo?" asked one of the mujahideen standing at the entrance.

"Yes," said the man draped in bandoliers of ammunition. "Can I speak to Omar?"

"He's not here."

"Where is he?"

"He did not say where he was going. You can speak to me. I'm in charge."

"I've brought the armour-piercing ammo for the American gun he asked for."

Ahmed picked up the heavy, cumbersome gun next to the door. "This one? It's a stupid weapon, always jamming, belonged to the Kafir who ran away."

"We have just seen his wife," said the ammunition man, divesting himself of the ammunition. "Khadija Abdul Rahman."

"What? That *sharmouta* is no longer in hiding? Where is she now?"

"We found her on the road."

"And you let her go? This is something Omar will want to know."

The sun was setting over the Arabian Sea at Bender Siyaada. The two dozen armed guards posted inside and outside Khadija's compound were less a show of concern for her security than of the self-importance of the half dozen Majeerteen elders who'd come to hear what she had to say. It was quite a turnout considering what short notice they'd been given, but Abdu Takar was insistent they respond wholeheartedly to their daughter's request for a council.

Her children, whom she'd fetched from various relatives in Bosaso, were now safely at home, and Khadija was upstairs tucking the last of them into bed. She had her hair tied back in a ponytail and she'd changed into black tight-fitting jeans, and a black T-shirt with the words "Terrorism has no religion" written across it in red, stylised Arabic.

"Can you please tell us the story of Queen Arawello?" asked her daughter Amina, who was eight years old, and the youngest of her four children. "She's the greatest Somali hero."

"Not tonight, Amina. We have important company downstairs."

"Oh please, mommy!"

"But you have heard that story so many times already," said Khadija, squeezing her daughter's cheeks then fluffing up her pillow.

"Yes, but I always like hearing it again. The way Grandma tells it is different than the way Uncle Abdu tells it. I like the way you tell it the best."

"That's because she tells us the *real* story," snapped her sister Layla.

"Well," said Khadija, "I guess I can give you the abridged version."

"Yay!"

"The great Queen Arawello was the last Queen of the Akisho, and she ruled Somalia five hundred years ago. Some say her kingdom stretched across the Horn of Africa, and that the Queen of Sheba and Queen Nzinga of Angola sent her gifts of gold to sustain her during her reign."

"What did she look like?" asked Amina.

"Arawello stood taller than most men. She was strong, with a muscular build, and kept her jet-black hair tied back to accentuate her aquiline features."

"Just like Mommy!"

"Just like me. Now, as legend has it, when she was a teenage girl her village was hit hard by drought and all the cattle and sheep died.

Arawello vowed she would feed her people, and, armed only with a home-made spear, she set out one day to the woods to hunt. Even after darkness fell upon the forest she continued to hunt, though she began to see strange figures in the tree trunks, animals dashing through the thorns, and feared she was the one now being hunted. There were many lions in that part of the forest."

"Could she kill a lion with her bare hands?" asked Amina, squirming under her covers.

"No she could not, little one," said Khadija, positioning herself on Amina's bed so she could stroke both her daughters' heads. "Nor was it a lion that leapt on her that night, though some people like to tell the story that way for younger ears. The truth is she was raped, by a man who had been stalking her. And this would stay with her for the rest of her life. They say it's the reason she resented men so much, and inflicted such cruelty on them during her reign."

"What did she do to them?" asked Layla.

"To hear a Somali man tell it," laughed Khadija, "she castrated them, and had an appetite for it, and that female circumcision is revenge for her wickedness." Both girls giggled. "The truth is Queen Arawello was a powerful, matriarchal ruler who was a breadwinner for all of society. She believed that the emancipation of women was a condition to establishing lasting peace throughout her kingdom, and overcoming famine."

"Which is why men say she castrated them," said Layla sardonically.

"OK, girls. Lights off! *Lala salaama…*"

"Oh please, Mommy, tell us more. Like, how did she die…"

"C'mon. Amina, Layla. Off to sleep now." She kissed them both goodnight, turned off the light and left, carefully closing their bedroom door behind her.

When she reached the bottom of the stairs she passed Nadif sitting stoically at the dining-room table, within earshot and view of the assembly of clan elders but strictly prohibited from speaking to it. The elders were seated on white plastic chairs in the living room, drinking mint tea, and sporting cotton prayer caps and dark, sombre *macawiis*. Khadija stepped over the debris still strewn across her disarranged living-room floor, to a position where she could address them all. "Do you see the writing on the wall?" she asked, but no one answered. Anyone doubting the seriousness of what she had to say was quickly checked by an intense glower. She wasn't playing. "Either you don't see it or you just simply choose to ignore it, but militant Islamism has invaded Puntland."

"Oh come now, Khadija," chuckled an elder, as he peered over his large spectacles. "There are no jihadists here. We have driven the Islamists underground."

"Are you blind? They're not underground, they're out, clearly visible in the light of day. Look at the state of my house, Did you read what they wrote on my gate? And this afternoon, on my way to Bosaso. What the hell was that? They killed my first husband, sent my second into exile, I won't let them take my son." She glanced at Nadif, who shifted uncomfortably in his chair but did not return her gaze.

"Isn't this a matter for the mullahs?" asked the elder.

"Who," snapped Khadija, "the Wahabi running our madrasas? They're the ones filling the heads of our young people with jihad."

"It's not so easy to stop them, Khadija," said Abdu Takar, raising his eyebrows and smoothing his brown *macawiis*. Over his shoulder he wore a burgundy shawl, from which he plucked small errant threads as he spoke. "You know how they work, Khadija. First they make generous proposals to build a new mosque or madrasa, saying they will pay for everything, but only on condition that we hand over the title deed to the land. After that we have no say about who they appoint as their imams and teachers."

"Right," snapped Khadija, "because they just want to brainwash our children into blowing themselves up…They are hyenas, preying on the most vulnerable in our society. Nadif is defenceless against them."

The most senior clan elder raised his hand. He had a thick fringe of kinky silver hair around the back of his head and his chin, and a brown spotty bald pate, which gave him the look of a large tiger cowrie. "Puntland does not tolerate Islamist militia," he said sombrely. "We have taken great steps to keep the threat of jihad out…"

"I see, and that's why there's an al-Shabaab base just thirty kilometres from this house? You're allowing fundamentalism to creep into our society, and turning a blind eye to the pirates while they mercilessly hijack ship after ship for ransoms that are only ever squandered."

"Khadija, let me speak, please. I agree we should not turn a blind eye to the threats you mention, and I am outraged by what has happened to Nadif...Let me speak to the imam at the madrasa."

"The man is an ignorant zealot! When I was young the Shaykhs were well educated men, well versed in the Quran, Hadith and Sunnah. I admired them. Nowadays any fool can put on a white robe, grow a beard and call himself a Shaykh. Some of these people can't even read the Quran, let alone interpret it, so you mustn't be surprised if they take it all literally."

Just then the heavy front door opened and Maxamid Malik stepped through it, carrying his Browning Automatic Rifle. "*Salaam alaikum,*" he said, staring wide-eyed at everyone, while propping the ungainly Second World War weapon against the wall. He had on a dusky camel leather jacket over a white shirt, blue jeans and pair of expensive Nike shoes, and he stood taller than the door frame.

"*Walaikum a-salaam,*" they responded.

"Where have you been?" asked Abdu Takar. "Mining salt at Aftal?"

"You know damn well where I've been," growled Maxamid, strutting into the centre of the room wearing a fearsome expression, "because you're the one who put me there."

"How can you accuse me of such a thing," asked Abdu, "when I spent the entire afternoon fighting for your release?"

"Don't play games with me, Abdu! You sold me out to the Coast Guard."

"I'm happy you've been released from prison, Maxamid," said Khadija calmly, knowing his anxiety was probably a result of him chewing *khat* all afternoon, "but as you can see we're having a meeting."

"That's OK," said the most senior elder. "We're all leaving now."

"No," snapped Maxamid, scratching his copper-wool goatee. "You will hear what I have to say." Khadija, realising she had been upstaged by her brother, shifted to a chair next to her son at the dining-room table. The elders sat back down, dumbfounded by his irreverent tone. "How many of you rely on contributions from the pirate gangs?" asked Maxamid. A couple of elders adjusted their positions in their seats, three cleared their throats, and another folded his arms across his chest. "Too many. We give you thirty per cent of our ransoms."

"Your takings were small last year," said the elder wearing spectacles, feebly toying with his *macawiis*. "We can no longer rely on your contributions."

Maxamid laughed. "You think you can survive without us? The *badaadintu badah* have defended this clan above all else."

"And, in return, we have defended you."

"Yet you can do nothing about the international maritime armada out there cracking down on us day and night, and the prisoners pouring into Bosaso and Aden jails. But do you think now you can just dispense with us?" Maxamid walked slowly towards Abdu Takar.

"Remember the clan code, Maxamid..." said the bespectacled elder.

"I'm telling you, it's all about survival now," he replied, staring down Abdu Takar. "I have a wife and six children in Hafun to feed, and if it comes down to my family or the clan code..."

"Would you all just listen to yourselves," yelled Khadija, leaping to her feet. "It's no wonder we live in hell when our *faraxs* behave like hyenas. *You should all be castrated!*"

CHAPTER SIX

"The Turks are very proud of this one," said Frank Paterson, the regional head of the World Food Programme. He was propped up on the edge of Maddy Jones's desk in her new office at Kakuma Refugee Camp, cooling himself with a rattan fan, a towering, portly, forty-something Australian with glistening jowls. Maddy hadn't expected a meeting with him on her arrival, but he was flying out on the same twin engine she flew in on, and only had minutes to spare. "It shows off their muscle in the Muslim world," he added, handing her a document, paper-clipped to a photograph of a large container ship.

"How much are they donating?" asked Maddy, examining the document.

"Two hundred thousand tonnes of food, and they want us to deliver the whole lot in one go. So, we'll be shipping it on the TSC *Tristola*, an ultra-large container ship, which is capable of carrying half a million tonnes of food."

"Where on earth are you going to put the thing?" asked Maddy, folding the paper, and then her arms, with incredulity.

"Mogadishu," he replied. "Not many people know this but, ever since Somali government forces recaptured the port from al-Shabaab, engineers have been busy deepening the harbour in preparation for this class of container ship. And there'll be more in the future. The upgrade will vastly cut down cost and increase our efficiency in delivering aid to the Horn of Africa."

Maddy stood stroking her chin. "And when can we expect this monster ship?"

"She'll sail from the Bosporus next Tuesday, clearing the Suez a day later, and cross the Gulf of Aden with an Indian Navy escort the day after that. That should bring her into Mogadishu port exactly a week from now. With any luck we'll have the trucks up here within two weeks. We'll be using a new tracking system called GT Nexus, which will automatically send you emails when the ship reaches key positions en route. That'll be for your eyes only, Maddy."

"You know you can rely on me."

"I should warn you, Kenya's invasion of Somalia has brought about a few changes at Kakuma. We're now operating under a total information blackout. There have been threats from al-Shabaab that they will strike at targets inside Kenya. We're all on high alert."

"And my first food distribution cycle is the day after tomorrow?"

"Yes. Baptism by fire, I'm afraid."

"You stuck your neck out for me, Frank," sighed Maddy. "Nonetheless, I'm on this one, mate. It'll be hard work but I'll give it a go. I won't let you down."

"You were the best candidate to apply for the job. You know that, don't you, Mad?"

Maddy gazed demurely at the floor. Frank had been her superior years previously, while she worked at the Christmas Island Detention Centre. She wasn't entirely convinced of his motives for endorsing her application for the job, as she hadn't even been aware he was on the World Food Programme's recruitment board.

"It's mostly logistics. The data you give us about how much food has been distributed at Kakuma has to be up-to-the-minute and completely error-free. The more accurate your information, the more mouths we feed. You'd do well to remember that."

"I'll do my best, mate."

CHAPTER SEVEN

"Beats the hell out of Kabul," said Lieutenant Simon Hay to a mate on his cell phone. "At least you can de-stress here." He was enjoying a Tusker beer and few moments' relaxation following two days of security briefings for aid workers in the conference room of the Fairview Hotel. It was his last afternoon in Nairobi. His flight to London was leaving at midnight. Despite his formidable size, he was dwarfed by the massive jacaranda and yellow-barked acacia trees that commanded the hotel's spectacular grounds.

He took note of the Israeli security guards patrolling the grounds. Their embassy was just across the street, and they were there with the hotel proprietor's consent to help keep this leafy block on Nairobi Hill secure from terror attacks. He acknowledged them with an almost imperceptible gesture. One of them smiled back and started to walk towards him. "All right, mate. Gotta go. I'll call you when I get into Brize Norton."

"Lieutenant Hay," said the security guard, with a strong Israeli accent, "can you come this way please. I'd like you to pass through the hotel metal detector."

"Don't worry," smiled Hay, "I have a permit for my Glock."

"I understand, Lieutenant. I would like to check for any others you might have concealed." Hay frowned but knew the routine and followed him to the metal detector located in the car park. An extra-large shirt concealed the weapon holstered in the small of the guard's back. Hay made the usual checks of the car park, but apart from two Kenyan askaris manning the gate, there were no other individuals in the vicinity. Every car was parked – no engines running.

He removed his Glock from its belt and handed it to the Israeli security guard who then instructed him to walk through the detector. As he did, he was struck hard at the base of his skull with his own pistol, and knocked out cold. A parked car suddenly started its engine and raced forward. The Israeli guard hastily picked up the massive hulk of Simon Hay and threw him in the back of the car. The askaris began shouting, and the two other Israelis scrambled to the scene, firing their Uzis through the thick foliage surrounding the car park. They were all quickly taken out by the rogue guard with his machine pistol. He then shouted instructions to the driver in Arabic as he dashed to open the crash barrier. Within seconds, they were gone.

Once in the vehicle, the captive was given a heavy dose of tranquilliser to make sure he offered no resistance. They quickly transferred him through a number of backstreets to an abandoned house in Eastleigh. A video camera was swiftly attached to a tripod. The captive was then dragged into a chair. A hood was placed over his head and his hands were tied behind his back. Three fighters gathered behind him, adrenaline pumping for the savage acts they were about to commit. Swords were brandished and placed at their captive's throat.

A fighter whose identity was obscured by his turban leaned close to his captive's ear and hissed, "When the blood of an Englishman is spilled, the world takes notice. But when hundreds of Somalis die they don't even make the news." With those words he called on God's will, and the beheading began. After a few excruciating moments, during which Lieutenant Simon Hay begged for mercy, it was all over. The video was posted on YouTube.

Derek, Johnny and Robert had been walking endlessly across badlands, mountain ranges, and the barren, unguarded frontier through which passes the borderline between Uganda and Kenya. They had begun to see vehicles in the distance, driving along on a road that ran parallel to the path they were following. Despite having no means of confirming it, they estimated they were less than ten kilometres from Kakuma Refugee Camp.

Robert walked behind, deep in his thoughts, while Derek and Johnny led the way, side by side. Derek was wearing a cheesecloth scarf around his neck, long-sleeved shirt and trousers, and trekking sandals, all in neutral bush tones, which camouflaged him in his surroundings. Johnny on the other hand had chosen an extra-large turquoise Hawaiian shirt to wear, which made him stand out like a battle standard. The terrain was flat and unchanging, with more anthills than acacia trees scattered across it, and the vegetation was mostly colourless shrubs and thorn bushes.

All around them was the sound of whistling. "The whistling thorn tree," said Derek. "See those bulbous swellings at the base of each spine cluster? Ants inhabit them and the holes they drill cause the wind to whistle as it blows through the tree. No one's sure if the relationship is symbiotic or not."

As they tramped the final stretch, questions began to mount in Derek's mind, things that didn't quite add up about Johnny's story. "Back in 1998, when you pulled your escape act out there on the Malindi-Watamu Bank, was I set up?"

"The truth?" asked Johnny.

"Yes please!"

"OK, after I quit the casino job, I needed out from the family, so I decided to stage my own abduction. I paid some dhow fishermen five hundred dollars to sail me up around the Horn, and *badda bing*, I disappeared. *Capisce?*"

Derek stopped in his tracks. "Holy shit! You bastard! I was your fucking patsy...and you left *me* to explain everything to your gumbas. I can't believe you set me up!"

"*Forgedaboudit!* I knew you'd manage."

"I thought there was something fishy about your story," said Derek, stomping indignantly onward across the rocky terrain while shaking his head in disbelief. "Somali pirates, right...But why go to Somalia in the first place?"

"It goes back to the Second World War. My grandfather Capitano Luigi Salvatore was stationed in Africa Orientale Italiana, today's Eritrea, Ethiopia, South Central Somalia and Puntland. Somaliland belonged to the British. Capitano Salvatore's division, the Granatieri di Savoia, under the command of Generale Guglielmo Nasi, was part of the force that conquered British Somaliland in 1940: Italy's greatest victory in the war. Then, while his unit was on patrol somewhere in the desert, they stumbled on a valuable antiquity. Right then and there all twelve men swore a blood oath never to tell anyone of its whereabouts."

"What was the valuable antiquity?" asked Derek. "Didn't your grandfather ever tell anyone?"

"He never got a chance. Eight months later, his entire unit got wiped out by British forces in Dongolaas Gorge. His name is among the many thousands of Italians who died in the Battle of Keren in Eritrea."

"May he rest in peace," said Derek, scratching his beard. "So, grandfather Luigi went to his grave without ever telling anyone about its location or anything?"

"So I was led to believe."

"Oh, the plot thickens..."

"You see, when I was growing up I was fascinated by the stories I'd heard about Nonno Luigi's treasure. When I was old enough, my grandmother gave me his letters to read. I studied them over and over again, and began to find clues written between the lines, anagrams and riddles. Obviously the men in his unit were screening every letter he wrote. Italians take their blood oaths quite seriously.

"I decided it must have been somewhere in Sanaag province. But my chance to go search for it didn't come until 1992 when Uncle Bobby invited me to run his casino in Malindi. After that I began to make regular trips to Puntland whenever work would allow."

"How did you know where to look?"

"All I had to go by were Nonno Luigi's letters. In them he makes many confusing references to 'a beady sardine', in English. I started asking around with the local fishermen and I found one guy who had heard about the discovery made by the Italians in the desert during the war. He told me to look near Bender Siyaada, which it turns out is an anagram of 'a beady sardine'."

"Cool, so did you find the treasure?"

"I sure did, then buried it again."

"Where?"

"Why the hell should I tell you?"

"Jesus, you've already strung me a whole load of half-truths to get me to follow you into the most inhospitable corner of Africa, you might as well give me something."

"*Forgedaboudit!*"

"C'mon," laughed Derek, mock-punching Johnny in the shoulder. "I was your patsy. You fucking owe me!"

"I'll tell you what," said Johnny, unclasping his watch and handing it to him, "you can have my Kobold."

"Wow!" sighed Derek, strapping the heavy chronograph to his wrist then holding it up against the sun to admire it.

"You can single-handedly invade Iran with one of those," laughed Johnny. "And that titanium bracelet screw-locks to prevent it being torn from your wrist."

Suddenly a loud cracking noise came from up ahead and Johnny let out a groan. Derek turned to see him staring in bewilderment at his stomach where a patch of red began to expand across the turquoise palm and surf pattern. He appeared to have been shot. Another shot followed directly and this time he dropped to his knees and collapsed.

"Take cover!" shouted Robert, dashing forward with frantic strides and then throwing his spear. Derek dived behind an anthill. There was a burst of semi-automatic gunfire and Robert tumbled to the ground.

Moments later, three tall Turkana tribesmen appeared from the thorn bushes, one carrying a rifle, the other two AK-47s, and walked over to the where the bodies of Johnny and Robert lay. Not one of them even glanced at the anthill where Derek was hiding. One of the Turkana drew his wrist blade across Robert's throat, and then he did the same to Johnny. Derek gasped in horror; he was sure they would come after him next. But the three men quietly walked back into the thicket and disappeared.

CHAPTER EIGHT

"What time do you call this, boy?" bellowed Derek's father, who was slouched in an armchair next to a dim floor lamp, barely visible in the gloom of their seaside apartment in Dar-es-Salaam. An opened envelope lay on his arm rest over which he held a tumbler full of whisky in his woolly hand, while his head bobbed up and down like a coconut adrift at sea.

"I was celebrating at the yacht club," said Derek, brandishing a sailing trophy. "Our crew won first place in the regatta this afternoon."

"You said you would be back before nine!" the old man slurred in a gruff Glaswegian tone, glaring at his son through bloodshot eyes. "When are you going to bloody learn to be responsible?"

"I could ask you the same question," replied Derek, walking into the room and picking up the empty bottle of Johnnie Walker Black Label from the coffee table.

"Don't give me your lip, boy! Or I'll give you the back of my hand – the one with my ring finger."

"I'm seventeen years old, Dad. I'm not a kid any more."

"While you're living under *my* roof," he snapped, "you'll obey *my* orders."

Derek retreated to the kitchen to defuse the argument. There was nothing he dreaded more than coming home to a drunken father. For three years they had lived together in Tanzania, just the two of them, and they were the worst years of his young life. Angrily opening and shutting cupboard after cupboard while looking in vain for something to eat, he muttered under his breath, "Fucking Scots hothead...*drunken, womanising git...*"

A skilled engineer, Bobby Strangely had emigrated from Scotland to Canada in the 1950s to build bridges in the Quebec interior. There he met Derek's mother, Genevieve, a beautiful young Iroquois woman, to whom he proposed. Even apart from their religious differences – he was Protestant and she was Catholic – they came from completely different cultures. Consequently, their union was disavowed by everyone in their respective communities. Nonetheless they married and relocated to Montréal to start a family. Born in 1962, Derek was the last of three children. Four years later, his father was sent to build more bridges, this time in East Africa, and the infant Derek moved with his family to Nairobi.

To begin with, life in the Tropics was sweet, touring the game parks, meeting nice people, collecting cowries on the reef at low tide. The lifestyle surpassed everyone's expectations, except Derek's. He didn't have any. As far as he knew this is what childhoods were meant to be like.

Tanzania had everything: the fossil remains of oldest man, the biggest and best game parks, Serengeti, Ngorongoro, Kilimanjaro, Zanzibar, Jane Goodall, and the most superlative beaches in the world. Expatriates were willing to put up with the irregular political machinations of the Tanganyika African National Union, which ran the country under President Julius K. Nyerere, for the sumptuous lifestyle.

Everyone scuba-dived, sailed boats or toured the game parks whenever possible, recounting their adventures to gasps of astonishment or roars of laughter at Dar's inescapable cocktail parties. Genevieve was in her element. She fitted in well with this racially diverse social set that gathered on the weekends in resplendent backyards, culminating every so often in huge, fairy-lit, diplomatic soirees, attended by everyone.

By all accounts, Bobby and Genny's circle of friends was a shade too dark, and they began to fall off more and more invitation lists. This upset Derek's mother no end, especially after she discovered her husband's motives for mixing with the locals were not entirely altruistic. It turned out his appetite for native women carried on long after they met. Once Genevieve knew of his betrayal, life in the Tropics turned sour.

Derek's sister and brother were away at separate boarding schools, and he was the only child still at home, a young teenager enrolled at the International School of Tanganyika. He spent his nights listening to his parents argue. After a while his education began to suffer; some days he didn't bother going into school. He thought about running away but that was hardly an option for an adolescent living on another continent, thousands of miles from his hometown.

Then he discovered pot. It was the escape he had been looking for. He found a ready supplier in an old Muslim woman who owned a bicycle-repair stand under an impressive baobab tree off the Bagamoyo Road. She kept a stash of marijuana in a tree hollow hidden behind the assortment of inner tubes that hung around her like rubber halos. The only other solace he found was in the wilderness, where he would regularly retreat in a blaze of bangi smoke.

Eventually his parents divorced and, at fourteen, Derek was faced with the choice of returning to Canada with his mother or remaining in Africa with his father. After much painful deliberation he chose the latter, which he would sorely regret. He never saw his mother again. Genevieve was killed in a road accident six months after she returned to Montréal.

Following her death Derek embarked on a path of rebellious self-destruction, involving substance abuse and delinquency at school, which provoked massive fights between him and his father. Bobby's attempts to discipline his son increasingly fell on deaf ears, and in due course Derek's respect for the old man completely evaporated. Lately, their clashes had become more abusive and even violent.

"Why didn't Patience prepare any dinner?" asked Derek,

bemoaning the dearth of food in the kitchen, his young features dramatically illuminated by the fridge light. "She always leaves something for me." Patience, their maid and cook, was considered part of the family. A demure Tanzanian in her early forties, she had been a sympathetic ear after Derek lost his mother, having once buried one of her children. There were times when he thought of her as his only family. His brother and sister never came to visit. Patience was all he had left.

"Because I sacked her!" growled Bobby.

"*What the hell?*" Derek slammed the fridge door and stormed back into the living room. "You can't just sack her. She's been with us for years."

"She was stealing my whisky, and watering it down to look like none had been taken."

"She doesn't even drink alcohol, you drunken old fool!"

"I'm Scots, you bastard!" yelled Bobby, swigging back the last of his drink and slamming the empty glass down on to the table. "Don't you think I know what a fucking Scotch should taste like?"

Derek walked despondently to his bedroom and lay on his bed in the dark. The prospect of losing Patience was devastating. How would he cope? He thought about looking for her. She lived in one of Dar-es-Salaam's many shanty towns, which he'd visited once because she'd taken him there, but he didn't think he'd be able to locate it again by himself. He was truly on his own. Succoured by the pulse of the Indian Ocean heaving against the coral cliffs outside his window, Derek soon calmed down.

He reached under his mattress and removed a dog-eared paperback, *The Taking of Pelham 123*. Then, thumbing to a page about a third of the way through, as though he was about to attempt reading it in the dark, he revealed instead a secret compartment: a cubic space about five chapters deep cut from the middle of the book that contained a half an ounce of uncleaned marijuana and some rolling papers.

After making a small, awkward-looking joint he then lit it and took a few puffs. Lying back on his pillow he noticed every window in his bedroom was closed, so he quickly leapt up to open them. This took considerable effort, as there were dozens of slats running parallel from floor to ceiling across most of the wall space, which could only be opened in groups of six. Zonked, he lay back down on the bed and gazed around his room.

The posters on his wall had changed over the years. Wildlife images were eventually replaced by broody shots of progressive rock bands on stage. In one corner, awash with moonlight streaming through the window, was his reflector telescope. His mother had given it to him for his fourteenth birthday. She was the one who had led him to astronomy, with her fascinating interpretations of the constellations. For instance, according to the Iroquois, the seventh sister in the Pleiades married a mortal so was forced to ride at the back of the basket, which was why she was hard to spot. Derek dearly missed her.

He remembered the last time he ever saw his mother, walking away with such dignity. She told everyone she was returning to Montréal to translate for the upcoming Olympics. But Derek knew otherwise. "Don't cry, dear," she sniffed. "You can come and visit me during the school holidays." After a long embrace, she wiped the tears from both their eyes then turned to Bobby. Despite everything that man had done to her, Genevieve still gave her husband a heartfelt hug and a kiss before boarding her jumbo jet.

She flew out of Dar airport the same day the Israelis launched "Operation Entebbe" to free the hostages who were being held by Palestinian terrorists at Uganda's international airport. Hence it was announced prior to departure that her flight to Heathrow on British Airways would not be landing in Entebbe as usual. This only added to Derek's anxiety. What if her plane got hijacked, or worse, shot down as it flew over Lake Victoria. Amin, who was aiding the Palestinians, had shown what he was capable of doing. Bobby told his son to stop worrying.

As his bedroom door creaked opened he quickly threw his joint under the bed. "What did I tell you about smoking that bloody *bangi* in my house?" bellowed Bobby, looming unsteadily over his son like a Gallic savage.

"Shit, give me a break, Dad," groaned Derek.

"I've given you too many breaks. That's your goddamn problem. But now…" He grinned and waved the opened envelope that had been lying on his arm rest. "…now, I'm finally getting rid of you. He he. You're going home, boy. You've been accepted at McGill."

"What? You opened my mail?" Derek snatched the letter away from him.

"I'm your father, goddamn it, and this is my home! I do what I want in my own home."

"Yes, you've demonstrated that quite clearly," said Derek, carefully reading the letter. He was not in the slightest bit pleased by the news. There was nothing in Canada for him.

"I'm putting you on the next flight back to Montréal," slurred Bobby.

"Well, I'm not going."

"Yes you bloody are!"

"Fuck you!"

"Why you!" Bobby lunged at him, but Derek ducked away, and the old man fell on to the bed. Derek stood up, ready for another assault, but his father just lay there face down on the pillow. He checked his pulse: it was hard to tell if his heart was still beating. Suddenly the old man let out a stentorian snore. Derek pulled a blanket over him, grabbed a pack, threw his stash, the trophy and a few clothes into it, then bolted out of the door.

Cycling beneath the streetlamps of Toure Drive with his knapsack on his back, he had a sense he was leaving home for good. Good riddance. He couldn't remember the last time his father had patted his back and said, "Well done, Derek". It was all he yearned for, fatherly approval, yet it was the one thing the old man consistently denied him. He pedalled his bicycle faster and faster. The more distance he put between him and that madman the better.

But where would he go? He loved Dar. Following the coast road ahead of him, through the balmy, moonlit night, Derek was too engrossed in his thoughts to pay much attention to where he was going. Along Oyster Bay the waves were breaking as far as the palm groves between the road and the beach. The sea breeze and salty spray on his face felt good. At the end of the bay he struggled up a steep hill, standing as he pedalled to get the most from his leg power. From the top of the hill he had a clear view of the dozens of cargo ships floating off shore. There they waited, sometimes for weeks, to pull into port. Although frustrating for the shipping companies, it was a wonder to behold at night, all lit up like a floating city.

Toure Drive turned away from the coast at Kajificheni Cove, so Derek took a right on to Kenyatta Drive which rejoined the sea on the other side of the cove, where the waves were more tranquil. A massive baobab tree, as wide as a house, was growing on the manicured grounds of an ambassadorial residence along the waterfront, a familiar landmark along a familiar road. Eventually he reached Salamander Bridge, which marked the edge of town. The neap tide meant the stench of lagoon water wafting over the bridge was not so overwhelming.

Once across, he stopped under the giant Air India sign, portraying a cartoon maharaja bowing and gesturing to the airline logo. Opposite was the turning that led to his old school, which brought back bittersweet memories. He recalled the journeys home on the IST school bus, a rare time and space between teachers and parents, when rampant student anarchy took hold and the bus driver had to struggle to keep his unruly passengers aboard. Derek straightened up his bike and continued on his journey.

It was not often he saw the town in such a deserted state. Dar was a tidy chaos of government buildings, Indian grocery shops, Swahili tea shops, sprawling marketplaces, and countless little dukas, all fringed by the meandering line of a contrastingly sleepy, palm-fronded seaboard, strewn with fishing dhows and canoes. The port's colonial past – both Arab and European – contributed as much to its culture as the Bantu who had assembled there over the centuries, whether or not of their own volition. It hadn't changed much in the seven years since the Strangelys moved to Tanzania. Except for the Kilimanjaro Hotel, few structures rose higher than the palm trees around St Joseph's Metropolitan Cathedral, built next to the harbour by the Germans at the turn of the century. Its white, austere Teutonic facade somehow fitted in with its surroundings.

In 1979 Dar was as safe as any city. Sure, burglaries occurred from time to time, but a white person could still walk unharmed through most parts of the city at night. The only apparent threats were claims that South African-backed RENAMO rebels, fighting a civil war in neighbouring Mozambique against the Communist FRELIMO regime, were stalking Dar's backstreets after dark like vampires, assailing innocent people for their lifeblood, so they could send back bags of it to their wounded comrades in the jungle. Or perhaps that was just government propaganda.

Instead of trying to find Patience when he reached downtown, Derek purchased a one-way ticket to Arusha on a bus leaving Dar at two that morning. After buying some parched corn, loading his bike on the roof, and journeying north through the rest of the night, he met up the next morning with his schoolmate Nathan, whose dad owned a safari lodge in Tarangire National Park.

Presently, they were seated atop a hybrid vehicle that Nathan had built, parked on an escarpment overlooking the Tarangire River. As the sun dropped between the hills, Derek smoked *bangi*, Nathan drank beer, and they both discussed what they were going to do with their lives. "I'm going to stay and run my dad's lodge," said Nathan. "I mean, *this* is the University of Life. You can't get a better education than this. Nature teaches you so much more than a university ever could, about history, sex, the environment, even politics."

"Or you can just enjoy it," smiled Derek, propping his heels on the Land Rover bonnet under which Nathan had replaced the original engine with a Toyota V8. "Alice", as the vehicle was known, also sported a Land Cruiser chassis attached to her four sizable Unimog tyres that raised her to an impressive height and gave her passengers a commanding view of their surroundings. "Pass me those bins, will you."

A troop of baboons was scampering up some trees behind them, screeching madly as they gathered on the treetops for the night. Down by the river two bull elephants were dancing between the acacias. And a mother cheetah had gathered her three cubs on the riverbank. One by one she picked up each cub up by the scruff of the neck and carried it to the opposite side of the river. She had nothing to fear from elephants, though she remained wary of crocodiles as she crossed the shallow water again and again with each member of her trembling litter between her teeth.

"I only wish I didn't feel so homeless," sighed Derek. "There is no place on earth where I feel more at ease than in the Great Rift Valley. I'd be an outsider in Canada. I don't know how to ski, I don't like hockey, and I cannot bear the smell of maple syrup."

"You're what they call a third-culture kid, *rafiki*," laughed Nathan, taking a swig of his beer.

"Forced to put down roots in so many places throughout his short life he doesn't even know where he belongs. I'm telling you, Nate, 'home' is a fucked-up notion..." A bluish-black bird of prey circled overhead. "What is that?" asked Derck, taking a long toke of his joint.

"Bateleur eagle," replied his friend. Everything Derek knew about the fauna and flora in East Africa he'd learned from Nathan. "Looks like it's circling over a kill, doesn't it, but it's only riding the last thermals of the day."

"I love how it flies with such agility, like, 'What, doesn't everybody fly?'...Seriously, though, I think I've got to find out for myself if Montréal is where I really belong."

"It's too damn cold over there, *rafiki*. You'll freeze your balls off in an instant. Your home is here in the African wilderness."

"I actually miss the snow."

"There's plenty of it up there on Mzee's head," said Nathan, pointing to the golden summit of Kilimanjaro, fading into the African dusk. "I can't imagine anything in the world could be more impressive than that mountain. Have you ever climbed Kilimanjaro?"

Wrapping himself in several layers of clothing, as they thumped along the endless potholed road, Derek tried to bundle up against the highland wind blowing through a broken window on the bus, a blustery chill which brought back unwelcome memories.

On that fateful day three years earlier, he had been due to fly out from Dar and spend Christmas with his mother, but a Canadian blizzard delayed his journey. It was a particularly nasty ice storm over the Eastern Seaboard that locked down everything and everyone, except Genevieve. She was driving back to Montreal that night, after visiting family in Quebec City, when her car skidded on black ice and slammed into a maple tree, killing her instantly.

Derek arrived at the Toure Drive apartment shortly after dawn, exhausted from his all-night, sleepless bus journey back to Dar-es-Salaam. He'd been away a fortnight and dreaded the reunion with his father. Nonetheless, it was time for reconciliation. He would enroll at McGill. At least that's what his mother would have wanted.

He quietly turned the key to the front door, half-expecting to meet his dad on his way out to work. Instead, when he opened the door he found the apartment completely empty. Not just Bobby had gone but all the furniture and appliances too. Except for a packed Samsonite suitcase and Derek's telescope in the middle of the living room, the place had been thoroughly vacated.

Atop the suitcase lay a manila envelope. He opened it and found his birth certificate, passport, a one-way ticket to Mirabel Airport via Charles de Gaulle, and a thousand Canadian dollars in twenty-dollar bills, but no note. In short, he was on his own. The old man had moved away, leaving no forwarding address. Derek never saw his father again.

CHAPTER NINE

Derek's heart beat frantically as he stumbled onward towards Kakuma Refugee Camp. Dust gathered in nimble twisters that danced across his path. He tried to establish his bearings but it was futile on the featureless savannah, and his judgement was plagued by mirages, fear, and the enduring image of his murdered friends. They were dead and there was nothing he could do for them except alert someone to the crime. And if he had remained there any longer the Turkana might have come back and killed him too.

A strong wind began to blow, whistling through the thorn trees, kicking up dirt, and battering him with dust and detritus. He was forced to take refuge in the shadow of a small hill. Again he tried to get a reading on his GPS unit but it refused to function, so he threw it away, as he had done with his large backpack. Surrounded by a howling maelstrom he wrapped his scarf around his head, and remained hostage to the storm.

As the wind began to die down he climbed the small hill and tried to determine his whereabouts. It was impossible to distinguish anything at first, but as the dust settled he could see hints of a vast human settlement, thousands of tin roofs crisscrossing an area many square kilometres in size. "I've made it," gasped Derek.

He was about to descend the hill when he heard a sound, like a rusty hinge springing open. There was no mistaking the stridulation that a scorpion makes before it attacks. In an instant the creature struck Derek's large toe with its tail and envenomated him. "Argh!" he screamed.

The United Nations officials guarding the gate showed no inclination to hinder Derek's progress as he limped into camp, followed by a pall of dust. He got as far as the reception centre and then collapsed. Maddy Jones came running to his aid. He was incomprehensible at first as he tried to explain what had happened to him. "I am a safari guide," he rasped, "We were…I was leading a client through the Rift Valley when we were ambushed. They came out of nowhere, three Turkana tribesmen. They shot my client and our local guide."

"Oh my God. Where did this happen?" asked Maddy.

"About five kilometres due west from here. I – I've been stung by a scorpion…" Then he blacked out.

As Derek came to, he found himself lying in a cot, in a large wall-less ward along with dozens of other patients. The odour of medication and defecation made him sit up. All around him were ailing, emaciated people, who looked as though their drips were siphoning the very essence from their bodies. Nearby stood a blonde woman weighing a tiny baby on a scales. "You're a…sight for sore eyes," said Derek, grimacing from the pain in his leg.

"So, the mysterious traveller awakes," she said, writing down the baby's details on a card. She turned to the child's mother and, carefully placing the tiny patient in her arms, said, "Four more days of supplemental feeding." Her assistant translated the diagnosis into Somali. "And how are you feeling, mate?" she asked, walking over to Derek's bedside.

"Fine, except my leg's on fire. How long was I out for?"

"Only a few hours," she said, holding his ankle in her hand. "Don't worry, it's not serious. The African black tail scorpion has a moderate sting. No anti-venom was necessary. You probably passed out from exhaustion as much as anything else."

"Are you a doctor?" asked Derek.

"No, but in the Outback it pays to know a thing or two about venoms. Maddy Jones is the name."

"Ah, an Australian. Even better. Derek Strangely."

"Nice to meet you, Derek," she said, examining his toe. "They've been searching for your murdered clients, but so far no trace of them. The police want a few more details before they talk to the Turkana elders about it."

"Really?" cried Derek, in a fit of anxiety. "Where's my rucksack?"

"Just relax," said Maddy, putting a hand on his shoulder. "It's only the venom making you anxious. Your things are safe in my office. I made sure they were locked away."

"I need my rucksack!"

"Shhh-shh!" She pushed him gently back into bed. "I'll go fetch it for you, mate."

Derek stared wide-eyed at the blue plastic roofing above his head. His mind was burning with questions. Why didn't the Turkana kill him? Why hadn't Johnny Oceans listened when he tried to warn him about the risk of taking a Karamajong along? How long before the authorities discovered he had entered the country illegally?

Maddy came back carrying a dusty backpack, handed it to him, and then returned to her duties. Derek sat up and examined the pockets. His money was still there, as was his passport, which he discreetly slipped into his pocket. He would have to keep that out of the hands of the police.

"Tell me, Maddy," said Derek, watching her Somali assistant pass her another baby to weigh, "do you sell them by the pound?"

"Actually, it's utterly heartbreaking. Sometimes they're just too slight. This morning I had to turn a mother away, and tell her to go and be with her infant while she died, because there was nothing we could do."

"That's a pretty tough call to make," said Derek.

"It's all part of my job," said Maddy, putting the baby on the scales.

"Which is?"

"Food distribution manager for the World Food Programme," she replied, glancing at Derek. She had stunning eyes, and long, wavy hair the colour of beechwood. Although she was wearing a lab coat, beneath it she had on a low-neck blouse, revealing ample cleavage.

"Do you know if there are any Majeerteen elders in this camp?" asked Derek, climbing out of bed. It took him a moment to finally place his bad foot on the floor for the pain, but he was determined to walk.

"Don't ask me," she replied, "I've only been here a couple of days." She turned to her assistant. "Abdulmajid, are there any Majeerteen elders in this camp?"

"Sorry," said Abdulmajid, with a lisp. "They don't keep Puntland pirates in this camp, only Bantu Somali. You have to go to Puntland, if you want to find them."

"What?" sighed Derek. "So what the hell was Oceans on about?"

"This is Addis Ababa," said Abdulmajid, leading Derek down a long dirt road between two rows of mud shops, "the Ethiopian market at Kakuma." Children followed closely behind in a playful group, calling after them and mimicking Derek's limp. "Half the people in this camp are Somali like me. A third are Sudanese, and the rest are from Ethiopia, Congo, Uganda, Rwanda and Burundi. We each have our own communities here."

Derek had never seen anything like it: a mud metropolis of tents, shacks, cardboard houses and tin-roofed huts. These were the Horn of Africa's truly marginalised people, the poorest of the poor, gathered in shoddy dwellings that had been organised in orderly rows, as though the world might be more inclined to rescue them if their destitution was at least tidy.

"That's the Unity Bar," said Abdulmajid, pointing to a brick building with tied curtains in the doorway that was painted lime green on the outside, "which has a beer garden in the back. It's a very popular place, owned by an Ethiopian refugee. Many refugees operate small businesses, sometimes selling Chinese goods which they trade for food rations."

Abdulmajid was slim and of medium height and in his mid-twenties. He did not fit the look of the archetypical Somali. His head was perfectly circular and was crowned by a tidy layer of closely cropped, tightly twisted hair. When he smiled, which was often, his eyes squinted, his broad nose concertinaed, and his lips rolled back to make way for a cavalcade of immaculately white, lopsided bucked teeth that he seemed proud to bear. This gave him a disarming quality. From the way he spoke, Derek imagined he'd been schooled in a remote outpost by an English teacher who put much emphasis on diction, despite having very little grasp of it herself. "Somehow, it is home."

"Do you all get along?" asked Derek.

"At least we all manage to live like good neighbours," laughed Abdulmajid, "but we are constantly being raided by the Turkana who rob us and rape the women. Sometimes thieves will squat in empty houses, with their guns and machetes, waiting to attack you, especially during religious holidays, like Eid."

"Why then?" Derek peered into a house that had blue UNHCR sheets for roofing and an odour of urine and decomposing flesh emanating from within. An old man was seated in the doorway next to a row of empty yellow jerry cans, staring at them with an expression that made Derek look away. The old man made a feeble gesture with his hand to shoe away flies and his unwelcome onlookers, who continued walking.

"Because that's when the criminals think that we have money," said Abdulmajid, weaving his way between the puddles in the road, "which our relatives have sent us. They break into houses at night and kill people for that money. My compound is fortified because, for all I have no family to send me anything, Bantu Somalis are attacked more than any other group at Kakuma."

"Why do they target Bantu Somalis?"

"Because we are the lowest-ranked in Somali society and excluded from the traditional clan protection networks – an easy target for those bandits. Even a Turkana will ask you your clan before he robs you, or rapes you. We don't feel safe here."

"How did you end up in Kakuma?"

"That is what is in my head every day, how did I get here. I am trapped and no one can help me. Even if they do want to help it takes time. Kakuma is a very difficult place to live. The average temperature is forty degrees Celsius, and the sun and the dust deliver beatings every day like angry teachers."

"I mean, what happened to make you flee your home?"

"You know, we Somalis, we don't like to talk too much about ourselves."

They overtook a young albino woman, who was carrying a load of wood on her head. With so few trees to offer shade anywhere, Derek dreaded to think how she coped in a place like Kakuma. Everywhere he looked he saw despondent people, some staring blankly at the ground, others off into the distance. Two Congolese men deliberately bumped into him as they passed. They were followed by three women in burkas who glared back at him from behind their veils. He then noticed a police officer scolding a boy and beating him with a birch, next to half a dozen Ethiopian men talking angrily between themselves. "Everyone seems a bit pissed off," said Derek.

"That is because we're in the black days."

"The black days?"

"People are only given rations every fifteen days. Those final few days at the end of each food distribution cycle, when people are most hungry, we call them the black days. "

"When's the next food distribution?" asked Derek.

"Tomorrow," said Abdulmajid.

They passed a new building made of dark mud walls and a roof fitted with shiny corrugated-iron sheeting. The sign outside read, Don Bosco Vocational Training Centre. "I am also learning computer skills in this place," said Abdulmajid. "The camp manager has tried to improve us with some opportunities to grow."

"At least you have a job here," said Derek

"For that I am so grateful. Masha Allah, my parents paid for me to have an education when I was a child. Working in the camp reduces the stress of being a refugee. I have something to occupy my mind."

"What's it like working for Maddy?"

"I don't know. The madame has just arrived at Kakuma. I don't know if she will be a good boss or a bad boss. But I think she is a very strong woman, and also very beautiful."

"You got that right..."

Suddenly, the wind began to blow, sending blue tarpaulins flapping, shutters slamming, and things flying everywhere. Derek used his rucksack to shelter his face from the dust. Others continued going about their business as though nothing unusual was happening. "We get these dust storms almost daily," shouted Abdulmajid. "It is impossible to keep anything clean."

He stopped before a large mud hut with a tin roof that rattled like a barking dog, and a yellow coat of arms swinging madly in the wind above the door, and said, "We have reached Kakuma Police Station." Derek and Abdulmajid stepped inside, out of the wind. They were met by Sergeant Okimu, who greeted them warmly, though it quickly became apparent that the smile was only sugar-coating for what he was about to say.

"Do you know how fragile the balance is between tribal chiefs and police chiefs in Kenya?" he asked, as a teacher might, putting the question to the simplest pupil in his class.

"No, sir," replied Derek resolutely, and with complete seriousness.

"It has taken us many, many years of painstaking work to reach the balance we now have between this office and the Turkana chiefs. Now, for you, I must disturb that balance." He wasn't through with the word "balance" and bounced it around his conversation like a beach ball. "Do you think I need things falling on my head? That's what happens when you disturb the balance. My job is keeping the balance, not disturbing the balance."

"Did you find any evidence of the ambush?" asked Derek, sheepishly rubbing his beard.

"*Did I what?*" Okimu leaned forward as if he hadn't heard a word Derek had said. "What, do you think this is CSI Miami? Tomorrow's food-cycle day and I don't have officers to spare to search for bodies in the desert. Do you know how much desert there is out there in which to search?"

"Please forgive me, I had no intention of…"

"Your passport!" barked Okimu, jabbing his hand out at Derek. "I lost it."

Sergeant Okimu raised his eyebrows. "*You lost it?*"

"Yes."

"Allah! Any proof of identification?" Derek shook his head. The officer kissed his teeth. "OK…" He retrieved a pen and notebook from the top drawer of his desk, and thumbed his way slowly and deliberately to the first empty page, whereupon he returned to his desk for a sheet of carbon paper. After some searching he eventually found one in the third drawer, removed it, tore it carefully in half, then placed the two halves under successive pages of his notebook. "What is your full name?"

"Derek Arthur Strangely."

"And your occupation?"

"I am a safari guide."

"In Nairobi?"

Derek hesitated. "In Kampala."

Sergeant Okimu looked up. "You came all the way here from Kampala?"

"Yes."

"Why?"

"It was my client's wish to safari on foot through Turkanaland."

The officer shook his head scornfully, scribbling all the information into his notebook. "Now," he said, straightening his posture and raising an eyebrow, while making little gyrations with the tip of his pen just above the paper, "tell me exactly what happened to you on your way to Kakuma."

"Come and meet my friends," said Abdulmajid, taking Derek through a room, resonating with a baby's cries, but too dark to reveal anything. He led them to an open-air space in the back where a dozen men were seated on mats on the ground in the shade of a single small acacia tree, enthusiastically stuffing their mouths with handfuls of leaves they plucked from large bundles of foliage laid out between them. Derek and Abdulmajid were greeted with offers of cups of tea, and a place to sit in the shade of an awning strung to the tree. "Have you ever chewed *khat*?" asked Abdulmajid.

"Yes," smiled Derek, sizing up the bundles as he made himself comfortable. "We call it *miraa* in Kampala. But there must be at least ten kilos of the stuff here."

"You chew the *khat* to forget your problems, and we have many problems."

"What part of Somalia are you from?" asked Derek, placing just a few leaves in his mouth.

"Kismayo," replied Abdulmajid. "And your birthplace?"

"Montréal. Do you know where that is?"

"Of course. Many Bantu Somalis have already been resettled in Montréal. *Inshe Allah*, I will go there someday, and see what snow is really like."

"Believe me, the novelty wears off pretty quick. So are all you guys Bantu Somali?"

"That is the name given to us by NGOs," said a man within earshot. "We never thought of ourselves as one group until the civil war and refugee situations arose."

"We are Gosha," laughed Abdulmajid, "people of the forest, stolen from our ancestral homes in Tanzania, Mozambique and Malawi in the 19th century and taken to Somalia as slaves by agents of the Zanzibari sultanate. That's why they also call us *adoon*."

"Who calls you that?"

"Somali nomads," said the man. "They are Jilec, and we are Jareer, because they have soft hair and ours is hard. They are the masters and we are their *adoon*."

"What do you call yourselves, then?"

"Bantu Somali," said the man, shrugging his shoulders and smiling. "It's easier to get resettled if you do, and they get confused if you tell them you're Zigua, or Ngindo, or Makua, or Yao, or Nyassa, or Zaramo, or Makale."

Derek was intrigued by a lithe ebony mask hanging on the tree. "What's that?" he asked.

"That is the face of our Zigua ancestor," said Abdulmajid.

"So, you don't follow Islam?"

"I am a Muslim," said Abdulmajid proudly, "but I still follow the traditions of my ancestors." He stuffed a handful of leaves in his mouth and smiled to the others. "All Bantu Somalis follow Islam, but most also still practise animism to appease their ancestors."

"Those Bantu ancestors sure got you locked in for the long-term, don't they?" laughed Derek.

"If there's one thing all Africans fear, it's the spirit world."

"Especially its dark provinces, although sometimes it's hard to tell the difference between the good and bad spirits."

"We fear them all!" laughed Abdulmajid. "The story of the Ugandans at Kakuma is a good example. They had been pushed out of northern Uganda by the war between NRM and Joseph Koni, and then fled to Kakuma. But when they arrived here they were severely beaten by the Somalis, some even killed. That is until Alice Lakwena arrived."

"Alice Lakwena, the Acholi witch?" asked Derek. "She was a refugee here?"

"Yes. In fact she died here. But because they feared her wicked sorcery, the Somalis were quick to keep their hands off the Ugandans after Alice arrived at camp. Africans unite in their fear of evil spirits."

"And wildlife," said Derek, recalling the strange behaviour of Robert, Johnny Oceans's so-called Karamajong guide.

"Ha, that is true of most Africans, but not me. Here they only have snakes and scorpions. But where I grew up in the Juba Valley there were many wild animals: lions, leopards, giraffes, cheetahs, hyenas, even wild asses."

"Ever encounter a lion?"

"Many times. We used to have plenty of lions, until warlords came and killed them all."

"Listen, I need to leave Kakuma pretty soon and head back to Kampala. What's the best way for me to do that?"

"You have to get a Movement Pass, co-signed by UNHCR and the Kenyan Government. If you were a refugee, I would say you have very little chance of leaving Kakuma any time soon. But it should be no problem for you. Just ask Daudi Hussein, the camp manager, and I'm sure he will grant you one."

"So, you take the world's richest people on safari, to the same spot where we rescue the world's poorest," laughed Maddy, putting down two Tusker beers on the table in front of Derek.

"Small world, isn't it," said Derek.

She sat down opposite, clasped her hands under her chin and gazed at him. "You really do look the part, mate, with your hair and beard, and those streaks of grey running through it. That scouting squint, and those well-weathered features..."

"You're not so bad-looking yourself."

"Did I say you were good-looking? My God, what an ego!" She threw back her hair with a toss of her head, and smiled flirtatiously.

"As vast as the savannah," said Derek, taking a swig of his beer.

It was after 10 p.m. and they had been drinking in the Unity Bar since dinner. The mud floor, dim fluorescent lighting, distorted bar tunes and din from the generator provided an enervating atmosphere, but that didn't bother them.

"Tell me, how does a nice girl like you wind up in the middle of nowhere?" asked Derek.

"Maybe it's because I'm from the middle of nowhere myself. Ever heard of Woop Woop, Australia?"

"No, I can't say I have."

"Exactly...Well, if you must know, I first became interested in this sort of work in my late teens, when I visited the Christmas Islands. You might have heard about the place a few years back: Afghan refugees adrift on a Norwegian ship called the *Tampa*?"

"I think I remember hearing something about it on the news."

"That's the reason I got into humanitarian work. I mean, I

wasn't keen on asylum seekers taking advantage of our shores, any more than the next Aussie, but I was appalled by the way we treated those people. Heaven forbid it should be me stranded on a sinking ship, and some other nation turns me away. So, I volunteered to help. I just wanted to redress the balance in some way, you know. Anyway, after uni I ended up working at the Christmas Island Immigration Detention Centre."

"Not just for Christmas, then," quipped Derek, taking a swig of his beer. "That must have been one hell of an experience."

"No, I loved it, the islands were beautiful and the pace was slow. The refugees were a bit ornery, which is why no one else wanted to bloody work there, but I stayed for five years. The pay was fantastic. By the time I returned to Brizzy, I'd saved enough money to do a Masters in Nutrition and Dietetics at Griffith University."

"Which was your ticket into food distribution. Nice one! I like a woman with a purposeful career path."

"What about you?" asked Maddy, taking a quick sip of her beer. "How did you get into your sexy line of work?"

"I grew up on safari," said Derek, running his hands through his hair. "My father came out to East Africa to build bridges in the late 1960s, and basically whenever the opportunity arose he'd take the family on the road. We went everywhere, covered literally hundreds of thousands of miles, and I guess I just couldn't stop."

"What an amazing dad!"

"Yes...Well, he was to begin with."

"I've always dreamed about going on safari," sighed Maddy. "The way you described drinking sundowners with your mate surrounded by elephants and baboons sent a shiver up my spine...What's your favourite game park, then?"

"Oh, hell," exclaimed Derek, "there are so many great ones...and I've visited dozens of them. Serengeti's arguably the most important one; I've been going there since I was a kid. In many ways it's the most exciting biosphere on earth. Kidepo always takes my breath away. I was just there with Johnny Oceans. And then of course there are the primordial forests that intensify the closer to the centre of the continent you get. I guess I'd have to say Tarangire is my favourite national park."

"What's so special about Tarangire, mate?"

"During the driest months it is second only to the Ngorongoro Crater for concentrations of wildlife. You see, in northern Tanzania you have this patchwork of spectacular game parks and reserves stretching from Lake Victoria to the coast, known as the Northern Circuit. Each one is almost entirely different from the next, a myriad of independent and interdependent ecosystems. Only the wildlife truly understands the significance of these domains as they migrate from one to the other. In the dry season you can pull up to a herd of buffalo drinking alongside elephant, zebra, crocodile and lion – all at the same spot on the Tarangire river. And with so many baobabs, the place looks like a fat farm for trees."

Maddy leaned forward and crooned, "Did anyone ever tell you that you have the most beguiling eyes?" Derek blushed and looked away. "There's an uncommon light in those eyes, like a beacon to the uninitiated. I bet you've taken your fair share of Karen Blixens out there, on the savannah."

"You make me sound like a game-park gigolo," laughed Derek.

"But am I wrong?" beamed Maddy.

"Truthfully," said Derek, blinking sincerely, "I'm just as happy sitting by myself next to a campfire, under the stars, enjoying the solitude..."

Maddy stopped suddenly and cupped her hand over her mouth. Something behind his head had caught her attention. "Oh my God!" she gasped.

"What is it?" he asked, craning around to see a BBC World News broadcast on the television that was reporting about a British soldier, whose photograph was up on the screen.

"I know that guy," she whispered.

"...*Lieutenant Simon Hay was kidnapped and murdered in Nairobi on Tuesday by al-Shabaab militants, who then posted a video of his execution on YouTube. He had been deployed by British Special Forces in Afghanistan, but had been in the Kenyan capital conducting security briefings for aid workers. The leader of the militants, Omar Abu Hamza, issued a statement claiming responsibility...*"

"I attended those security briefings..."

"Poor bastard," said Derek, scratching his head.

"Security is getting worse around here," said Maddy, clutching her shoulders. Suddenly the generator cut out. It took them a moment to adjust to the gloomy quietude. Before long they could see each other's faces again, and hear the hum of tens of thousands of indigent souls going about their nightly routines without electricity.

"C'mon," he said, taking her hand. "Let's go look at the stars." They grabbed their drinks, stepped out into the beer garden, with crickets chirping all around them, and looked up into the blackness.

"Oh my God," gasped Maddy, "I've never seen so many."

"That's Venus," whispered Derek. "It's higher than it's ever been. And Jupiter...Hang on!" He retrieved his iPad from his pack and launched the Planets app, which showed a chart of the heavens that was digitally gimballed to whatever position he held the tablet, identifying the exact position of every planet and constellation in the sky at that moment. "Isn't this the shit," laughed Derek, holding the tablet aloft like a digital prophet.

"Amazing! So that's Orion the Hunter," she said, pointing to the prominent hourglass shape on the tablet then to the actual constellation overhead.

"Yeah, I think he's stalking me," smiled Derek, switching off the iPad and putting it away. He then extended his arm around her shoulders and pulled her closer, whispering, "We really are in the middle of nowhere here." They turned to face each other. The universe came to a standstill. They kissed. And the celestial motions resumed.

"Welcome to my humble abode," said Maddy, squeaking open the corrugated tin door to her quarters and switching on a rechargeable floor lamp. The room comprised a spartan arrangement of desk, bed, chair and table, a row of jerry cans lined up by the door, and one window, with tin shutters. "I've not really had a chance to unpack yet," she said, attempting to tidy up. It looked as though a bomb had exploded inside her suitcase. "They told me these were just temporary quarters, and I'd be given a proper house next week."

"I'm used to staying in all kinds of places," said Derek. Maddy stopped and glared at him. "What? *As a safari guide...*"

"I hear there's a thousand-dollar-a-night lodge not far from here, mate. In the meantime..." She threw her laundry aside, reached out for Derek, who nudged the door closed with his foot, and pulled him into her arms. They then began kissing passionately while frantically trying to undress each other. "I shouldn't be doing this," said Maddy, pulling back from Derek then throwing her arms around his neck again, and kissing him all over his face. "It's my first ... food ... distribution ... tomorrow."

"Nothing sexier," gasped Derek, kissing and squeezing her breasts, "than a woman ... who can feed ... tens of thousands ... of hungry people ... in one day."

"Let me see if I've got this right," said Maddy, staring at the ceiling, with her head on the pillow, her right hand behind it, and her blanket pulled up to her chin. Derek lay symmetrically beside her. Both were glistening with perspiration. "Your mate, Johnny Oceans, dead for years, suddenly returns, but only long enough to get killed again? And all because he needed to find a Majeerteen elder in Kakuma, who was the only person capable of saving Puntland from the Islamists?"

"I know, it sounds like a potboiler," said Derek, turning to face her.

She brushed her hair from her eyes and stared at him. Her face was that of a little girl gazing into a magical box. "But why steal across the border?"

"And why drag me along?"

She laughed. "I mean, why not take a bus from Nairobi? Busloads of famine tourists arrive here every day."

"None of it makes sense," sighed Derek. "There aren't even any Majeerteen in the goddamn camp. One thing I've learned: in Africa, nothing is what it appears to be." He followed the lines of her exquisite features with his finger.

"That's quite a two-bob watch you got there, mate," said Maddy, stroking Derek's arm and then running her fingers around the watch face.

"Johnny gave it to me," said Derek, "immediately after he told me about the treasure."

Maddy sat up, revealing her full, round breasts. "Treasure?"

"Yeah, just before he got shot, he said something about a treasure his grandfather had found in Somalia during the Second World War. He never got a chance to tell me anything more about it. But he did give me this Kobold Phantom Tactical," said Derek, unclasping it from his wrist, "which was a wedding gift from his brother-in law, who's a pirate in Puntland."

Maddy took it from him and examined the exquisite timepiece. "Sure is heavy."

"Apparently you can single-handedly invade Iran with one of those."

"Look. It's got an inscription on the back."

"Really? Give it to me."

"Wait, let me read it. '1051 Lynx and Fez, Uptown'. What do you suppose that means?"

"Damned if I know. He was an enigmatic guy, as you've heard. Let me have a look."

"Sounds like a Manhattan address..." said Maddy, handing the watch back to Derek.

"As far as I know," he said, reading the inscription, "there's no Lynx and Fez in New York City, certainly not Uptown."

"Lynx and Fez are an odd combination," laughed Maddy, gazing at the corrugated tin ceiling. "A lynx wearing a fez uptown is a jaunty vision. I suppose you could have a lynx-skin fez..."

"Maybe it's some kind of riddle. Johnny told me his grandfather's letters were full of riddles and anagrams."

Maddy's face lit up. "Struth, I love riddles..." She jumped out of bed and came back with a pen and paper. "What's the address again?"

"1051 Lynx and Fez, Uptown." Jotting down the letters in random order, she then began crossing them out. "It is an anagram, mate! See, why else would it spell 'Land of Punt'?"

"Holy shit, you're right!"

"Eliminate those and you're left with '1051 ynx ez, w'."

"It doesn't make sense," said Derek, scratching his head.

"Riddles often don't. Why is a raven like a writing desk?" Maddy scribbled down the letters in a different order then scowled at the paper. "I still can't find an anagram for those letters. Maybe they're coordinates. Look, there's an N and an E, which may be a reference to north and east..."

"Of course!" cried Derek, leaping out of bed. He slalomed around the scattered clothing and retrieved his backpack on the other side of the room. Back in bed with Maddy, he removed his iPad, opened up Google Earth and zeroed in on the Horn of Africa. "Well, what do you know, 10° N and 51° E are coordinates within Somalia, which just leaves 'w, x, y, and z'..."

Maddy looked at him with puzzlement. "...the last four letters of the alphabet."

"Maybe they correspond to the minutes and seconds of the coordinates, 23, 24, 25, 26. If I put them in after the degrees..."

"X marks the spot!" cried Maddy, clapping her hands. "Do you think that's where the treasure's hidden?"

"I don't know, it's a couple of kilometres off the coast of the Hafun Peninsula..." Derek stared blankly at the screen for a moment. Then his eyes widened and he slowly put his hand over his mouth. "Of course. Trust Johnny Oceans to bury it at sea."

"Daudi Hussein, Camp Manager?" asked Derek, timidly knocking on a door that was slightly ajar. It was bright and early the next morning and he wasn't sure he'd find the camp manager at his desk. He nudged open the door a little wider. The office was as rudimentary as anything he'd seen at Kakuma: mud floor, handmade furniture, tin walls Sellotaped with posters that offered advice about avoiding cholera and malaria, and a bright blue desktop calendar from the

UNHCR. Seated behind it was the camp manager, a stout, balding man, who stared over his spectacles, and left all the smiling to the Kenyan president on the wall. "Uh...I'm Derek Strangely. I've come about my Movement Pass."

"Please sit down," said the manager, pointing to a white plastic chair. He was visibly bemused by Derek's visit.

"No need," said Derek, unfolding a piece of paper on his desk, then tapping it with his forefinger. "I wouldn't want to take up any of your precious time..."

"Have a seat," insisted Daudi. Derek gradually lowered himself into the chair. The camp manager removed his spectacles and placed them carefully on his desk. "I've consulted the elders in Lodwar," he said, "and they know nothing of your ambush. Worse still, your claim has upset the delicate balance in our relations with the Turkana."

"I see," said Derek, hunching forward with eyebrows raised, hands clasped together, and elbows on his knees, which caused his watch to cascade down his forearm. "I can assure you, Mr Hussein, in all sincerity, that it was never my intention to cause any trouble. I just wanted to see justice served for my client. That has obviously been done to the best of your ability. Now, if you don't mind, I would like to go home."

"You, and eighty-four thousand, two hundred and forty-nine others at Kakuma, Mr Derek."

"Huh," chuckled Derek, reclining back into his chair. "That's a lot of Movement Passes..."

Daudi Hussein touched the tips of his fingers together a couple of times and stared coldly at Derek. "When I started as camp manager at Kakuma, security was poor, and there were attacks *every day* by armed Turkana. Now we have twenty-four-hour patrols, law and order has been established, and the camp is totally free from attacks. This is down to the work of this office, the Kenyan Police, and in particular the local Turkana community. It's taken us years to earn their trust..."

"Yes, I can imagine that community relations would be a major factor..."

"Then you can also imagine how your accusation was received by the Turkana, especially after they learned you have come here from Uganda. It's a wonder you're still alive." He picked up his glasses and began cleaning them with his tie. "Why did you come to Kakuma with your story? You're a safari guide. This is not a safari destination. Why not take your problem to the Kenya Wildlife Service?"

"This was the very first place I found. Look, all I ask is that you counter-sign the Movement Pass that the UNHCR has already approved, and I'll be out of your hair before you can say anything more about it."

"Without a passport, Mr Derek, you have absolutely no chance of getting a Movement Pass." He put his glasses back on his face and scowled at Derek.

"I beg your pardon?" cried Derek. "How am I supposed to get to the Canadian High Commission in Nairobi? They're the only ones who can issue me with a new one."

"You should have thought of that before you wandered into my refugee camp. This is now a matter for the Kenyan Ministry of Immigration and Registration. And you will remain here at Kakuma until we are satisfied that you are who you say you are."

"As you wish," said Derek, standing up.

"Wait," said Daudi, retrieving a notebook from his desk. "My colleagues in Nairobi have asked me to confirm when and where you entered the Republic of Kenya: the date, time, and border crossing."

"Sure. I can do that...Let's see. It was Malaba, the day before yesterday, at around 3 p.m." Derek was certain it would take them at least a couple of hours to discover he was lying, by which time he might have found a way to escape. "Anyhow, I've most likely taken up far too much of your precious time already, Mr Hussein. After all it is food-cycle day."

"What's your hurry?" asked Daudi, now forming an approximation of a smile. "I see you have quite a precious timepiece strapped to your wrist. I might be persuaded to sign your Movement Pass if you were to make a gift of that watch, let's say as a token of your gratitude for my hospitality at Kakuma."

Derek examined the overpriced adornment dangling from his arm and wondered how long would it be before he was forced to pawn it anyway. He never wore a watch, preferring to check the time on his phone instead. He was about to satisfy Daudi's request but stopped short of unfastening the Kobold from his wrist. "Am I really that thoughtless? My old friend Johnny Oceans's last mortal deed was to give me his watch, a priceless heirloom. And it's the only thing I have to remember him by." He also had a sneaking suspicion there was more to the gift than his old friend had let on. It seemed an incredible coincidence that Johnny was killed only seconds after he removed it from his wrist. "I'll take my chances with Kenyan immigration," he said, smiling back at the camp manager as he stepped out of his office.

"Maddy, you've got to help me," cried Derek, trying to keep up with her as she dashed back and forth between a queue of refugees, thousands of people long, each waiting for their handout of rations, and a counter with an open laptop. Everything was covered in a layer of flour. A large chalkboard, with the words "World Food Programme Distribution Dept. All food weighed in kilograms" written across the top, kept track of the amount of cooking oil, maize, pulses, maize flour, wheat flour and salt that had already been handed out to the refugees. It was being updated every few minutes by Abdulmajid.

"What can I do, Derek?" demanded Maddy, transcribing the new total on the blackboard into her computer. "If Daudi says you have to stay, then you have to stay, mate. He's the camp manager."

"He was fishing for a bribe."

"Look, I wish I could help," she said, brushing her hair back from her face as she began furiously twiddling the trackpad. "This bloody software's supposed to keep track of the food distribution, but it isn't working. To make matters worse we'll soon run out of emergency supplies. They tell me I've got to somehow make this lot stretch for two food cycles. I mean…Oh, what is it now?" She dashed over to the front of the food queue to quell a disturbance.

Derek sidled over to her laptop and glanced at what she'd just been reading: an email marked "For Your Eyes Only". It was composed of the itinerary and manifest for the next World Food Programme shipment, including the name of the ship, port and date of departure and arrival, and a full description of the cargo. He made a mental note of the ship's name then quickly stepped back from the computer.

"I can help you escape." He spun around to see Abdulmajid standing behind him.

"How?" asked Derek, trying to look nonchalant.

"Two forged Movement Passes," he whispered.

"I only need one."

"You must take me with you."

"No way! How far would you get?"

"I'll take my chances. I cannot stay another day in Kakuma."

"Where's the next town?"

"Lodwar."

"OK. You can come with me to Lodwar, but from there you're on your own."

"Whatever you say, boss."

"Right. What do I have to do?"

"Pay me five hundred dollars," said Abdulmajid, "and meet me in an hour at the Don Bosco Vocational Training Centre."

"Fine. Here's the money. Don't even think about double-crossing me."

CHAPTER TEN

"When will I see you again?" asked Maddy, standing with her hand on her hip in the doorway of the Unity Bar. She smiled thoughtfully while stroking his grey and black hair. "I bet you forget me the minute you return to Kampala."

"Not likely, sweetheart," said Derek, gently lifting her chin with his forefinger. "I'll take you on a dream safari to Tarangire."

"It'll have to wait until I get some R and R," she said, looking back over her shoulder at the queue of people waiting to receive food. Two Turkana were arguing with a refugee over a sack of food. She turned back and sighed. "Look, I can't hang about."

"You know, Australia's not the first place I'd go looking for a woman as compassionate and appealing as you."

"What the hell's that supposed to mean?" she yelled, pushing him backward.

"That's more like it…" he laughed, pulling her into his arms.

Greeted by all he passed, camp manager Daudi Hussein walked down the main drag of his refugee camp with self-important strides and gestures of gratitude. He relished his position, as it put him in everyone's favour, especially the orphaned girls. His regular promenades through the camp allowed him to garner admiration for his largesse, and see what beauties were out and about. On this occasion he was accompanied by Sergeant Okimu.

A large crowd of Turkana were making their way ahead of them, dragging goat carcasses that they hoped to trade for food from the distributed supply. Daudi was repulsed by the putrescent odours. Food distribution cycle day was the only time the Turkana were allowed to visit camp. He wasn't keen on them being allowed in at all. They disrupted order and generally lacked the hygiene of the refugees. But for the sake of community relations he capitulated, insisting they could only gain access to Zone 2.

His cell phone rang and he answered it with a supercilious "D'afta noon!", smiling and waving at a passer-by as he did. "...Who?...Yes, he's still here..." He stopped abruptly and furrowed his brow, so deeply it cast a shadow. "...I see." Another smile for another well-wisher, then back to the frown. "Well, I will have him arrested immediately!" Daudi hung up, and turned to Sergeant Okimu. "Mr Derek is an illegal alien. Immigration have no record of his entry into Kenya."

"Allah!" yelled Okimu, drawing his night stick. "I just saw him in the Unity Bar now-now." The two men turned and marched back in the direction of the bar.

"Shit!" cried Derek, spotting Daudi Hussein and Sergeant Okimu marching through the crowd of Turkana towards the Unity Bar.

"Hurry," cried Maddy, ushering him towards the beer garden, "I'll keep them occupied while you escape out the back."

Derek dashed into the garden and climbed over the wall, glancing back at Maddy who blew him a kiss before he leapt over. She then turned towards the two men who were just entering the bar.

"Where is he?" demanded Daudi.

"Where's who?" asked Maddy, smiling casually as she strode towards them.

"Derek Strangely," said Daudi.

"I saw him come in here," added Sergeant Okimu.

"Oh, right, yes, he was just here, but I think he said he was going to see you. Something about trading his watch for a Movement Pass."

"He said that?"

"I'm pretty sure that's what he said he was going to do. Quite an expensive watch too."

"C'mon," cried Daudi, turning on his heels. Sergeant Okimu followed.

Derek and Abdulmajid skulked through the complex of administrative buildings clustered around the entrance to the camp, trying to look nonchalant as they surveyed each car in the parking lot. They spotted a navy blue Land Cruiser with its keys still in the ignition. Derek slipped into the driver's seat and Abdulmajid, the passenger seat. Inside the car was scorching from the afternoon sunshine and they made a commotion trying not to get burnt by the vinyl seats. This caught the eye of the sentry standing guard at the main gate, though he did not react. Derek started the engine, put the car in gear and drove up to the barrier.

"Where are you going?" asked the sentry, stepping up to his window.

"To Nairobi," said Derek.

"Your passes, please!"

Derek handed over the two forgeries Abdulmajid had acquired for five hundred dollars, and the sentry examined them. He then went into his cubicle and checked them against a roster before returning and handing them back. "You may go," he said. The barrier was lifted and they began to drive on.

Daudi Hussein appeared, running with Sergeant Okimu towards the gate, shouting at them to stop. The sentry blew on his whistle and tried to lower the barrier, but Derek already had his foot down on the accelerator and it came down on the rear bumper, knocking it loose. He sped away to the main road, leaving behind a cloud of dust. Daudi, Sergeant Okimu and two other officers scrambled for their police vehicles, a Land Rover and two motorcycle choppers, and took off in pursuit.

A large number of Turkana and their cattle were gathered outside the camp, forcing Derek to slalom between them. He barely missed cattle, sheep, children, which caused cries of protest from the Turkana, especially after his bumper flew off and struck a lamb. He then turned left sharply on to the main road, fishtailing the Cruiser out on to the opposite kerb, before taking off due east in the direction of Lodwar. The police were in hot pursuit, with the Rover in front and the two choppers following close behind, side by side.

As he raced through the town of Kakuma, all at once Derek hit a speed bump at high speed giving to the Cruiser's suspension a painful whack. The police were not so foolish and slowed down, which Derek also did for the second, third, and fourth bumps, opening up only after Abdulmajid assured him there were no more. "Sorry," he cried when they hit a fifth and took off skyward. The car hit the ground with a racket that warned them the chassis would not take much more abuse.

As they passed the airstrip on the edge of town the number of pedestrians began to dwindle until there were only a few lone individuals walking along the roadside. Derek looked over his shoulder. The Rover was only about three hundred metres behind them and picking up speed. He accelerated the Cruiser to one hundred and twenty kilometres an hour.

They were surrounded by flat, barren, treeless terrain, with a few thorn bushes and termite mounds scattered across it. Everything to the horizon, where a small range of mountains rose, was bathed in amber by the late afternoon sun. "I think it might be a good idea if we found a back road," said Derek.

"There are no back roads," said Abdulmajid.

"But, surely the police will put up a blockade at the next town."

"There is no next town," laughed Abdulmajid. "Lodwar's at least a hundred kilometres from here, and there's nothing in between."

Derek checked the petrol gauge. The tank was nearly empty. He knew they would soon run out at that speed, but he kept the pedal to the metal just the same, as their best chance for escape was in outrunning the police. The road was desolate and perfectly linear so there was no need to slow down. Every kilometre or so they passed small groups of Turkana walking east, mostly women and children, carrying loads of food and cooking oil they'd traded for livestock at the camp.

He was suddenly forced to slow down as they came up behind a dawdling lorry. Loaded so high with people, its centre of gravity appeared to be somewhere above the vehicle. Derek tried to overtake but the road was suddenly inundated with oncoming traffic. He remained behind, swerving out occasionally to look for a way around the wobbling, brimming rig that was otherwise obstructing his view of the road, but every time he pulled out, he was almost hit by another car. "This road was fucking empty a minute ago!" cried Derek. The countless passengers aboard the lorry, who by now had spotted the police coming up behind, began to laugh, wave and cheer on the fugitives.

Derek took a chance on a fleeting gap and accelerated around the lorry, missing an oncoming minibus by a hair's breadth. He spotted a crossroads a few metres ahead, with a sign that read, "Lokitaung 140 kms," and swung left sharply on to the new road, hoping the police had not seen him and would overshoot the intersection. The tarmac quickly disintegrated into dirt. "I don't know how much longer this rust bucket will keep moving," shouted Derek, over the din.

"They're still on us," cried Abdulmajid.

The two motorcycles had given up, but the Rover continued in hot pursuit. "Jesus, they're persistent bastards," cried Derek. The farther up the road they headed the more it deteriorated. Behind them a pall of dust obscured their rear view and they could no longer be sure if they were still being pursued or not. Even so, Derek kept driving at high speed, while the Land Cruiser felt like it was about to fall apart.

"Looks like rain," said Derek. Across the tops of the hills into which they were headed were gathering clouds, the first anyone had seen in a while.

"The rain will only fall in the Kalulenyang Hills," said Abdulmajid. "Down below it will remain dry. Unless there's a flash flood, which can sometimes happen."

"Another cruel joke..." laughed Derek, checking his rear-view mirror. "Are they still on our tail?"

"I can't see anything..." coughed Abdulmajid.

The fuel gauge began flashing. Derek spotted a right turning ahead. "I'm getting off this road," he said, spinning the steering wheel clockwise with such force the vehicle's two left tyres lifted off the ground. When they returned to earth the impact snapped the rear suspension block, after which the car began to shudder like an Apollo re-entry. At the same time the cab suddenly became infested by a swarm of flies, biting their arms and necks. "Tsetse flies!" screamed Derek, trying to maintain control while striking his legs. "They're everywhere!"

"*Allah!*" shouted Abdulmajid, slapping the back of his neck. "I'm being eaten alive!"

The vehicle came to an abrupt halt, and they both leapt out to beat off the flies. The tsetse invasion seemed more directed at the car than them, so they ran away from it, then stood at a distance, rubbing their bites and taking stock of the situation.

They were on the top of a small sandhill. Behind them the road was barren. "Looks like we managed to lose the cops," said Derek, "but where the hell are we?" He looked up, as he thought he'd seen something out of the corner of his eye, a glint in the sky, but it was gone. Nor was there a soul anywhere to be seen in the vicinity.

"What do we do now?" asked Abdulmajid.

"Well, it's only a matter of time before they figure out we made that turning. But as this vehicle is no longer capable of providing transport, we have no choice but to continue on foot."

"There are plenty of spitting cobras and scorpions around here," said Abdulmajid, scoping shadows around the large rocks.

"We'll just have to be on our guard, that's all." Derek removed his iPad and checked their location, then scanned the valley below. The ashen landscape, crisscrossed by cattle tracks, resembled an old bull elephant's hide, and was pierced by the long shadows of the hills they were in the midst of. He referenced the satellite image of a dried-up riverbed on his device with one snaking across the landscape below. "That's Lake Turkana in the distance," he said, pointing at a shimmering expanse of water on the horizon. "We can follow the riverbed to the lake, where we'll camp for the night before making our way into Lodwar in the morning. I should be able to catch a bus to Nairobi from there. But we better get a move on because it'll be dark soon."

Seeing the sun was about to set, Abdulmajid stopped, rolled out his prayer mat and asked his travelling companion for some privacy so he could pray. Derek looked at his watch and was about to say something about making time, but decided against it. Abdulmajid's prayers were brief, but before setting off down the slope towards the empty river, he first picked up a stone and neatly placed it at the start of their descent. "Don't worry," laughed Derek, "I doubt we'll be back this way again soon."

"No," replied Abdulmajid, "it is not a marker. In Turkana tradition, to protect himself from evil in the valley, a person who descends a mountain must lay a stone at the commencement of his journey."

The wind picked up, peppering their faces with sand and blowing through the ant-addled thorn bushes with an ethereal tune. With dusk descending, warm air off the lake was searching out weather depressions in the hills. Derek wrapped his scarf around his face. After clambering over lava rocks and down crevices, in due course they found themselves on the riverbed, walking side by side midpoint between the waterless riverbanks. "What else do you know about Turkana tradition?" asked Derek, unravelling his scarf from his face.

"What I have learned is mostly about their mythology."

"Like?" asked Derek.

"The Turkana believe hills and mountains are occupied by spirits," replied Abdulmajid. "What they call *ngipean*, who are monsters that can change their shape as they wish. People have seen them and have even heard them talk and laugh, but the only trace they leave is large footprints."

Derek checked the riverbed for footprints, but saw only the

teardrop forms of pristine overlapping layers of sand, recalling the watercourse that recently flowed through it. "Do they believe in God?" he asked.

"Yes, they believe in one God, Akuj, who lives near the tops of hills and mountains, and who is the sky itself. If Akuj is happy he will give rain, if he is angry he will withhold it."

Derek heard a crack of thunder in the distance and said, "Akuj speaks."

"No, no, he is not the thunder nor the lightning, because those occur without rainfall. But there can be no rain without Akuj."

"So Akuj controls the rain," said Derek. "The Turkana must think Akuj is pretty pissed with them right now."

"Do you hear that?" asked Abdulmajid, putting his hand to his ear. Derek stopped. "That rushing sound?"

"Yes, I hear it," said Derek, shaking his head in bafflement. They searched the surrounding landscape which was quickly losing its features in the fading light, but they could find no indication of what was making the noise, nor where it was coming from. It was unrelenting, getting louder and louder with every second, like an avalanche. "*What the hell is that?*" Then they saw it, swiftly cascading towards them: the forward surge of an immense flash flood.

"*Allah!*" screamed Abdulmajid. "I cannot swim."

"Quick!" cried Derek, making a mad dash for the nearest riverbank, more than ten metres away. The fast-moving wall of water swelled ever larger as it raced towards them, drowning everything in its path. They needed to take just a few more strides to reach the bank. Derek mustered all his strength and a dose of adrenaline to take one long jump on to the edge of the riverbank, but Abdulmajid was knocked off his feet before he could reach safety and got carried away swiftly downstream. Derek then quickly dived in after him, grabbing hold of Abdulmajid just as the torrent began to drag him under. He pulled him to the surface and into a half nelson to keep his mouth above the water.

Derek put all his energy into trying to remain afloat, furiously kicking his legs while looking for something to grab on to with his free hand. It was like white-water rafting, but without the raft. He tried to lodge his feet on the riverbed, but the flood continued to drag them headlong towards the lake. Floating in the torrent alongside them was the detritus of the flood's destruction: thorn bushes, tree trunks, even animal corpses. Derek grabbed hold of a passing hippo carcass and instructed Abdulmajid to do the same. As they continued heedlessly towards Lake Turkana, he then began to worry about Nile crocodiles. The lake boasted Africa's largest population.

Gradually the riverbed began to widen and the flash flood to dissipate, and they were finally able to get ashore. "Thank you, my friend," sputtered Abdulmajid, sitting on the riverbank, coughing and spewing out water as he tried to recover. "I owe you...a debt of gratitude for diving in after me and saving my life."

"You owe me nothing, *rafiki*," said Derek, gripping Abdulmajid's shoulder.

"Where are we?" asked the Somali, unable to make out anything in their immediate surroundings.

In attempting to answer the question Derek made a horrifying discovery: his backpack was no longer strapped to his shoulders. "NO FUCKING WAY!"

"What is it?"

"My backpack. It's gone. It had all my money in it, my passport, my iPad, everything..."

"*Allah!*"

"Shit, now we're *really* in trouble."

Night had fallen and they needed to find somewhere to camp. The lakeshore was still a way off, yet the smell of sulphur blowing across the flats from Lake Turkana was overwhelming. Their surroundings were astonishingly serene, and there was not a wisp of cloud anywhere in the sky. Billions of stars were scattered across it, of such magnitudes they lit up the earth more vividly than a full moon. It was as though the universe had flipped and they were standing upside down in a stellar millpond. Although sodden, their clothes were quickly drying in the warm, parched air. "There's definitely an otherworldly quality to this place," said Derek, wringing the water from his scarf.

"I know," said Abdulmajid. "It scares me."

"Somewhere near here is where they found Nariokotome: Turkana boy, a one-and-a-half-million-year-old hominid."

"Who?" asked Abdulmajid.

"*Homo ergaster*, one of your earliest ancestors."

"Your ancestor, maybe," laughed Abdulmajid.

"I'm telling you," insisted Derek, "this is one ape you'd be proud to call Grandpa. He was an incredibly fast runner, and the stone tools he used were far more advanced than anyone expected to find from that far back in time."

"I guess Nariokotome liked his high-tech gadgets just as much as the next guy," grinned Abdulmajid.

"You could be kicking some of Nariokotome's bones around as you walk."

"It certainly feels like a graveyard."

"What the hell's this?" gasped Derek, stopping suddenly. Spread out before them, across an area ten by twenty metres in size, was an array of stone pillars averaging a metre in height and protruding at different angles from a layer of smaller stones. "Sure is one incredible sight out in the middle of nowhere," he whispered, touching the tops of the shiny basalt monoliths as he walked between them. Some had pebbles on top of them, laid out in figures of eight. "I would say this place definitely serves some sort of scholarly purpose," he added. "Look at the way they're all arranged. It's like a miniature Stonehenge."

Abdulmajid wasn't as keen to go wandering through them. "Could these be the Dancing Stones of Namaratunga?" he asked, scratching his chin.

"The dancing stones of what?"

Just then a voice spoke from the darkness beyond the pillars. "The Turkana believe they were dancers who were turned to stone after they mocked a malevolent spirit." Derek and Abdulmajid both looked up in amazement. Making his way towards them was a slender old man dressed in an orange and blue tartan fabric tied around one shoulder, and carrying a stick and a small wooden neck-rest-cum-stool in his hand. "Hello. How do you do? My name is Gabriel Lokonyi," he said, extending a lithe hand.

Derek hesitated, then reached out and shook the man's hand. "Derek Strangely."

"You speak like an Englishman," said Abdulmajid, coming as close as he dared. "Are you a guide here?"

"You could say that," chuckled Gabriel, grinning toothlessly at the two of them while puffing on a clove cigarette. "I'm a palaeontologist. As for my accent, I got that serving in the King's African Rifles during World War Two."

"Ah, a war veteran. You have my greatest respect. Abdulmajid is my name."

"Thank you," replied Gabriel.

"I'm curious to know the story behind these stones," said Derek.

"It's an observatory," he replied.

"You see," laughed Derek. "I knew they served a purpose."

"Each stone corresponds to a different point on the horizon where seven star clusters rise," he continued. "Or, should I say, used to rise, in 300 BC."

"Wow! A two-thousand-year-old observatory...out here in the middle of nowhere. I had no idea such a place existed."

"Was it the Turkana who made this?" asked Abdulmajid.

"No," said Gabriel, raising his eyebrows. "They were here when the Turkana arrived. We don't know much about who made them. Maybe Borana cattle herders from Ethiopia, as they were noted astronomers."

"Which selected stars do they correspond to?" asked Derek.

"Ah, a fellow astronomer, I see," said Gabriel, reaching into his tartan and removing a card to show to Derek. It was a simple diagram showing the positions of the pillars transected by long arrows, delineating lines of sight to the points on the horizon where each star rose. "The seven harvest stars from the Borana calendar," said Gabriel, who then proceeded to point to each object in the sky as he read its name on the card: "Bellatrix, the belt of Orion, Saiph, Sirius, Aldebaran, Pleiades and Triangulum."

"I can see why they would build an observatory here," breathed Derek. "There is just so much horizon, bound to an almost perfect semi-sphere of celestial night sky."

"And plenty of fish in the lake," added Abdulmajid.

"Nile perch, crocodile, hippo, soft-shelled turtles," laughed Gabriel. "Who wouldn't want to settle here?"

"There's something of the supernatural about this lake," whispered Derek.

"Anam is a sacred spring," said Gabriel, seating himself on his little stool, with his back against a pillar, "the beginning and the end of all rivers." He gazed out across the flats to the lake, a distant placid sheet that mirrored the sky in every detail. "It was once a vast oasis, you know, a much wider lake that drained into the River Nile. Eight thousand years ago it would have been lapping at our feet."

"Why does it all seem so strangely familiar?" sighed Derek, sitting down beside him. Abdulmajid remained standing.

"All human beings possess a memory of this place," continued Gabriel. "It's midpoint on the path our gracile ancestors took out of the heart of Africa. From here you can see everything, both in time and space, and in any direction." Derek glanced at Gabriel. The twinkle in the old Turkana's eye suggested a fondness for riddles, and did much to compensate for his complete lack of teeth. "Come," the old man laughed, "let us make a fire to dry your damp clothes. Are you hungry?"

The faces of the three men were aglow from the blaze of thorn bushes and acacia logs as they sat close to it, leeward of a sirocco breeze that blew steadily from the hills towards the lake. Dinner had consisted of a dozen small cakes made with powdered milk, dried wild berries and cows' blood, called edodo. Abdulmajid savoured his as if they were special treats. Derek wasn't so keen. They smelt unpleasant and tasted off, but because he was hungry and didn't wish to offend the old man he nonetheless ate his share, smiling all the while. Convinced Gabriel was a Turkana tribal elder, he then went on to retell the story of the ambush outside Kakuma. After he had finished Gabriel stared contemplatively at the sky. "I heard about that attack..." he said, solemnly. "The bodies were disposed of and the perpetrators dealt with, after which the elders sought to cover the whole thing up."

"I knew I wasn't losing my goddamn mind," cried Derek.

"You have a duty to fulfil, my friend," said Gabriel, rising to his feet. "You must go to Puntland in Somalia, and deliver the news of Johnny Oceans's death in person to his widow."

"Actually," chuckled Derek, as he also stood up, "I kind of hoped to take the first bus to Nairobi from Lodwar tomorrow morning."

"You cannot go to Nairobi," protested Gabriel. "Kenyan immigration will nab you the moment you get off the bus."

"I agree with Gabriel," said Abdulmajid.

"But Puntland's miles away," moaned Derek.

"Fifteen hundred kilometres, as the eagle flies," smiled Gabriel. "It will take you three days to get there."

"Really, how?" asked Derek, "I'm broke, I don't have a car, and I'm in the middle of nowhere."

"You can take my sailboat," beamed Gabriel. "It's moored in Ferguson's Gulf, not far from here."

"You have a sailboat?" laughed Derek, scratching his beard inquisitively, as his long grey hair blew about his face in the warm breeze.

"I love sailing on this lake," grinned Gabriel, "and have done for years."

"What made you think I could sail?"

"You are obviously a celestial navigator. Why else would you need such a skill? I prefer sailing at night too, under all those navigable points. It's an ancient art."

"So, you're saying we should just get in your boat and sail the hell out of here?"

"If you sail north, you'll cross the Ethiopian border at the Omo

River Delta, about a hundred kilometres from here. With a fair wind, and there's one tonight, it'll take you four, maybe five hours. Then, simply follow the Omo River to Omorate. You can leave the *Argo Navis* tied up there and I'll fetch it in a few days. From Omorate you'll easily find a lift to Addis Ababa. And from Addis there are daily flights to Bosaso. I'm sure your embassy would be willing to lend you the airfare, or you could pawn that watch. I venture to say you could make it to Puntland in just two days."

"*Argo Navis*?" laughed Derek. "Isn't that the ship Jason and the Argonauts sailed to fetch the golden fleece?"

"I named mine after the ancient constellation, Argo Navis."

Derek wasn't sure where he wanted to go. Reflecting on the past few days he couldn't figure out why Johnny Oceans had made up the excuse of needing to contact a key tribal elder in Kakuma. What had the American really been after in Kenya? Derek thought about the Land of Punt treasure. Based on what he and Maddy had worked out, he pretty much knew where to find it, if indeed that's what the riddle meant. He had already begun to have second thoughts about going home. Even if he somehow managed to avoid being arrested, there were not too many opportunities waiting for him back in Uganda. He turned to his travelling companion and asked, "What do you know about the Hafun Peninsula?"

"Only that it's full of pirates."

"Good enough for me..."

"Splendid!" said Gabriel, handing them a bundle wrapped in cloth. "Here is some more edodo to sustain you on your journey." Derek and Abdulmajid thanked him. He then swept his hand across the sky, and said, "Just follow the stars. You'll find your way."

CHAPTER ELEVEN

"What's up, Frank?" asked Maddy, munching on a carrot stick while speaking to her boss on a secure line in the World Food Programme's private communications centre.

"G'day, Maddy," said Frank. "Listen, we need you to be the supercargo on the TSC *Tristola* leaving Istanbul Port the day after tomorrow for Mogadishu."

"What's a supercargo when it's at home?"

"You oversee the cargo from port to port."

"Struth! But I've got my hands full here, mate."

"No you don't. Food cycle's over. You're free to do this. This is important, Mad. You will only be away from your post for a week."

"Surely you can get someone more qualified."

"We haven't got anyone else to spare. Everyone's occupied with something at the moment. As you know, at any one time WFP has fifty ships at sea, sixty planes in the air and seven thousand trucks on the move. It's the only way to maintain an unrivalled deep field presence in the most remote locations on earth, Mad..."

"No need to preach to me about how great the World Food Programme is, Frank. What I'm worried about is sailing through the pirate-infested Gulf of Aden."

"You have little to worry about, mate. Piracy around the Horn is way down on what it used to be. And you'll be escorted by the

Indian Navy frigate the INS Shivalik. You'll even have the Aussie Air Force buzzing overhead. What could go wrong? Anyway, I seem to recall you worked aboard a couple of refugee ships that sailed through pirate-infested waters off Indonesia."

"You got me there. What do I have to do?"

"Fly back to Nairobi this afternoon and catch the Turkish Airways flight out of Jomo Kenyatta tonight. I've already bought you a ticket, and the twin engine's on its way to pick you up now. Throw a few things together and be out at the airstrip in half an hour."

"You haven't given me much choice in the matter."

"I knew you'd agree. You're my Jillaroo on this one, mate!"

CHAPTER TWELVE

"Did you see that?" asked Derek, with his hand on the tiller, glancing up at the sky while preparing to change course around a sharp bend in the river.

"See what?" asked Abdulmajid.

"Up in the sky. A glint...Coming about!" he cried, releasing the mainsail. "Sit down," he added, just before the boom swung around. Abdulmajid complied, though he had yet to grasp the dangers of sailing. "When I say 'come about' you have to sit down."

"You told me to look at the sky," barked Abdulmajid. "So, I was looking." Derek scanned the wide blue yonder but the object had gone.

With her sails fluttering in the morning breeze, the *Argo Navis* was a pleasure to behold. Across her mainsail was a pale blue drawing of the ancient constellation, and her jib was solid eggshell blue. She was well-weathered, a typical twenty-foot wooden weekender. Inside her small cabin the aroma of clove cigarettes pervaded, and most things, like the stove and compass, were held down by gimballed fixtures. There was also a table littered with navigation charts and star maps, weighed down with a tarnished brass sextant, magnifying glass, and an astrolabe. Derek hadn't seen one of those outside a maritime museum.

They had been sailing since the early hours before dawn,

following a course that took them lengthwise up the middle of Lake Turkana to where it meets the mouth of the Omo River. High winds and a dark night had made the journey perilous but brief, and they had slipped surreptitiously into Ethiopia at daybreak.

Now, in the first light of day, they were meandering up the Omo's fertile delta towards the town of Omorate, through a land that was in stark contrast to the barren terrain they'd left the previous day. The banks of the river were lush and verdant, fed by its regular floods, and there were many more people living on them, their cows and goats grazing green pastures between shambas growing maize and beans in the rich Omorate soil. Around every bend in the river was another settlement. Although arranged in much greater density, their dome-shaped houses were similar to the Turkana's, made from a frame of branches, and covered with hides. Many people ran to the river's edge as they passed, evidently astonished by the sight of a sailboat navigating upriver at the hands of a white man.

The riverine activity began to intensify. Every canoe they passed steered closer to deliver a warm greeting from its canoeist and satisfy his or her curiosity about this strange dhow sailing upriver with a black man and a white man aboard. Many of the adults had a small, square silver plate pierced through their lower lip, reflecting the sunlight appealingly as they smiled. It reminded Derek of the Congo River.

A group of teenage girls were at the water's edge, giggling and taunting each other. "*Allah!*" said Abdulmajid, standing up to wave at them. "Those are some bathing beauties." They waved back, calling out in a language he could not understand. It seemed they were enjoying themselves at his expense, but he didn't mind. They were all similarly adorned with layers of blue, red and yellow bead necklaces that matched the patterned wrap-arounds tied to their slender waists. Their hair was shaved back from their foreheads and braided or teased into various styles. Some wore headdresses made of bottle caps and beads. Each one was stunningly beautiful, and naked from the waist up, their pert breasts catching the morning light like dark chocolate kisses. "Is this heaven?" Abdulmajid sighed.

"Coming about," cried Derek, but the Somali paid no heed. This time the boom struck him roundly at the back of his head and he fell forward. He would have dropped straight into the river if Derek hadn't grabbed him by the back of his shirt. "I warned you," he said. All at once the girls began to squawk exuberantly. Abdulmajid was still conscious but struggling to regain his wits, and his pride. He smiled back, gesturing for more applause with one hand while rubbing the back of his head with the other. "I think I saw a first-aid kit down below, if you need to put something on that."

Abdulmajid bade farewell to the girls and went down below. "It was kind of Gabriel to lend us his sailboat," he said, lisping with abandon as he rummaged around the cabin, "though he certainly was a strange old fellow." He picked up a brass disc as wide as his head that looked like a clock with mysterious markings around the edges. "What's this?"

"It's an astrolabe, an ancient GPS unit," said Derek. "With that instrument alone, and a sky full of stars, the ancients could pinpoint their position anywhere on earth."

"OK," said Abdulmajid, scratching his head. "In Somalia we use a Kamal, even when travelling on land. I would expect a Turkana elder to be knowledgeable of such things, especially one living so remotely, but an astro-blade...I don't think so."

"He certainly was a strange egg. But I've met characters like him before, throwbacks to colonial times whose eloquence and knowledge are of little consequence when dealing with the harsh realities of Africa."

Abdulmajid climbed out of the cabin with the first-aid kit under his arm, sat down next to Derek then unzipped the bag. "I think he was sorcerer, a *ngipean*. I've heard tales of crocodiles turning themselves into humans, so they can walk among us undetected."

"I didn't check if he left large footprints," laughed Derek. "Well, at least he was kind enough to give us his food, which doesn't strike me as very crocodilian behaviour."

"Do you think there are crocodiles in this river?" asked Abdulmajid, searching the banks for any tell-tale signs.

"Judging from the build-up of human habitations, I'd say no. But the lake we just crossed is the most croc-infested on the continent."

"*What?*" gasped Abdulmajid, scrabbling through the bandages and creams for something that might lessen the pain in his head. "*Masha Allah*, you didn't tell me that last night, while we were sailing in those high winds. There were times I thought we were going to tip over."

"Capsize," corrected Derek.

"I've never checked," sighed Abdulmajid, throwing a couple of painkillers down his throat. "Why? Do you think I should wear one?"

They heard a voice cry, "Ag man!" Out in the middle of the river a white man and his dog were adrift in a canoe that was sinking. "We're taking water!" Derek steered the *Argo Navis* towards them, slackening the jib to slow it down as he approached. In a moment they were alongside and Abdulmajid grabbed hold of their boat. The dog, a Ridgeback, began barking nonstop at him, for which his master reprimanded him with a slap to his nose. "This bloody pirogue is about to sink to the bottom of the Omo River," he cried, with a staccato South African accent, rolling his r's and spitting his t's. "Can you give us a lift?"

"Sure," said Derek.

"Thank you so much," said the man, struggling to climb aboard with a cooler in one hand and a .308 hunting rifle with a powerful scope in the other. Although tall, broad-shouldered and in his early thirties, he had an enormous beer belly that strained the tensile limits of his safari shirt. His face was darkly tanned, at least the parts that weren't carpeted with unkempt curly black hair. He wore a brown cowboy hat with a real leopard-skin band around it, and khakis exactly the same shade as his dog. Both gave off an unpleasant odour, like dirty wet socks.

"*Aweh*, I'm Ryan," he said extending his hand to Derek, "and this is my not-so-bright dog, Helder." He handed his cooler to Abdulmajid.

"Welcome aboard ship." Ryan only nodded at the Somali; Helder growled. "Please sit down", said Derek, shifting closer to the tiller to make room for him. But before the South African could do so he had to first remove the binoculars and dog whistle from around his neck, then the hunting belt from his waist, which had attached to it a leather scabbard for his axe, another for his Bowie knife, and a flask. He detached the flask, unscrewed the top and took a long swig, wiping his beard with the back of his hand then offering some to Derek, who declined.

"Nice idea," said Ryan, examining the boat while still standing, "sailing up the Omo. I wish I'd thought of that."

"Well, we kind of stumbled on it ourselves," laughed Derek.

"Is that so?"

"Yes. We're trying to get to Addis Ababa."

"Ha! Well, you're in luck. I'm driving up there today. I'll gladly give you a lift to Addis if you take me and Helder to Omorate."

"That's very kind of you. Please sit down," laughed Derek. "So, what brings you down here, to the Omo Delta?"

"This," laughed Ryan, sweeping his hand across his field of view, and ducking each time the boom swung around, "is what brought me to the delta. Everything you see around you is new land. Whether it's due to silt coming down the river, or a drop in the levels of Lake Turkana, or both, no one's bloody sure, but in the last fifteen years the Omo Delta has expanded by over five hundred square kilometres, even extended into Kenyan territory. That's a lot of fucking reclaimed territory where before there was none, something you don't often get in Africa."

"What do you have in mind for it?" asked Derek.

"There's real potential for hunting here. That's what I do, I organise hunting safaris, out of Arusha. I'm over here scouting around for new opportunities."

"Really. I'm also safari guide – gorillas mostly – out of Kampala."

"Looks like we both had the same bloody idea," grumbled Ryan, finally sitting down. "Too much competition in our industry, bra."

"We're not exactly here on safari," smiled Derek, "more like, just passing through."

As the river widened the terrain on the riverbanks became less vegetated. On the right bank they saw evidence of urbanisation, proper cement buildings with tin roofs, commerce, people in Western clothing, bicycles. An Ethiopian man standing among a small crowd of people on a cement wharf was waving frantically at them, inviting them to come ashore. "You can moor here!" he shouted. He seemed to be expecting them.

Derek flipped the bumpers over the starboard gunwale and came alongside the wharf. Positioned on the bow, Abdulmajid threw a rope to a longshoreman who, with a few swift figures of eight, secured the *Argo Navis* to the wharf. Derek grabbed the bundle of supplies and climbed up on to the wharf. The aromas coming from it were intoxicating: the smoke from food stalls roasting corn, goat meat, and spices mixed with tar and petrol fumes. "Welcome to Omorate," said the man who had come to meet them, helping each one ashore. "I am Ibrahim."

Ryan and his dog refused any help. Once on the wharf they ambled over to a merchant who was roasting a dozen ears of corn on a skillet. "Who wants parched milee?" asked Ryan.

"Oh, yes please," said Abdulmajid.

"Wasn't asking you," snapped Ryan, "but, I suppose you can have some. Helder likes it too. Four pieces. Chop chop! We'll eat them on the road."

"But I have organised a lift to Addis for you," said Ibrahim, smiling while rubbing his hands together.

"They already have a lift," grunted Ryan, "in my car."

"Hold on a second," laughed Derek, tucking his bundle under his arm. "If our Ethiopian friend here has gone to the trouble of organising transportation, then it might be rude not to accept."

"Suit yourself," said Ryan, paying for the corn. "C'mon, Helder, let's let Derek travel to Addis with his black friends." He then marched up the road and turned out of sight.

"Can't say I'm sorry to see him go," sighed Derek, turning to

Ibrahim. He felt a cold steel ring slam against his right wrist then heard the unmistakable sound of metal locking on to metal. He'd just been handcuffed to Abdulmajid.

"You're under arrest," said Ibrahim, grabbing Derek under his left armpit, "for entering Ethiopia illegally." Another man from the crowd roughly took hold of Abdulmajid. "Come this way, please." They were joined by two more officers who escorted them up the street in the same direction in which Ryan and Helder had departed.

Suddenly, from around the corner came a fast moving vehicle. It was Ryan in a beat-up, grey-and-white Defender, driving directly at them. The police officers ran for cover while Derek and Abdulmajid just stood there stupefied. The Defender came to a halt in a maelstrom of dust, just centimetres in front of them. "Hop in!" cried Ryan, leaning over to open the back door. Helder already occupied the front passenger seat so they raced around to jump in the back. Derek threw his bundle before him and was the first to dive in, but Abdulmajid had not even managed a foothold before Ryan hit the accelerator, forcing the Somalian to run as fast as his legs could carry him beside the open door, shackled to Derek.

"Hang on, goddamn it!" yelled Derek, who was in danger of being dragged out. Ahead of them a gormless calf had wandered into the road, on a collision course with Abdulmajid, whom Derek rescued just in time. The door struck the calf with a force of impact that slammed it shut. The Defender took off at high speed. Derek looked behind. The animal was stunned but still standing. There was no sign of the police. He leaned forward and put his left hand on Ryan's shoulder and said, "Mate, I'm sorry..." But he was hit by a nasty olfactory assault from Ryan's shoes propped up in the divider, and forced back into his seat.

"That you're a kaffir lover," laughed Ryan. "I knew that black bastard wasn't genuine." He held up two pieces of roasted corn for them, prompting a moment of chaos as Derek and Abdulmajid grappled with their handcuffs while trying to grab their individual cobs, and Helder incessantly barked his disapproval.

"Yeah, well, thanks for rescuing us just the same," said Derek, biting into a row of kernels.

"*Masha allah*," murmured Abdulmajid, knowing he wouldn't be there if he hadn't been attached to Derek.

The Land Rover bolted across the barren countryside at breakneck speed, so fast the distant mountains hurtled past. Ryan and Helder stared straight ahead, their expressions fixed, while Derek and Abdulmajid gazed through their windows at the wide-open countryside. They passed a herd of zebra grazing at the roadside. "What do Derek and a zebra have in common?" asked Ryan.

"I'll bite," said Derek. "What?"

"Neither of you can decide whether you're black or white!" Ryan roared with laughter, and Helder started barking nonstop again, for which he received a wallop. Even Abdulmajid found it funny.

"That's not true," protested Derek. "I know I'm white. I just don't think race is important. I respect other people's cultures, traditions and beliefs, but I don't think the colour of their skin is in any way relevant – certainly not to me, though it may be to them."

"Get off your high horse, bra," roared Ryan, patting his dog on the head. "You're a nigger lover."

"What the fuck..." cried Derek.

"Don't get me wrong, bra," laughed Ryan, looking in his rear-view mirror, "I love black pussy just as much as the next *muzungu*. Ag man, there's this amazing bar in Addis, called the Bäre, that I've been frequenting for the past couple of years, with some of the tastiest whores you've ever seen. You won't believe me when I tell you this, but they've got septuplets working there, seven non-identical twins who are the most stunning piccaninnies you've ever seen in your life. Their grandfathers were Italian and their grandmothers Ethiopian. I'm telling you, bra, there's nothing hotter than an eight-some with this lot. Four of them look like well-tanned Mediterranean supermodels, the other three like coloured goddesses. I'm telling you, never have I had so much fun in my whole fucking life. I'll take you there, bra. We'll have the best time. You can even bring your kaffir friend here."

"Jesus! I don't believe what I'm hearing…" groaned Derek. With Helder staring him down, he donned his Ray-Ban Wayfarers and sunk back into his seat. The journey to the Ethiopian capital was going to be uphill the whole way.

Some time later he was awakened by a popping in his ears and the uneasy feeling he was being watched. It took him a moment to reacquaint himself with his situation: shackled to Abdulmajid, in a Land Rover driven by racist white hunter and a dog that had too much attitude. Derek removed his sunglasses with his free hand and surveyed the landscape outside. An escarpment loomed over them like a breaking tidal wave. The road had begun climbing towards the town of Arba Minch, winding around hairpin turns through of a lush alpine forest where a light rain was falling.

When they reached the plateau, it was as though they had gone up an octave in the geological aria that began in the Omo Delta. Still in the Great Rift Valley, they were now in the "overlap zone" between the Ethiopian and Gregory rifts, comprised of the oldest volcanic rocks and basins found in the East African rift system. It was an entirely new kind of terrain: graben like in other sections of the Rift, rolling savannah formed over eons from the ash and weathering of nearby volcanoes, but much older and more eroded than elsewhere.

A local radio station was playing an Ethiopian pop song, a swinging ballad with melancholy lyrics sung by a male vocalist, backed by a subtle mix of funky bass, organ, guitar, and plenty of horn. For the next seven minutes the song rolled along like the landscape.

"*Good afternoon. You're listening to Arba Jazz 87.1 FM. Our guest this afternoon is Master Sergeant Peter Seuss, who oversees AFRICOM's operations in Ethiopia. Welcome to the show…Sergeant Seuss.*"

"*Glad to be here. You can call me Peter.*"

"*Now, it was reported recently in the Washington Post, Peter, that the US military is operating a base at Arba Minch airport. Can you explain the purpose of that base?*"

"*First of all, it's important I clarify something: there is one, and only one, US military base on the African continent, and that's Camp Lemonnier in Djibouti. Now, from Arba Minch we do operate a squadron of UAVs, but the airport still operates as a commercial airport for the town, and we have only deployed a limited number of US personnel to this post. Our presence here is totally non-invasive. And, I might add, we will only continue to operate in your country as long as the government of Ethiopia welcomes us.*"

"*Can you please explain to our listeners what a UAV is?*"

"*Sure. UAVs are aircraft piloted by remote control, often from as far away as the United States. They are sometimes used for intelligence-gathering, sometimes for attack. But out of Arba Minch we fly Reaper drones for surveillance purposes only.*"

"*What about the invasion by neighbouring Kenya into south Somalia? Have you not been providing air support for the Kenyans with these drones?*"

"*The United States is in the Horn of Africa to tackle radical Islamism and piracy – dual threats to the stability of Ethiopia. However, there is no relationship between our aircraft operations in Ethiopia and the Kenyan operation in Somalia. As I said, the squadron of drones at Arba Minch airport are not involved in any air strikes. They are used solely for information-gathering.*"

Ryan turned off the radio and muttered, "Go Team America!"

"That must have been what I saw this morning from the river," said Derek, "and the day before after we abandoned the Land Cruiser, a fucking Reaper drone."

"I've seen plenty in Somalia," sighed Abdulmajid.

"The Yanks send them to spy on pirates," said Ryan, looking up between beats of his windshield wipers to see if he could spot any.

"So, why is this one spying on us?" asked Derek. "And has been since yesterday."

"Maybe Abdulmajid is a terrorist," laughed Ryan.

Abdulmajid smiled. He was at least grateful that the man had called him by his name. "You want to know how I ended up at Kakuma Refugee Camp?" he said, his voice faintly quivering. "I witnessed the stoning to death of a rape victim accused of adultery in Mogadishu, and reported what I saw to the authorities. I've been on the run ever since."

"Who are you running from?" asked Derek, staring out of the window.

"Al-Shabaab," said Abdulmajid.

"Seems like everyone's on the run from the Islamists," said Derek. Just then he glimpsed a dark, wooden statue glaring back at him from the trees. The tilt in its head and the way its face had been carved, with sunken eyes, elongated nose and a pendulous lower lip, gave it a haunting, soulless expression. Even though he'd lost sight of the thing in an instant, such a sinister image made him shiver and remained engraved in his mind. He wondered who put it there, so close to the road, and for what purpose.

"I see a lake," said Abdulmajid.

"That's Lake Chamo," said Ryan, "in Nechisar National Park."

"Do you think we could stop somewhere and try and get these handcuffs removed?" asked Derek. Abdulmajid nodded his agreement with enthusiasm.

"Don't worry," replied Ryan, "we'll be in Arba Minch in twenty minutes. I'll pick up a pair of bolt cutters in the hardware shop." He kept his eye on the lake as he drove, shaking his head and kissing his teeth. "They cleaned out that park completely, with illegal fishing and poaching. I'm telling you, it's irresponsible the way these people live. They're just ignorant, greedy bastards."

"Really?" asked Derek, leaning forward. "And what did your ancestors do? Weren't there once lions on the Cape? Boer farmers extirpated all the animals that got in the way of their progress. Yet you still feel justified coming up here to tell these poor people that their wildlife must be protected and, in fact, is more valuable than they are."

"You say you're a safari guide," laughed Ryan, "yet you defend the bastards who're doing you out of your livelihood."

"I certainly don't think my livelihood is more important than theirs. I'm all for pristine wildernesses, but not at the expense of the local people. This is their traditional land, for Chrissakes."

"Which earns them nothing, bra. Revenues from hunting could help revive this national park, now a shadow of its former self, and the communities around it. There's a few zebra, gazelle and hartebeest left, and a load of crocodiles, but nothing else."

"What's your solution?"

"Clear the locals out."

"What the hell kind of solution is that?" hollered Derek

"The only one. Problem is, they're well-armed and not willing to go without a fight. So we have to take a different approach with these chaps. All I'd need is a few of the guys I fought alongside with in Angola, and I could clear them out in a week."

"Your approach to wildlife conservation is just another form of racism, an excuse to take pot shots at poor black people for the sake of game. It debases the people and the wildlife."

"You're talking a load of bullshit, bra," said Ryan, looking angrily over his shoulder. Helder began barking nonstop, for which he received no further rebuke.

"*No, man, you're talking a load of bullshit!*" cried Derek.

"I should drop you both right fucking here by the road..."

"Bull!" cried Abdulmajid.

"What's that, kaffir?" roared Ryan, raising his arm to give the Somali a dose of what Helder had been getting.

"In the road!" screamed Abdulmajid, pointing straight ahead. "You're going to hit a bull!"

Ryan whirled around to see a large brown bovine creature with enormous red eyes staring him down from the middle of the road. The Landy was doing at least eighty kilometres per hour and it was too late to hit the brakes. Derek and Abdulmajid gripped their arm rests in terror, as Ryan tried to swerve around the beast. He lost control of the car, careening into a drainage ditch that sent them corkscrewing through the air.

No one uttered a sound as the vehicle pirouetted skyward, on a trajectory that went on seemingly forever. The dog, Ryan's shoes, Gabriel's bag of edodo, and the heaps of litter on the car floor all became weightless. Everything else was strapped in.

Derek was overcome with regret. They would have been much better off in the hands of the Ethiopian police. Now he was about to die at the hands of a lunatic, while shackled to Abdulmajid. With an almighty crash, the car returned to earth upside down, then continued hurtling forward on its roof until it had expended all of its momentum.

One by one they climbed out of the tangled wreckage, which took considerable effort on the part of the handcuffed fugitives, and examined themselves. They were in the middle of a bean field. With its wheels spinning aimlessly in the air, the Landy looked like a distressed beetle lying on its back. It had no front screen, no wing mirrors, no back window and its roof had been crushed in. Ryan reached in and cut the engine off, then retrieved his hunting rifle. The dog scampered around the vehicle. with his tail between his legs, trying to figure out why this thing had disciplined him. Except for plaintive birdsong, rustling leaves and the rumble of a coming storm, there was silence.

"Wow," laughed Derek, "Close call! At least no one was injured. And, you know, with a bit of body work and a touch of paint…"

"*It's a total fucking WRITE-off, you bastard!*" bellowed Ryan.

"Oh, I don't know…"

"That Landy's been my transport for over twelve fucking years. I should never have given you *poes lickers* a lift. " Ryan aimed his .308 directly at them. "Start running!"

"What?"

"Start running before I change my mind. Go on! Get the hell out of here, or I'll shoot you both! You and your bloody kaffir!"

"But we're in the middle of fucking nowhere," protested Derek. Ryan fired two shots over their heads. Derek and Abdulmajid needed no more persuading, and legged it down a mud road towards Lake Chamo, bound at the wrist. Ryan might have pursued them if he hadn't been barefoot.

"If you're looking for eats," he shouted after them, "stick to the lakeshore. You'll eventually find a market…" He then began laughing hysterically and fired a couple more shots into the air. "Helder! Fetch me my shoes!" The dog scampered back into the wreckage where he found his master's sneakers lying among the broken glass strewn across the ceiling. He was about to pick one up with his teeth when he spotted a scorpion climbing into it, prompting him to retreat to a safe distance. "My shoes, mutt! Where are my bloody shoes!" Helder tilted his head and raised his ears, but for once the dog was silent.

CHAPTER THIRTEEN

The port of Aden was bathed in intense morning sunlight, illuminating its oldest and darkest recesses. Tucked away in a backstreet in the old town of Ma'alla, in an al-Qaeda safe house that served as the terminal of his telegraph line, Ali al-Rubaysh was seated in the bedroom of a small ground-floor apartment.

In the corner of the windowless room was a wooden chair and desk. On top of the desk, taking up the entire surface, was an elaborate brass and wood antique. Its base resembled a harmonium that had the letters of the alphabet written across its keys, and fastened to its lid was an array of speed governors, cogs, wheels, and large painted enamel cylinders. The words "W.U. TELEGRAPH CO. NEW YORK, G. M. PHELPS Maker" were stamped on a steel plate fastened to the largest cylinder. Unable to follow Morse code, Rubaysh had replaced his simple brass sounder with a printing telegraph that he found in an antique bazaar in Aden.

He was waiting for a communiqué from Omar, and kept his eye on a large spool of ticker tape at the back. It began to whir and rattle with an incoming telegram, printing at a rate of five characters per second. "Confirmation US Navy intel STOP Also Mehemet Abdul Rahman is dead STOP."

"*What?*" yelled Rubaysh. "That was never in my plan!" He kicked aside the chair and paced the room. This was not good news.

He knew Abdul Rahman had been close to uncovering the whereabouts of the Land of Punt treasure, if he hadn't already. That's why he tried to have the American kidnapped, not killed, so he could relinquish the information. The key to all his designs was locked away in that treasure, his desire to join the people of Yemen and Somalia for the sake of global jihad, as he'd done with the telegraph line, to part the sea of infidels with a reprimanding strike from a wrathful staff of God. He sat back down and sent a reply, spelling it out angrily with one finger. "Who killed him STOP."

"What does it matter STOP The Kafir is dead STOP."

"It matters a great deal to *me*," hissed Rubaysh.

"Should we dispose of his wife STOP," continued the message.

"NO!" yelled Rubaysh, slamming his fist down on the antique keyboard. He then bashed out a final message. "You will not go near her, nor anyone else who knew him STOP Understand STOP Leave them to me."

"I must get my hands on that treasure," rasped Rubaysh, reclining on cushions in the living room, unremittingly chewing khat as he pondered his options. Few were aware of its existence; he knew everything about it except its whereabouts. He'd been careful to conceal his quest from his fundamentalist collaborators, knowing they could only misconstrue his intentions. Islamists were not motivated by such mundanity as hidden treasure. Even so, he was of the firm belief that whoever possessed this holy relic, which had been imbued with the power of Allah himself, would have the means to crush the Kafir once and for all.

He reached into his robes and pulled out a photograph of an old walking stick. On the back was written an inscription in Arabic:

"*The Staff of Musa. Allah has vouchsafed the power of his Rod* only three times in history. *We were godless fools the first time, fresh out of Eden, using it to cross Bab-el-Mandeb with less understanding of its might than if it had been an ape's walking stick. The second time the prophet Musa was given the power of the staff, both to invite the pharaoh to accept God's divine message as well as to help the Israelites escape Egypt. But the staff was wasted on the Jews as they were unwilling to fight the Canaanites once they reached the Promised Land.*

"After the prophet's death, the staff was moved to Jerusalem. Many comers then tried to get their hands on it but all were denied even the chance to shift it from the stone where it lay entombed. The third and last time Allah bestowed the power of his staff was on the 13th-century Muslim Sultan Baybars, who was allowed to remove it from Jerusalem, as it was otherwise destined for the hands of Frankish barbarians. He placed it in a nondescript box, and took it to the Land of Punt where it was reburied in the desert. And there it has remained, hidden away under the sands of time..."

Rubaysh sighed and replaced the photograph, whispering, "That is until Mehemet Abdul Rahman found it." He refused to believe the Staff of Musa could fall into the hands of an American. That was never the will of Allah. News of Johnny Oceans's death confirmed it. But as a result he was now farther from finding its location than ever before.

Following his communiqués with Rubaysh in Aden, Omar ordered a meeting of his mujahideen commanders at the al-Shabaab safe house in Bosaso. They were seated around a glass coffee table drinking tea, dressed in white robes and *kufi* caps. Omar was holding forth with real determination in his face. "Now that the American's out of the way, we are closer to achieving a Mujahid nation of Somalia."

"That Kafir was close to the pirates," said Ahmed, a stately mujahideen with angular features and a razor-sharp beard. "We can only guess what he was up."

"Praise be to Allah, his wicked conspiracy has failed," said Dahir, who chuckled as he spoke. His forehead and jowls were glistening from perspiration and every so often he used his *keffiyeh* to wipe the sweat away. "May Allah the almighty give us success."

"OK, down to business!" snapped Omar. "Shabaab is by no means defeated, regardless of what the Western media is saying. We still control large areas of south central Somalia. And we can still launch attacks in Mogadishu and Kismayo. Our alliance with al-

Qaeda in the Arabian Peninsula means we no longer have to rely on port taxes, and we're still earning good money from charcoal. We will continue to come under attack by AMISOM in the south, but our presence in the north here remains unchallenged."

He regarded each of his commanders, narrowed his eyes then lowered his voice. "Conditions are right to launch our plan for jihad in Puntland. The Combined Task Force 150 has seriously weakened the might of the pirates at sea, which has led to resentment among the Majeerteen, while Shabaab has grown stronger on land. CTF 150 does not realise it, but in the past year it has created a fertile ground for jihad among the Majeerteen pirates. It's time for us to nurture their discontent."

"How do you propose we do that?" asked Ahmed. "We're already in the madrasas. If we provoke the local authorities any more they will surely raid our base in Galaga again, only this time we could lose our foothold in Puntland once and for all."

Omar tapped the side of his nose, retrieved a piece of paper from his pocket, carefully unfolded it, and then placed it on the table in front of his fellow mujahideen. "This is from Yusuf Ali al-Rubaysh, commander of AQAP in Aden. He wants us to launch attacks on the pirates and make it look like they were carried out by CTF 150."

Ahmed picked up the diagram and chuckled. "So, we attack as usual only this time we don't claim responsibility. In fact we make it look like our enemies carried out the attacks on the Majeerteen, thereby pushing them closer to jihad."

"They like to think they're impervious to it," continued Omar, cracking a rare smile, "but what we will inflict on them in the coming days will bring the Majeerteen to their knees, begging for mercy."

Rubaysh was ready to cross the Gulf of Aden himself to the port of Bosaso and find out what he could about Oceans's last movements. Khadija, his wife, had already been spotted in public. Maybe she would tell him what he needed to know. But there were drones in the sky day and night, photographing Yemenis and spying on them wherever they went. The Americans no longer concerned themselves with apprehending al-Qaeda suspects, nor bringing them to justice. The moment they had a clear shot, they simply took them out with a Hellfire missile. Consequently people had begun avoiding weddings and private functions, fearing they might unwittingly find themselves in the sights of a Reaper drone.

US reconnaissance was Rubaysh's greatest nemesis, but he had learned to evade it through various labyrinths of deception. SIM cards and sat phones were regularly replaced or rotated out of service. Sending out false information was another way he deceived his enemy. On one occasion he gave his sat phone to a foot soldier, and instructed him to take it to al-Mukalla but not switch it on until after he'd reached the port. Two hours later he heard the port had been bombed, and the soldier killed, by a drone.

He sent a text message to his cousin saying, "*Masha Allah*, I will attend your glorious wedding in Shibam today." Then, donning a light blue burka and stashing a second black one beneath it, he left the Ma'alla safe house disguised as a woman and moved across the port of Aden on foot. He made one stop, a money broker on the Hawala network, with whom he deposited five thousand dollars that he would redeem on the other side of the Gulf. When he reached the harbour he boarded a boat with a different destination to his, and then disembarked just before it departed, now dressed in the black burka. From there he transferred by bus to the airport and, using a false passport, embarked on a flight to Djibouti.

At least the Americans would be faced with a choice of targets, and that would be enough for him to evade their drones this time. In Djibouti he lost the burkas and paid a fishing dhow to take him to Puntland. Thus he arrived in Bosaso port late afternoon, undetected by the Puntland Intelligence Agency, and took a room at the Hotel Huruuse in the old quarter of town.

CHAPTER FOURTEEN

"I say it's essential we stick to the lakeshore," said Derek, as he and Abdulmajid struggled along in the mire that led through Nechisar National Park. Mud-leaping was all the more precarious when shackled to another person. It had begun to rain and, judging by the clouds in the distance, it was about to get much worse. In the rolling squall, the storm bubbled, and the trees began to totter and collide, sounding disturbingly like the previous day's flash flood.

"We should have stayed on the main road," said Abdulmajid.

"And deal with that lunatic, Ryan? No, *rafiki*, best we stick to this road." Derek examined his shoes. They had tripled their mass with mud. "It's certainly doing a pretty good job of sticking to us."

"I say we go back to the road."

"No longer an option, Abdulmajid! Don't worry, I'm sure we'll find help soon enough."

"But we can catch a lift on the road. This way could lead to more danger."

"Look," smiled Derek, "trust me, I'm an experienced safari guide. We'll be fine. The first rule of finding your way out of nowhere is to follow the watercourses. Now in just a hundred metres or so we will reach the lake. From there, we'll be able to find the market."

"I don't believe there is a market down there."

"Let's just keep going and see what we find."

Lake Chamo was about ten kilometres wide and surrounded by mountains. As the squall picked up the lake grew choppy, and the sky darkened, making it more and more difficult to find their way across the ashen terrain. Then it began to pour. With the wind and the rain beating them back, they struggled along a beach that was scattered with large grey logs, barely visible in the downpour. Derek pointed to a craggy hilltop up ahead and Abdulmajid nodded.

"It's not easy negotiating your way around these timbers," cried Derek, trying not to trip on one. He was suddenly yanked to a halt. "What?" he snapped, shielding his brow with his free hand to try and see what had caused the Somali to stop so abruptly.

"They're not timbers," said Abdulmajid through chattering teeth. His gaze was transfixed by something on the ground. Derek looked around and quickly came to the realisation that they were actually standing in the midst of at least two dozen Nile crocodiles. And, having reached the middle of the congregation, there was no apparent way out. The crocodiles remained perfectly still and silent in the downpour, not even a hiss. Their instincts were to wait until their prey was close enough for an ambush.

"So this is what Ryan meant," cried Abdulmajid. "A crocodilian market."

"The power of the croc's bite is ten times that of a great white shark," said Derek.

"Now's not the time for Discovery Channel, Derek!"

"Actually, there are a few things you should know about them. They're not hard to outrun while they're slithering on their bellies, but as soon as they rise up and start 'high-walking', look out. Also the muscles they have for opening their jaws are extremely weak, so if you do get in a tussle make sure you keep that snapper shut." Abdulmajid began to pray. With the rain pouring off his chin, he might even have been crying.

Two crocodiles started slowly slithering towards them. "OK, if we don't leave soon, they *will* attack," rasped Derek.

"We'll be eaten alive!" cried Abdulmajid.

More of the crocs lying in the sand began to stir. "Fuck it!" said

Derek. "Let's just make a run for it."

"Are you out of your mind?"

"If we take long, raised, rapid strides we'll cover as much ground as possible with the least number of footfalls. It's our only chance. Now or never. C'mon, on three..."

"*Inshe Allah*," whispered Abdulmajid.

Positioned with his right hand extended back to where he was connected to Abdulmajid and his left foot forward, Derek scoped the surest route. His head was reeling from a plethora of poor options. He swallowed hard, counted aloud, "One...two...*three*," then took off in a mad dash, with Abdulmajid in tow. The crocodiles were all in motion now, high-walking and snapping their formidable jaws. "Holler at the top of your lungs," cried Derek. "That's worked before."

Yelling and screaming as they ran through the frenzied nest of crocs, they managed to dodge every one, some by just a hair's breadth. They had nearly escaped the danger when they then spotted one last crocodile blocking their path: a six-metre-long male, its enormous mouth agape, waiting to eat them both up whole. "I'm not about to stop now," cried Derek.

"No!" screamed Abdulmajid, but before he knew it, Derek had spring-boarded off the brute's snout, slamming it shut, then bounded down the length of its body. Abdulmajid followed and they did not stop running until they had reached higher ground.

"Close call," laughed Derek, trying to catch his breath.

Abdulmajid was in much better shape but not at all jubilant. "That crocodile could have eaten you, and I would not have been able to escape the same fate. I cannot believe you did that."

"*We*...did that, *rafiki*. Extraordinary people...do remarkable things...in tough circumstances."

"I had no choice in the matter, which is something I'm used to. Being a refugee teaches you endurance and pride. It requires courage, but I never take unnecessary risks. You, my friend, just want to die."

"OK, fine. Let's try and break free of these cuffs. And then you won't have to go along with all my decisions any more." Derek looked around and found a piece of volcanic rock, about the size of a grapefruit. "Are you right-handed?"

"No, left-handed."

"Great, so they shackled us *both* by our good hands." Derek placed the chain connecting the two cuffs across another rock. "Let's hope I don't miss then..." Abdulmajid winced as his fellow captive raised the stone and, with a sharp intake of breath, brought it down hard on the chain. There was a loud bang, a flash of sparks, and the rock broke in two. But when Derek examined the results the metal had not even been dented. "I guess we need a blacksmith," he sighed, standing up. "Let's keep heading north."

While continuing to aim for the hilltop, they steered well clear of the lakeshore, following a muddy inland game-viewing track through Miombo woodland. The rain had stopped and the flora glistened as the sun broke through swiftly moving clouds, turning the puddles into strobe lights. The chatter of a thousand weaver birds erupted from the shrubs and trees around them, in a feverish cacophony that seemed to oscillate in decibels relative to the intensity of sunlight.

They were still shaken after their narrow escape from the Crocodile Market, though, except for the occasional warthog, they encountered no more wildlife. "We'll never reach Puntland at this rate," moaned Derek, checking his watch. "It's already midday and we're not even in Arba Minch."

"I'm hungry," moaned Abdulmajid.

"Yeah, me too. Haven't eaten anything since that parched corn Ryan bought for us in Omorate. I really wish I hadn't left Gabriel's care package behind."

"Can we order a big plate of *injera wot* when we reach Arba Minch?" asked Abdulmajid, rubbing his belly.

"How will we pay for it?" replied Derek.

"You're a *muzungu*. I'm sure they'll believe whatever jazz you tell them..." Abdulmajid began to scan the sky. Above the din of the weavers he had heard a familiar sound. "Look," he cried, pointing south. Flying low above the trees, like a giant grey heron, was a long, thin aircraft with a vast wingspan. "Allah," cried Abdulmajid, "it's a drone, and it's going to crash into that hilltop!" The aircraft lowered its hydraulic undercarriage, barely missing the top of the hill before disappearing behind it.

"C'mon," said Derek. "Let's see if it landed safely."

When they reached the summit, they saw that the drone had touched down on a paved airstrip running parallel to another lakeshore, about a kilometre below the hilltop where they stood, which according to a sign was the "Bridge of God" separating Lake Chamo from Lake Abaya. Derek cupped his hand to his ear. Fading in and out on the wind was a familiar guitar riff: Blue Oyster Cult, "Don't Fear the Reaper". "That must be the US airbase at Arba Minch," he said. "Let's go check it out."

Without their usual payloads of six missiles suspended beneath them, the gangly wings of the four MQ-9 Reapers taxiing over the bumpy runway oscillated aggressively as they prepared for take-off. Powered by a single propeller, situated aft of a triangular set of tail wings, the unmanned ariel vehicle was designed for endurance and not speed. Its fuselage was long and narrow but broadened to an inelegant bulbous hood at the nose: the nub of all its surveillance technology. The whole aircraft was a uniform drab olive, with tiny United States Air Force insignia painted in black on its side. Angled aerodynamically atop the fuselage, slightly forward of the wings, was a fin-shaped antenna with a tubular top.

"A perfect handhold," said Derek. He and Abdulmajid were concealed in the shadows of a pine wood surrounding the airport.

"What?" asked Abdulmajid.

"Shhh!" said Derek, pointing out that they now had company. Wholly unaware that two people had just infiltrated their drone base, two uniformed American airmen, one redhead and one Latino, were standing nearby, enveloped in a cloud of marijuana smoke.

"The Wing King said we're going LATN on this next four," said the redhead, passing a joint to the Latino. "They're headed to Camp Lemonnier."

"What the fuck is Sergeant Seuss up to now?" laughed the

Latino, letting out the smoke.

"I think he's testing some new surveillance equipment." The redhead took a few last hits on the joint then stubbed it out with his boot. "C'mon! Let's get back before Sergeant Seuss hears a who."

Derek watched as the lead aircraft made a one-hundred-and-eighty-degree turn at the end of the runway, then he turned to Abdulmajid. "Imagine hitching a ride on one?" he chirped. "That would get us to Puntland in a hurry."

Believing Derek was speaking hypothetically, Abdulmajid laughed. "Allah! Where would we sit?'

"On the wings, of course, either side of the fuselage. We could secure ourselves to that antenna with our handcuffs."

"Surely, they would find us there," sneered Abdulmajid.

"I doubt it," insisted Derek. "All that surveillance equipment is designed to scan the ground below, not the aircraft itself. Our presence would cause a bit of drag, sure, but no more than if it was armed with missiles." Derek began to move stealthily towards the runway. "Don't you think it would be cool, hitching a ride on a Reaper drone?"

Abdulmajid suddenly realised he wasn't kidding. "Cool?" he cried, yanking at the cuffs in a vain effort to free himself from the madman. "No, not cool. Suicide!"

"What are you talking about? We'll be fine!" insisted Derek. Despite Abdulmajid's efforts to restrain him he was determined to get closer. "You heard what that guy said. They're flying this squadron low to the ground."

"I didn't hear them say that!"

"That's what LATN means: low altitude tactical navigation. We'll hold on for a couple of hours, then when the drone swings around on its final approach into Djibouti, we'll jump into the drink."

"I never heard such a ridiculous idea. Why don't we just appeal to these guys for help, or some blacksmithing skills?"

"Listen, if we walk into that base handcuffed, we'll be arrested. And that'll just open up a whole new can of whup-ass. These guys are likely to render us blindfolded to a forgotten hellhole still stuck in the Arab Winter and hand us over to a sadistic homosexual prison commandant. And I, for one, sure as shit don't want to be rendered to the Middle East."

"Don't you think they'll be even angrier once they discover hitchhikers on their drone?"

"They won't."

"There is no way I am flying on a drone all the way to Djibouti."

"Do you have a better idea?"

The last drone had reached the end of the runway and Derek knew it was now or never. Using the midday shadows of the pine forest as cover, he and Abdulmajid dashed along the perimeter of the runway until they were about five metres directly behind the Y-shaped tail fins of the Reaper. The "pilot", sequestered in a dimly lit control room somewhere on the base, prepared his aircraft for take-off, manipulating the flaps, then revving its rear propeller to full throttle.

Trying to stay out of sight of the camera secured to its belly, the pair snuck up behind. But before they could reach it, the aircraft began to move down the runway. Derek gestured to Abdulmajid that they should chase after it. As the drone began to accelerate, they put all their effort into running alongside its left side so they could climb on to the wing, which was at eye level for Derek but above Abdulmajid's head. The fuselage was vibrating so violently on the uneven runway it caused the craft to flap its spindly wings like a bird. There was nothing to grab on to.

Running as fast as he dared, lest he cause Abdulmajid to trip and fall, Derek moved away from the fuselage towards the tip of the wing. Then, raising his shackled arm high enough to pass over the wing, he ran ahead. As the drone took off his weight dragged Abdulmajid forward, on to the wing, while he hung below the aircraft, his legs rotating aimlessly above the ground. He was in danger of pulling Abdulmajid off again, but the retracting undercarriage gave him the means to hoist himself up.

The aircraft then began to tilt sideways. "Quick! Climb over the fuselage!" he yelled. "We have to balance the weight!" Abdulmajid manoeuvred his legs over the centre of the aircraft and, as Derek had suggested, used the communications antenna to secure them to the plane. And then, like a broken bronco, the Reaper took to the sky, with two stowaways on board.

CHAPTER FIFTEEN

It was not yet dawn when Maxamid parked his white pickup truck by the water. He and Nadif stepped out on to a secluded beach a few kilometres up the coast from his sister's house in Bender Siyaada. Nadif was dressed in a manner befitting a young Islamic scholar, with a white skull cap, long-sleeved beige cotton shirt, matching long trousers and leather sandals. Maxamid wore rolled-up jeans and an unbuttoned blue shirt, and no shoes on his feet. His lanky form appeared to be sprouting from his garments. He stashed his BAR behind the seat. He would not be needing his weapon at sea today.

From the rear of the vehicle they gathered two boxes of fishing line and bait, a harpoon, a bucket of chopped fish, and a bundle of fishing rods, and carried them to a long, thin skiff beached at the high-tide mark, its white fibreglass hull faintly reflecting the orange and blue horizon. Maxamid was eager to launch. For the first time in weeks high tide coincided with daybreak and the sea was calm.

They placed the fishing tackle in the forward hull. Maxamid lifted each one of a half dozen red gasoline tanks to determine its contents. "There's enough fuel here to take us to Aden and back," he said. With its two 250-horsepower outboard engines, his twelve-metre skiff could fly across the water and outrun the fastest coast-guard vessels. He checked the fittings on the six rod holders secured along the gunwales and made sure his fish-killing club was under the stern.

Nadif laid a mat down on the sand and faced Mecca for sunrise prayers. Maxamid continued organising the tackle. This wasn't the first time they had gone fishing together, though he couldn't remember the last time. It was his sister's suggestion. She thought the boy might benefit from spending time with a father figure. At first Nadif refused, claiming Islam forbade fishing for amusement, and only agreed after Maxamid assured him they would either eat or sell everything they caught.

Maxamid's phone vibrated. He pulled it from his pocket to see who was texting him. Nadif looked back with consternation then continued with his prayers. It was the same anonymous message as an hour earlier: "*Tuna shoals off Abdul al Kuri. Masha Allah, they're only there for you, Maxamid.*" Fishermen sometimes sent messages indicating where the fishing was good. But no one knew this number. "*We-hel,*" he cursed. That he could leave his boat and fuel unguarded on the beach was indicative of the respect and fear Maxamid inspired among his fellow Majeerteen, including the *badaadintu badah*.

He ignored the message and returned his phone to his pocket, then, seeing Nadif was through with his prayers, snapped, "C'mon, boy, grab hold of the gunwale, let's go." Taking advantage of the back flow from a large wave, they eased the skiff into the water and climbed aboard. Nadif sat on a cross bench close to the bow, Maxamid at the stern. He lowered the engines into the water, squeezed the gas-line bulb, then from the console turned over the ignition. The propellers spun into action. He pushed the throttle forward then sped his skiff away from shore.

Acquainted with a fisherman's routine, Nadif carefully secured lures to lines on rods while his uncle motored on in silence. Once the sun had ascended a quarter of the sky they were on a familiar bank in the Gulf of Aden, surrounded by undulating swells. Without cloud, vessel or coast in sight Maxamid switched off the engines and let the boat ride the waves. It was impossible to tell what, if any, prizes circled around down there, but the bank was as good a place as any to start.

He wasted no time casting a hook into the deep blue sea. Once the line had reached an adequate depth he rapidly reeled it in again, hoping to lure a passing tuna with its animation, then repeated the process. Nadif followed his uncle's every move. The two of them continued "deep jigging" in this way for a while.

"Is this how Majeerteen fish?" asked Nadif.

"How should I know," came the reply.

"But you are a fisherman, aren't you? And a Majeerteen."

"I may be Majeerteen but I was born in Kismayo, and I grew up in Kenya. Your stepfather taught me how to fish like this."

"Is that the reason you have no knowledge of the Quran, because you went to Kafir schools?"

"C'mon, Nadif. Let's just try and enjoy ourselves."

"The Prophet says it is unlawful to pull fish from the water with a hook for no other purpose than to amuse yourself."

Maxamid took a sharp breath then said, "Believe me, there's nothing amusing about fishing with a teenage fanatic."

"What?"

"Why don't we pray for a strike, eh?" asked Maxamid. "*Inshe Allah.*"

"There is no need to mention Allah's name when fishing. Fish are after all automatically halal after they die."

"Do you know the fable of the tuna fish and the dolphin?" asked Maxamid, casting his line as far out as he could. Nadif shook his head. "One fine day while hunting for sardines, a tuna fish accidentally swam into a bay belonging to a bad-tempered dolphin. The dolphin spotted him chasing after his sardines, and splashed through the water at speed to stop him. Realising his mistake the tuna fled, but the dolphin persisted, gradually gaining on him. When close enough to seize his prey the dolphin pounced, but the force of his attack sent the tuna hurtling on to a sandbank, and without a moment's thought the dolphin leapt out after him. Suddenly they were both beached. The tuna looked up with a smile and said, 'I'm happy to die now, knowing the one who killed me will suffer the same fate.'"

Maxamid felt his phone buzz again. "How?" he asked. "We're out of network range..." It was the same message, only this time it gave the exact coordinates of the tuna shoal.

"Who is texting you?" asked Nadif.

"Some anonymous messenger telling me there are tuna shoals off Abdul al Kuri."

"Why don't we go there?"

"Forget it," laughed Maxamid. "Abdul al Kuri is more than three hundred kilometres away, in Yemeni waters, and shark-infested. It's also where the task force is most active. I have no intention of going anywhere near it."

"But we're skunking here."

US Navy Commander Steve Musgrave scanned the ocean with his binoculars as his ship, the *Loreto*, headed east from Bosaso on her way to Socotra on routine patrols. The mission was considered low risk; accordingly his crew were inexperienced and the ship was equipped with only minimal defensive weapons. The rest of the task force, stationed at Camp Lemonnier, was designated to aid all patrol boats if necessary, but there was no need that morning. Pirate activity off northern Somalia had dropped to a fraction of what it had been.

"Sir, patrol cutter approaching from the southwest" declared the seaman manning the radar equipment.

The commander picked up the radio handset. "Marine vessel, state your purpose."

The radio crackled to life. "*This is Commander Sharif of the Yemeni Coast Guard cutter Fatuma No 35683, requesting immediate assistance from the* Loreto. *Is Commander Musgrave on board?*"

Commander Musgrave examined the approaching vessel. It was a standard Navy cutter, typical of the CTF 150 patrols in the Gulf. The call sign checked out. "This one says she's friendly but we can't be too sure." Again he spoke into the handset. "*Fatuma*, what is the nature of your emergency?" There was no reply. The *Fatuma* began to gain on them. "Man your stations! Full speed ahead!"

"Full speed ahead, Captain," cried the seaman at the helm. The rest of the crew scrambled breathlessly for the ship's guns. But as the *Fatuma* drew closer they saw none of her crew on deck, none of her guns manned. Nor did they see the two blue drums bobbing in the water ahead of them. Commander Musgrave thought he saw someone wearing a gas mask on the cutter's bridge.

"What's that smell?" cried the radar operator. "Like rotten eggs..."

"Chemical attack!" cried their commander as he leapt for his gas mask. But there was no time to act. In an instant the ship was enveloped in a cloud of hydrogen sulphide gas, and after a few gasping moments of asphyxiation, everyone on board was killed. The commander was the last to die as he struggled in vain to send out a distress signal.

Despite her skipper and crew lying dead on her decks the Loreto continued on her phantom course, while the Fatuma kept pace alongside. Only after the air around her had cleared and the deadly toxin had dissipated was she boarded and commandeered by al-Shabaab.

"Yelee!" cried Maxamid, as his nephew hauled another prize catch into the boat. "It's yellow-fin genocide!" The tuna were jumping and Maxamid was at the helm of the skiff idling in over the swells in a zigzagging pattern, trolling a spread of six, the lines at different angles to simulate a school of baitfish. It was mid-afternoon. Their morning on the bank had not yielded a single strike, and so consequently they decided to risk sailing to the coordinates off Abdul al Kuri. After only an hour they had already caught five yellow-fin tuna. "This is truly great fishing!"

"Allah is great!" laughed Nadif. "He has provided again." The boy was overcome with spiritual joy as he clubbed to death his fifth tuna. Not since learning the Quran had he experienced anything quite as exciting. "How much will these fetch?"

"Maybe three hundred dollars each. Bad-weyn is bountiful."

Rising and falling like a laughing sultan the sea was throwing fish into the skiff. The spread of lines dangling from their stern was catching the afternoon sun and everything under it.

"Fishing is such a honorable pursuit, Uncle. How can you be a *badaadintu badah?*"

"I'll tell you why," said Maxamid, steering the boat into a large swell. "Because of what happened in these waters. When I started out fishing was a prosperous livelihood, but during the 1980s and 1990s the stocks plummeted at the hands of illegal foreign trawlers, who knew no limits to their ravage."

"I've heard that folklore too many times, Uncle. So why now, when there are no more foreign trawlers in these waters, does your piracy continue?"

"Are you mad? Our seas are swarming with foreigners, here only to protect their interests. Yet despite this so-called 'combined task force', illegal fishing and waste-dumping continues in Somali waters. Not a single perpetrator has ever been brought to justice. And our own Coast Guard is too stupid and corrupt to do anything. Who else but the *badaadintu badah* will protect Somalia?"

"Weren't you once in the Puntland Coast Guard?"

"Yes, for a time in the late 1990s, after our government hired a British security firm to train up a proper maritime protection force that could effectively patrol the Puntland coast. Hart Security taught us how to use sophisticated radio equipment, GPS, satellite phones, boarding techniques, special undetectable vessels, and mother ships, as well as Internet resources to locate illegal trawlers in Somali waters. But the government had a change of heart, and got rid of them in favour of a Somali company based in Dubai. After that things went downhill and pretty soon there were fifteen hundred highly trained maritime paramilitaries out of work."

"That explains the *badaadintu badah* better than your creation myth," laughed Nadif. He was a bright boy. Both his father and grandfather had been intellectuals.

"You want to hear something really funny?" asked Maxamid, turning his skiff around.

"What?"

"Hart Security now provides most of the anti-piracy security for ships coming through the Gulf."

Nadif smiled then gazed out across the sea as he slowly reeled in his line. "My stepfather is dead, isn't he?"

"Who, Mehemet? Nonsense. He is a capable man. I'm sure he's safe."

"I heard it in the madrasa..."

"You cannot believe the rumours you hear in the madrasas, Nadif."

"You would rather I believe nothing, like you?"

Maxamid did not reply. There wasn't much he believed in. He'd never made a pilgrimage to Mecca, despite having the means, only ever observed Ramadan when the going was good, and rarely went to mosque. But if there was one thing he was convinced by, it was the stamina of his old friend and brother-in-law Mehemet Abdul Rahman. Despite all the rumours, he refused to believe that man was dead.

"Let me tell you something about your stepfather," he said, leaning forward and putting his hand on the boy's shoulder. "He had mad skills like no other man. Did you know that, before he came to Africa, back in Miami, he used to be a smuggler?"

A look of utter disbelief came over Nadif's face. "Mehemet? But he tried to put a stop to Puntland piracy."

"That was not always the case," said Maxamid, toying with his hennaed goatee. He was unsure about just how much he should reveal to his nephew. "You have heard of vessels that sink in fair weather, with suspicious cargo on board, send no mayday, crew vanish?" Nadif nodded. "Well, back in 1999, there was one ship that came to these shores from Italy..."

Just then a line at the bow of their skiff began screaming off its spool. Clearly a massive fish had struck. Maxamid leapt forward to grab it, pushing his nephew aside. "Take the helm!" he shouted, strapping on his fighting belt and arranging his lanky frame optimally for the match. Nadif tried to steer the skiff in such a way that his uncle could reel the monster in over the gunwale. "This is going to be back-breaking," growled Maxamid.

He thrived on adrenaline in uncertain situations, and always welcomed a battle between equals, but there was nothing more invigorating than having it out with nature. The fish circled back. It was a very big circle and he fought with all his strength to shorten it, rocking and reeling while the massive creature rose steadily in ever tighter rotations. He then let the spool of line feed smoothly off his rod as it dived again, and took a break from the fight.

All at once the line slackened, and he wondered if it had snapped. Not likely with a breaking strain of four hundred kilograms. There was only one other explanation. "Quick, the throttle!" he yelled to Nadif, who shoved it forward as far as it would go, causing the engines to scream. At that moment the hooked fish surfaced right next to their skiff. Maxamid staggered backward, marvelling at his prize. It was a blue marlin, and looked to weigh over three hundred kilograms. As quickly as it had surfaced the fish submerged. Holding the rod firmly, he felt it dive deeper and deeper into the deep blue ocean.

It took another thirty minutes' fight before he managed to reel the marlin to the surface again. This time he made sure it took the thrust of his harpoon. The creature twisted its body in agony, then dived, taking the harpoon and line with it. In no time the ocean began to bubble with half a dozen swiftly moving grey dorsal fins. "Tiger shark!" cried Maxamid, struggling with his rod. He knew they would destroy his catch. He looked out across the water and sighed.

"Don't worry, I can outrun the sharks," said Nadif. But no matter how much he tried to evade them the sharks maintained their pursuit of the skiff. "Keep reeling him in, Uncle! You've almost got the monster."

Maxamid now had a change of heart. Whether it was down to the exhaustion or the heat, he wasn't sure, but in his mind he could see his blue marlin sailing happily away to the Spice Islands, in a big samosa-sailed dhow, and making it in time for mint tea under the big shade tree. Holding his rod firmly in one hand, he reached down with the other and picked up the knife. Then raising the blade to the line, he said, "I owe this to you, my friend."

"No, wait!" cried Nadif.

"Too late," said Maxamid as he cut the line.

"Why did you do that?"

"Respect."

"But you have denied it its Sharia purpose..."

"Don't question me, boy. Do you think I just..." He caught sight of another skiff just beyond the swells, belonging to a fellow pirate. Half a dozen people were on board. "Damn! We don't need any competition."

"Are they *badaadintu badah?*" asked Nadif.

"Yes, but they won't fuck with me." Just then a siren sounded, followed by a fog horn. Two larger ships were in pursuit of the pirate skiff. "*We'el!*" cursed Maxamid. "Maritime police!"

"We should go," said Nadif.

"No, stay cool. Worst they can do is fine us for fishing in Yemeni waters without a licence. Let's just cut the engines and wait until they're finished dealing with these other guys." The other skiff came to a halt in the water and the two ships pulled up on either side of it. From a hundred metres away Maxamid and Nadif could see the sailors on board the ships were aiming their weapons at the skiff, but they were unable to hear the instructions they were issuing its occupants. "Looks like a US Navy ship and a Yemeni Coast Guard cutter," said Maxamid. Then, for no apparent reason, the sailors opened fire on the skiff.

"*Uncle Max!*" cried Nadif. "*They just killed those people in cold blood?*"

They then poured gasoline over the skiff and set it alight, causing the survivors to leap about in a dance of agony that was brought to an end by more gunfire. The two maritime ships then pulled away from the blazing skiff and sailed towards them. Nadif began to pray. "Don't be afraid," whispered Maxamid.

In a moment the vessels were alongside their skiff. "Cut your engines!" ordered a man standing on deck of the cutter, who spoke in Arabic through a megaphone. Nadif did as he was told. "Don't move! Put your hands in the air!" Sailors aboard both ships cocked their weapons and aimed them at them.

"We're unarmed," cried Maxamid, throwing up his long arms as high as they could reach. Nadif did the same. It was obvious they were just fishing. The only weapons on board were a knife, a club, a harpoon and six rods. And at their feet lay five large tuna in a pool of blood, one or two still showing signs of life.

In all his time at sea, Maxamid had never before seen maritime police massacre their prisoners in cold blood. The poor bastards didn't even get a chance to explain what they were doing. At that moment all he could think of was his Browning Automatic Rifle. At least if he had that weapon in his hands he would be spared a dishonourable death. He caught a whiff of a strange odour, like rotting food, coming from the Yemeni cutter. There was also something odd about the American ship. The crew may have been wearing US Navy uniforms, but they looked Somali: brown, lanky and curly-haired like him.

Standing back from the large, tinted-glass window on the bridge of the *Loreto*, so as to remain unseen, Omar scrutinised the skiff with merciless eyes. He was dressed in the uniform of a US Navy commander, and beads of sweat had gathered on his forehead and shaven upper lip. Hunting pirates was hard work. They had murdered dozens that day, pulling up alongside unsuspecting skiffs, opening fire, then torching their boats.

These two may have been unarmed, and only fishing as they claimed, but there was no mistaking a pirate's skiff, with its twin 250-horsepower engines. While two of his mujahideen held on to the boat with grappling hooks, four others had their fingers on their triggers, eagerly awaiting his order to open fire. But Omar hesitated. He recognised these two. It was Maxamid Malik, brother-in-law to the American, and his nephew Nadif. The boy was a potential new recruit to al-Shabaab. What better way to spread the word among the madrasas of Puntland than to let him return with his story? Besides Rubaysh wouldn't want them killed.

"Let them go!" said Omar, staying concealed on the bridge of the Loreto.

Ahmed, who was standing nearby, looked back at his commander with incredulity. "I thought you said kill every pirate we find."

"No," said Omar. "Let these two return and tell others what they saw here today."

CHAPTER SIXTEEN

The Reaper did not fly very fast, hence Derek and Abdulmajid had been airborne for hours, hanging on with the last of their failing strength, sunburnt, windburnt, exhausted, hungry, and thirsty. The drone had been following a chain of scintillating lakes through the Ethiopian Rift Valley, the final and most ancient stretch of the Hominid Highway that led to Bab-el-Mandeb, the Gate of Tears. On either side of the valley, spread out across plateaus, was a patchwork of ancient smallholdings separated by sheer canyons, deep wounds in the landscape that gave it an upside-down appearance.

Every minute of the journey had been hair-raising, as the aircraft kept to three hundred metres above the ground, over the most vertical terrain in Africa. Once during the flight, Abdulmajid had fallen off and Derek had to struggle to pull him back on. Consequently, their wrists were now mangled and bloody.

Derek searched ahead for the other three drones in the formation, but could only make out one against the mid-afternoon haze. Abdulmajid clutched his stomach with his free hand and, speaking loudly enough to be heard over the wind and propeller, asked, "What are the chances of a meal when we reach the sea?"

"Pretty good, if you're a shark," laughed Derek.

The Somalian threw his head back with exasperation. "Look," he said, "flying up there." Derek used his free hand to block out the sun. A large bird, with a vast wingspan and a ruffled breast of rusty feathers, soared directly above their heads, and it appeared to be holding something in its talons. "It's an eagle," said Abdulmajid.

"Actually, that's a lammergeier vulture," said Derek.

"Doesn't look like a vulture to me and, believe me, I've had many of them circling above my life. You're not a very good safari guide, are you? At least I can tell the difference between a vulture and an eagle. Eagles have feathers on their heads, like this bird, vultures are bald."

"I'm telling you, it belongs to a minor lineage of vulture that sports a feathered head. Looks like the front end of a griffin. You should be more concerned about the object it's carrying in its claws."

"What is it?"

"A bone."

"Why should I be worried?"

"Because it looks like it's about to drop the bone on our heads..."

"*Allah!*"

"That's what it does, scavenges bones and then drops them from a great height, so it can smash them open and get to the marrow. For some reason it thinks this Reaper is a dropping spot. Just keep a watchful eye on him and make sure it doesn't let go of that bone."

"Too late!"

Pulling each other in opposite directions like bound and confused cattle in an abattoir, Derek and Abdulmajid engaged in a frantic struggle to dodge the falling object. By sheer coincidence, their handcuffs took the blow of the lammergeier's osseous missile, exactly where it counted, and they were instantly freed from each other. "*Finally!*" exclaimed Derek, swinging his arm around like a propeller.

"*Masha Allah*," cried Abdulmajid, rubbing his wrist.

"Boo yakka!" cheered Derek. "Mother Nature strikes a bullseye!"

The valley had given way to what looked like a vast dried-up river delta. Derek recognised it as Ethiopia's Afar region, a desert abutting Djibouti and one of the hottest places on earth. It was exactly the direction in which he expected them to fly, which hadn't varied since taking off from Arba Minch airport. He was about to point out the proximity of their destination to his fellow passenger when the drone suddenly began banking steeply to the right, out of formation. They each grabbed hold of the antenna, this time with both their hands.

"What is happening?" asked Abdulmajid, eyes darting in every direction.

"We're turning east," replied Derek, "to Somalia."

In a dimly lit operator's cockpit, the airman assigned to monitor the formation of UAVs headed to Camp Lemonnier was seated in a large tan leather flight chair nonchalantly clicking through video feeds while sipping from a US Air Force mug filled with black coffee. Like most MQ-9 Reaper operators, he was attached to the 42nd Attack Squadron at Creech Air Force Base in Nevada. The Reapers' onboard sensors were sending back real-time data from the ground below, including vivid images of the landscape, which the distrait airman noted was becoming increasingly parched and gnarled as the flight progressed.

Most UAV missions flown out of remote locations switched operators shortly after take-off to Creech. This being a non-combatant mission over friendly skies, there was no need to station more than one service member in the 'cockpit' of the four aircraft as they followed a fixed northeasterly flightpath to Djibouti.

He picked up the issue of *Scientific American* and returned to the article he was reading by Yohannes Haile-Selassie about human origins. He propped his feet up on the instrument panel and leafed through the photos of fossil finds and rock formations in the Afar Triple Junction. It took him a moment to realise that he was reading about the very same place the squadron of UAVs was flying over at that moment. "Hmm," he smiled, "I wonder, if I zoom in, whether I might be able to find a fossil of my own." He leaned forward to turn the knob that operated the zoom. "That's odd," he said, noticing one of the gauges was indicating that the rear UAV in the squadron was armed. "There are no missiles on this drone..."

Suddenly a beeping red light on his control panel indicated the aircraft had fallen out of formation. The video feed confirmed it was on an entirely different flightpath. He immediately telephoned his commander. "Sir, I no longer have positive control of one of my aircraft. It's heading east over Oromia into Somalia."

"Roger that, airman. We verify command of your UAV has been compromised." After the video feed on his console went dead, the commander spoke again. "Airman, stand down, your aircraft has been requisitioned for a classified mission."

"Why do you suppose those sailors killed everyone on the skiff?" asked Nadif, gazing despairingly at the horizon where the ships had sailed. Until then, he had been sitting in stunned silence. What had started as a relaxing day fishing had ended in nightmare. Now they were adrift at sea, beyond Ras Asir, the apex of the Horn of Africa, which rose from the coast like the withered hand of an emaciated continent in the throes of death.

"I doubt those maritime police were legitimate," growled Maxamid. He tried again to spark the ignition. Nothing.

"Americans and Yemenis..." whispered Nadif. "They killed everybody, without mercy. Are they at war with us?"

"There are many out to destroy Somalia – even Somalians," said Maxamid. "We should never have sailed into Yemeni waters."

"It's what the imams have been telling us all along. They want to destroy us."

"Yeah, well, you are a smart boy, Nadif. You need to think for yourself."

"There is no question that we must defend ourselves."

"We've got more important things to think about," growled Maxamid. "This catch is in danger of going off in the hot sun and salty bilge."

Accordingly Nadif continued bleeding, gutting and removing the gills of their tuna, after which he put them in a cage and returned them to the cool water to keep them fresh. Attracted by the scent of tuna blood, the tiger sharks began to come back. Maxamid cursed them, and yanked the cage back into the boat. Soon, like waterborne hyenas, the sharks were caught up in a feverish hunt, moving swiftly yet erratically around the skiff.

A familiar humming made them both look up. A small aircraft was approaching from the west over Ras Asir. "*WE'EL!*" cried Maxamid. "A fucking drone, and it's heading straight for us." He'd endured enough attacks to know what to look out for, like heavy ordinance hanging from the wings. But on closer inspection of this drone he saw something quite unimaginable. Aloft on the wings of the aircraft, waving their arms in the air and shouting, were two passengers.

Maxamid rubbed his eyes in disbelief. Was he being pursued by demons? In desperation he tried the ignition once more and the engines finally started. He pushed the throttle forward and sped the skiff away, but when he looked back, the drone had adjusted its flightpath to keep him on target, while its frantic riders screamed louder and louder. As much as he tried to shake it, the flying monster kept on coming after him.

"Americans are invading Somalia!" yelled Nadif. "We're going to die in holy jihad!"

The drone descended to just ten metres above the water then buzzed their skiff and began turning on a tight arc, at which point its two screaming passengers jumped into the sea. The aircraft then circled for three hundred and sixty degrees before continuing on its way. Maxamid raced towards where the two hapless swimmers, a farenji and a Jereer, were struggling to stay afloat. The tiger sharks were closing in. Once alongside, he dashed forward to help Nadif. Without a moment to spare, they hauled the two men aboard, rescuing them from the hungry jaws of sharks. It was then that Maxamid noticed the *farenji* was wearing a large black watch, the very same one he'd given Mehemet.

Chapter Seventeen

As Khadija's newly arrived guests gravitated towards her dining room at Bender Siyaada, they found two female servants laying out dinner on a large oval table. First the women brought out baskets of dates and mangoes, jugs of fresh milk, water, and hot xawaash tea spiced with cardamom and cinnamon bark, then clay bowls filled with injera bread. Derek and Abdulmajid did little to disguise their appetites when the main dishes arrived: pots of spaghetti and basmati rice, grilled goat and chicken spiced with cumin and turmeric, and a stack of barbecued tuna steaks, the result of the day's catch.

Khadija sat at the head of the table smoking a cigarette. Behind her an offshore breeze wafted through the large dining-room picture window and flung her auburn hair in and out of moonbeams bouncing across the sea. Though the news had already reached her before his dramatic arrival, she appreciated that Derek had travelled a great distance and faced enormous challenges to tell her in person of the passing of her husband.

"Johnny, sorry, Mehemet," said Derek, stuffing a piece of goat meat in his mouth, "died at the hands of warriors, with his boots on, in the wilderness. Hell, I can't think of a better way to go. He didn't suffer; death was instantaneous."

She was even more beautiful than he imagined she'd be. Her eyes, lips and complexion were each a shade of Indian Ocean spice, and she radiated a youthfulness that belied her wisdom. She listened stoically to his account, while displaying no outward emotion, then asked, "Where's his body?"

"Couldn't find it," said Derek, "but that's not unusual in the wilderness. You'd be surprised how quickly a pride of hungry lions can…" He stopped, mid-sentence, realising he was being insensitive. Khadija remained impassive. One of her servants brought out a soapstone incense burner shaped like a medieval chalice. "Ah, I love that smell," laughed Derek. "Reminds me of Catholic mass."

"It's *luubaan*," said Khadija, wafting the smoke with her hand, "what you call frankincense or olibanum. It's tapped from the Boswellia tree by slashing the bark, and allowing the exuded resins to bleed out and harden. Puntland is one of the few places in the world that produces it. The Roman Catholic Church has obtained its supply from us since the 1st century. But we've been producing the stuff for much longer than that. There's a mural on the walls of Queen Hatshepsut's temple near Luxor in Egypt, depicting sacks of frankincense traded from the Land of Punt that dates back to the 13th century BC."

"Awesome," said Derek, rubbing his wrist where his watch was strapped. "I had no idea." Hearing her mention the Land of Punt reminded him of the treasure. He wondered how much the gathered family members knew about it. Khadija undoubtedly did, though she'd said nothing when she first noticed her late husband's Kobold Phantom Tactical attached to his arm, except, "I'm thankful you didn't leave it behind."

"So, you came all this way just to tell us the news of Mehemet's death," said Maxamid, laughing contemptuously and shaking his head. "Well, you and your Jereer can go home tomorrow. There's a flight to Djibouti leaving in the morning, a manned flight."

"Maxamid, please!" said Khadija firmly. "This is my home and these people are welcome here for as long as they wish. You must forgive my brother. He was raised by a fishing rod."

"Yes I was. Until outsiders came and took away my livelihood."

"You're a Puntland pirate, right?" asked Derek. "I fully support what you guys do. How the hell else are you gonna protect your tuna stocks, right, *rafiki*?"

"What *rafiki*? I ain't your *rafiki*. And don't use that Jereer language around me. Here we speak Somali, not Kiswahili..."

"I'm afraid you have arrived at a very turbulent time in our country, Mr Strangely," interrupted Khadija. Nadif, who was seated adjacent to his mother, looked up. She took a contemplative drag from her cigarette then continued. "The Islamists have been pushed from the south, out of Mogadishu, Kismayo, Baidoa, and Beledweyne, and are now moving into Puntland. What used to be a peaceful semi-autonomous region of Somalia has become a target for al-Shabaab and al-Qaeda, and no one here seems inclined to stop them."

"How can we defend ourselves against terrorists?" asked Maxamid.

"With courage and fortitude," replied Khadija, "The Majeerteen sultanate was once a powerful enclave, but we have been mellowed by the sea and Somalia's creeping nihilism. Today we're nothing more than common criminals. All we think about now is hijacking ships and holding their crews for ransom."

"How else do we defend Somali waters from overfishing?" asked Maxamid.

"The problem of overfishing has always been there," said Khadija. "It doesn't mean you can take the law into your own hands."

"At least *badaadintu badah* provide for their people," said Maxamid, proudly nodding his head.

"What? You think we need khat and AK-47s? We need schools, Max, not drugs and guns, and ones that do not teach our children to blow themselves up."

"Somalia Muslims are weak," said Nadif, tearing off a piece of injera bread from a bowl in the centre of the table. He had a peculiar smile and spoke with a cracked voice, His soft brown eyes and symmetrical diamond-shaped face were offset by pimples and a patchwork of facial hair sprouting insufficiently from various places on his chin and cheeks. He addressed each of the guests with uncommon pubescent self-assurance. "It's because we're weighed down by the accumulated intellectual baggage of Sufism."

"Listen to how the boy talks," sneered Maxamid.

"I would hate to see us do away with any school of Islamic thought," said Khadija, stubbing out her cigarette and turning to her food, "but I refuse to allow the rule of one ideology over another. Why can't Somalia be a country with a broad range of doctrines and ideas, an all-embracing society?"

"Because Salafism demands intense commitment from its followers," insisted Nadif. "If our reform movement is to succeed, we must only follow the original teachings of the Prophet Muhammad."

"It's not a reform movement," said Khadija, putting a forkful of basmati rice in her mouth, "it's a revolution that aims to destroy the way Islam is practised in Somalia."

"That's not true!" said Nadif. "We simply want people to accept *al-salafia*. Somalia needs strict discipline to bring it out of its clannish stupidity."

"And if they don't follow your doctrine, what then?" asked Khadija, raising her eyebrows. "Hmm?" Her boy stared blankly back at her. "Nadif, Somalis will always be clannish, chew *khat* and practise Sufism no matter who tries to reform them, and to whatever degree. Salafism is just another kind of clan. And it's not what I brought you up to believe. "

"But I want to be part of something that inspires strength and solidarity."

"I can understand that," said Khadija, leaning across to stroke his hair. "All I'm asking is that you balance what you hear with what you were brought up to believe. Seek your own theological answers from the Quran. That's all." Nadif smiled at his mother in acquiescence, and she leaned closer and kissed him on his cheek.

"Could you explain Salafism?" said Derek. "I'm a bit of an infidel."

"Certainly," said Nadif, cheerily. "A salafi should only eat with the right hand, as Muhammad did. Women should cover themselves.

Men should grow beards. A salafi also despises these 'innovations' of Islam such as Shiism and Sufism, with their silly rituals and ridiculous adulation of the saints."

"Why are you so opposed to Sufis, Nadif?" asked Maxamid.

"Because there is only the way of the salafs," snapped Nadif.

"What about the massacre we witnessed today off Abdul al Kuri? You saw for yourself what your salafs are capable of. I say they're nothing but cold-blooded killers."

"You keep insisting those people were al-Shabaab," cried Nadif, "when it was clear from their boats and uniforms they were Americans and Yemenis."

"Whoever they were," said Maxamid, raising his eyebrows and eyeing the guests at the table, "they were out to eliminate the Majeerteen."

"Sounds like a bad dream," said Derek. "How has the community reacted?"

"Americans and Yemenis," laughed Nadif, "intent on killing Majeerteen. Jihad is now unavoidable. The pirates will fight back."

"If it comes to it," said Maxamid, speaking with a mouthful of chicken, "yes, we pirates will fight to the death to maintain control over these waters. But it's one thing to get your skiff impounded by a corrupt Coast Guard official and quite another to be beheaded in the name of jihad. I for one don't wish to die in the name of religion."

"That's just the sort of talk that Shabaab mujahideen love to hear," said Khadija.

Abdulmajid glanced around the table smilingly, thrilled simply to be eating a home-cooked meal, his first since longer than he could remember. Bender Siyaada was such a lovely place with such a gracious and lovely host, the nicest Somali woman he'd ever met. The others weren't as ready to make a Bantu Somali feel welcome but they were gradually coming round. How would they react if they knew his true past? "I thought it was shameful," he said, speaking up for the first time, "what Shabaab mujahideen did to those Sufi grave sites in the south."

"It is forbidden to make shrines out of graves," retorted Nadif.

"Sufism is nothing but a carnival. Somalia needs a more authentic sharia..."

"OK, son," said Khadija, "you've had your say. Now let's change the subject."

"Meanwhile you can say whatever you like," laughed Nadif, staring wildly at his plate, "shame yourself on the Internet in front of tens of thousands of people. They're calling you a porn star."

Khadija glared at her son. "Who's calling me that?"

"The students at my madrasa. The imam says you are an unchaste woman, unclean, a shame to your whole community...And I agree with him."

"Nadif! How dare you! I forbid you to return to that madrasa!"

"You cannot tell me what to do!" said Nadif, throwing down his napkin. "I'm not one of your damn Twitter followers."

"You will not speak to me like that in my house!"

Nadif stood up and spat, "*Sharmouta!*" then bolted upstairs to his room.

"Nadif! *Nadif!*" Khadija shoved back her chair and rose to her feet. Derek hadn't noticed quite how incredibly tall she was until now. After a moment she slowly sat back down again. "Please forgive my son. His father was killed when he was an infant. My nation is filled with boys just like him. The imam at his madrasa knows he's vulnerable and is taking advantage of his state of mind, filling his head with fundamentalism. It's as if no one cares in this community. They're all just walking blindly towards jihad."

"He does have a point," said Maxamid.

"I beg your pardon?" cried Khadija.

"About your reputation. I mean, you are drawing lots of attention to yourself." Maxamid regarded his sister and shrugged his shoulders. "Somalia is not ready for the Arab Spring."

"That's where you're wrong," laughed Khadija. "Have you read what they're saying about me?"

"I'm sure your Internet friends are all in agreement, but other people are offended and despise you, cold-blooded people...You should at least wear a headscarf."

"Absolutely not!" protested Khadija. "The expression of free will is the one thing the Islamists fear the most. By not wearing a hijab, I exercise my right to free will. It's the only way we're ever going to emerge from this mess."

"I'm worried about your safety, Khadija," insisted Maxamid. "Bender Siyaada is in the middle of nowhere."

"Mehemet told me things were bad up here," said Derek, taking a sip of water.

"Well, they've become much worse." Khadija caught her breath and lifted her napkin to her lips. "Please excuse me," she said, then got up to leave the room.

After she had gone, Maxamid leaned forward, wedged his bony elbows into the middle of the table, then loosely clasped his hands together in front of his face, glaring intimidatingly over the tops of his knuckles at Derek and Abdulmajid. "You're not welcome here," he growled.

"And you've made that patently clear," said Derek, rubbing his chin, "so we'll be out of here in no time."

"Your sister has made us feel welcome," said Abdulmajid.

"*Shut up!*" snapped Maxamid. "I don't want to hear you speak, Jereer! Understand?"

"What's eating you?" asked Derek.

"I see you're wearing his watch," said Maxamid. "Did you take it from his corpse?"

"Good God, no!" cried Derek. "I would never do such a thing. He gave it to me just before he died."

"Well, I want it back!" Maxamid leaned closer. Derek clenched the timepiece on his wrist and leaned back in his chair. Maxamid thrust out his hand. "Give it to me! You know nothing of its origin."

"Why don't you tell him about the ship," chuckled Abdulmajid.

"Ship?" said Maxamid, stroking his goatee, reclining in his chair.

"What ship?" asked Derek, turning to his friend.

"The Turkish ship carrying all that food," said Abdulmajid. "The one you saw on Miss Jones's computer."

"Shit, you know about that...?"

"We can look it up on my database," said Maxamid, rising from the table. "I'm curious about this ship." He stood up and walked slowly into an adjoining room to fetch his computer.

"Did you have to tell him about that?" whispered Derek, clenching his jaw. "The man hijacks ships for a living, goddamn it."

"He was going to take your watch," breathed Abdulmajid. "I had to distract him somehow."

Maxamid pulled up a chair between Derek and Abdulmajid and placed his laptop on the table in front of them. In a moment all three were huddled in the glow of the computer screen reading the details of the ship. "...*Vessel: Tristola. Container Type: Ultra Large Container Ship. Booking # 2899489. Customer: World Food Programme. Carrier: Turkish Shipping Company. Shipment: 200,000 metric tonnes of sorghum wheat. Port of Load: Bosporus Harbour. Port of Discharge: Mogadishu.*"

Maxamid leaned back, clasped his hands behind his head and smiled. "Three hundred and seventy metres long, fifty metres wide. We'el! Not even the Pirates of the Caribbean could take a ship that big."

"Too big?" asked Derek.

"Too well-defended," laughed Maxamid. "You wouldn't believe the anti-piracy technology those things have on board. Fire hoses, long-range acoustic devices, boat traps, electric fences, optical laser distractors, dazzle guns, slippery foam, robot anti-pirate boats, and maybe even an active denial system."

"What's an active denial system?" asked Abdulmajid.

"It's a heat ray. It uses millimetre-wave electromagnetic energy to heat up people like cups of coffee in a microwave. The United States military spent millions of dollars developing the technology, which means a heat ray doesn't come cheap to the shipping company. But the pirates have figured out a way around them anyway."

"Really? How?" asked Derek.

"We wrap our bodies in aluminium foil blankets and the heat ray can't harm us. We find ways around all their defences. Still, a ship this size bearing such an important cargo will probably have a whole flotilla protecting it during its sea voyage, especially through the Gulf of Aden. We need to find a way to distract them..."

"Does this mean you're going to take the ship and hold the crew for ransom?" asked Derek, anxiously biting his nails.

Khadija stepped into the light with a cup of coffee in her hands. "We'll take the ship," she said, "but not for ransom, for its cargo. With the *Tristola* we will feed our people and demonstrate to the world what miracles can be performed in the failed state of Somalia."

CHAPTER EIGHTEEN

For the first time since he could remember, al-Rubaysh felt safe walking down the street. No one in Bosaso recognised him. During his two days in port he had managed to carry out his enquiries in the open, audaciously and without the threat of drone attacks. Widespread fear among Majeerteen fishermen, aroused by the recent spate of attacks on pirate skiffs, helped loosen the tongues of those he consulted. The conspiracy to foment jihad in Puntland through a terror campaign at sea, a plan he'd dreamed up, was working fine. So far he had gleaned useful bits of information about Mehemet Abdul Rahman. Now he needed to connect the dots.

It was eight o'clock in the morning and pedestrians were streaming through traffic, moving swiftly through the shadows of the old quarter's cavernous streets. Every building on Osman Street, at least the corners and cornice mouldings, was painted a candy shade of pastel. Fragrant whiffs of frankincense poured through open doorways. And at each cross street a clutch of shops displayed sacks of fresh spices. Rubaysh was on his way to find an old man who once worked for the American.

There was no need to bluff his way through harbour security today. He'd been told to ask around on the west side of the port under the shade trees, where the fishing boats were kept. In due course he found the old man leaning against his skiff and using a fishbone needle and nylon cord to mend a damaged fishing net. Tawny, weatherbeaten and misshapen, his true age was hard to fathom. He was wearing a pair of tortoiseshell Wayfarer sunglasses that when removed revealed a pair of pterygiums growing in the corners of the his eyes, the result of too much sun.

"Good morning," said Rubaysh, smiling and extending his hand in a salesmanlike manner. "Are you Mohamud Farole?"

"What do you want?" asked the old man, bluntly refusing the offer of a handshake. "I don't talk to strangers."

"My name is Aden Ali, and I'm from Hodeida Port Authority."

"I know the port well. Never seen your face before." While the old man continued to mend his tattered seine, fingers moving across the weave like ballroom dancers, his peculiar eyes never left Rubaysh. "Besides Hodeida's nearly a thousand kilometres from here. What are you doing in Bosaso?"

"There's a very simple explanation for my being here. I believe you used to do business with the American, Mehemet Abdul Rahman, also known as Johnny Oceans."

"Never heard of him."

"It's just that, well, he died recently, and a container full of goods he arranged to have shipped here from France is now stuck in my port. Maritime authorities in my country have slapped it with a 'deceased cease order' until I can find someone in Bosaso to whom we may deliver it."

"Why don't you ask his widow?"

"Ah, so you did know him then."

"Yes, I knew him." Mohamud dropped his gaze. "Mehemet was a good man, a Majeerteen in all but blood. He helped many fishermen along this coast retain their livelihoods, so they did not have to become badaadintu badah."

"Really? How did he do that?"

"With small loans that we paid back within a few months. I bought a smoking machine with mine so I could process my fish for export to Dubai. I don't know another foreigner like this man. An American who would rather help us than kill us."

"A great man indeed, this Mehemet must have been. Did you ever work for him?"

"Yes."

"Doing what?"

"Why do you ask so many questions?"

"It's a rather delicate matter, and I'm not actually at liberty to discuss it. Let's just say the contents of Mehemet's container have led us to believe he may have been involved with organised crime."

"Mehemet was not a gangster."

"How can you be sure?"

"Because I used to run errands for him."

"Errands?"

"To Djibouti. He would give me a package and I would take it there by boat."

"What sort of package?"

"Always the same thing: a locked black box."

"I see. And who was your contact in Djibouti? Who did you meet there?"

"An American Navy officer from Camp Lemonnier, who always gave me a different black box in return."

Rubaysh's eyes sparkled, and he began toying with his beard. "So Johnny Oceans was a spook," he hissed. "Thank you, Mohamud. You've been very helpful. By the way, do you happen to know if the widow Khadija still lives at his same address, in Bender Siyaada?"

Khadija pulled her Land Cruiser over in front of the harbour entrance and deposited Derek, Abdulmajid and Maxamid on the curb. "I'll pick you up after I fetch Nadif from Friday prayers. Should be about two thirty this afternoon. Good luck." She then drove a few blocks to the Arawello Internet Café and parked on the street directly in front of the entrance. Juggling car keys, her phone and a coffee thermos she locked the car and stepped inside. "Good morning, madame," said a young woman seated at reception wearing a blue hijab.

"How are we doing?" asked Khadija.

"Lots of customers as usual, madame. But number seven and

number twenty-three are not working today."

"Did you call Hassan?"

"Yes, madame. He said he will be here after prayers."

"Why can't he come before?" But the girl had exhausted her knowledge of the situation. "Never mind." Khadija glided through her establishment, between rows of booths occupied by dozens of people huddled over working computers. They paid a thousand Somali shillings – about sixty American cents – for a half hour at a work station. When the business was operating at capacity, like this morning, she could earn the equivalent of five hundred dollars a day, albeit in a currency that fluctuated like a weak heartbeat. Still, it was enough to provide for a family of five.

She closed the door to her office, and booted up her computer. By the time she had lit a cigarette and poured herself a cup of coffee she was all set up to start recording a new video blog. "Because we are ever-present in the African diaspora," she began, looking directly at the web camera, "in refugee communities around the world, Somali women are exposed to the world's hatred more than any other group of people. Take Sweden, where a Somalian was recently forced to pour milk over herself in order to symbolise that she should be white. But what about here in our own country, Somalia?"

Huddled around a table in a street-side food hall that featured half a dozen kitchens serving different Majeerteen dishes under one roof, were Derek, Abdulmajid and Maxamid, along with two fellow pirates, just released from prison. Mustafa was in his early forties, lanky and had a laterally receding hairline that left a fuzzy peninsula at the apex of his forehead, which he accentuated with henna. The diminutive Faraad's flat, bald head appeared to have been sledgehammered into his neck.

The front of the hall was completely open except for a waist-high tin wall painted blue and nailed up against a row of wooden posts. From where they sat they could watch the movement of cargo coming in and out of Bosaso harbour. Derek looked around to see if anyone in the restaurant was watching them. But the din of happy eaters, busy cooks, and a sound system playing a string of Eighties hits, was enough to make their conversation inaudible to anyone but them.

"Don't worry, it's cool here," said Maxamid. "Everyone loves the badaadintu badah in Bosaso."

"Especially since the massacres," said Faraad, twitching his head. "The Americans killed two dozen Majeerteen fishermen in three days."

"I'm telling you," said Maxamid, "I saw them, and they were not Americans, not Yemenis, but Somali Shabaab."

"Why then does Shabaab refuse to claim responsibility for the attacks?" asked Faraad, twitching his head again. It was a nervous tick he'd acquired in the line of duty.

"Shabaab always claims responsibility for its attacks," said Abdulmajid.

"You see!" laughed Faraad, gesturing to the Bantu Somali. "Your Jereer knows what I'm talking about."

"I heard drones took out those rogue cutters this morning," said Mustafa.

"Because the Americans do not want us to find out the truth," insisted Faraad.

"At least, for once, they did us a favour," said Mustafa.

"Do you guys come under a lot of drone attacks here?" asked Derek.

"Listen to the farenji," laughed Mustafa.

"Drones are everywhere," hissed Faraad, lifting his hands above his head as if to swat one away. "They follow us all the time, giant wasps in the sky that peer into our lives, watching our wives in their bedrooms at night, before dropping bombs on our innocent children in their beds. This is how we live in Puntland."

"Faraad likes to exaggerate," said Maxamid, turning to Derek. Just then the song "We Are the Champions" by Queen began playing on the sound system, and it was obvious from all the lip-syncing going on around the table that Freddie Mercury was something of a celebrity among the pirates. "I still don't believe that guy was gay," sighed Maxamid, stroking his hennaed goatee.

"Tell us about your ship, Max," said Mustafa.

The lanky pirate lord grinned, his gold teeth glittering, then leaned in closer to the others. "Everything synchronises nicely: the tides, weather, details of the vessel. The only thing we don't know is the extent of the Tristola's defences and the course she intends to take. We can at least rely on the fact that the World Food Programme flatly refuses to allow armed guards on board its ships. We just have to distract her convoy."

"What navies will be escorting her?" asked Mustafa. "It makes a big difference."

"We're still trying to find that out too," replied Maxamid, "but foreign navies can't be everywhere at once, and as you know there are no over-the-horizon defences in a convoy. With everyone saying the threat of piracy has all but disappeared, no one will be expecting this."

"I don't know," said Faraad, pulling a sheet of paper from his shorts pocket. "These days they've got all kinds of defences on board. I found this on the Internet. See, even small yachts are equipping themselves with these protectors, which provide 'comprehensive threat detection and a counter-measures system enabling twenty-four-hour situational awareness and a robust yet non-lethal first line of counter measures...'" He looked at the others and shrugged his shoulders.

"We must hit them with the unexpected," continued Maxamid, "in this case rapid, organised manoeuvres, and a large-scale coordinated assault."

"What exactly do you have in mind?" asked Mustafa.

"The key is in the diversionary tactics. We need to create a big enough distraction, like an attack on an oil tanker just beyond the horizon, to draw the bulk of her convoy away." He waited until the other two pirates had nodded their approval before continuing. "And then we must force her to change course in the direction of our ambush."

"Are you saying we will have to launch an attack just to create a decoy?"

"The *Mikanos* has anchored off Socotra for the past seven months. We'll sail her out to sea, and then set fire to one of her oil tanks."

"What if the *Tristola* has air support?" asked Faraad with a furrowed brow, darting worried glances at the others.

"That's a possibility we have to plan for," replied Maxamid. "We should certainly be wary of drones."

"And how big a ransom are we going to demand?" asked Mustafa.

Maxamid stroked his chin and smiled. "We're not going to demand a ransom."

"What?" laughed Mustafa, shaking his head in disbelief.

"You're joking, right?" said Faraad, sitting back and folding his arms.

"No, I'm not kidding. We're going to hijack the *Tristola* just for her cargo."

Faraad dismissed the idea with a wave of his hand. "We never concern ourselves with cargo."

"How can we possibly get paid without a ransom?" asked Mustafa.

"We don't get paid," replied Maxamid.

"Now you're sounding *crazy*."

"What exactly is her cargo?" asked Faraad.

"Sorghum wheat, two hundred thousand metric tonnes of it," said Maxamid, staring blankly at them. The two men began to laugh. "Wait! That's enough to feed four million starving Somali families for a whole month. Think about it. We offload the cargo and distribute it to them ourselves."

"What? Forget it! I might have been convinced if it was diamonds, gold, or even better *khat*. But food?"

"You're wasting our time," said Mustafa, getting up to leave.

"Now wait a minute," said Maxamid, "sit down and hear me out. When was the last time either of you got paid anything? It's not like it used to be out there. Since the maritime community cracked down on us, we've lost sixty per cent of our business; the Combined

Task Force is thrashing us at sea. But it's not as if anything landside has changed. We're still struggling in Somalia." Mustafa sat back down slowly. Faraad leaned forward and propped his chin up under his elbows.

"Like me, you were both driven to the cause of the *badaadintu badah* by foreign vessels overfishing and dumping toxic waste in Somali waters, right? Yet, ask yourselves, have any of you ever actually tried to address the problem?" The two men stared back at him. "With this humanitarian act, we could convince the rest of the world to crack down on illegal fishing in our waters, and get back our livelihoods as fishermen."

"But if this ship is destined for Mogadishu," said Mustafa, "why don't we just let her sail and the food will reach the same hungry people."

"Not all of it," said Derek. "Much of it will fall into the hands of al-Shabaab."

"What's to stop them taking it from us?" asked Faraad.

"People power," said Derek. "The audacity and nobility of the act will be so overpowering that no one will dare obstruct its progress. Have any of you heard of Live Aid? No? Well, for sake of the starving in Ethiopia, Bob Geldof convinced a bunch of pop stars to appear in two stadium performances, one in London and one in Philadelphia. The publicity they generated for the cause was unprecedented – a media extravaganza that has yet to be matched and a high-water mark for public altruism. Hijacking the *Tristola* for her cargo so that you may guarantee its delivery to starving Somalis will be the pirates' Live Aid. You'll be the champions."

"What the hell are you talking about?" asked Mustafa.

"When you picture Freddie Mercury do you see him in a white cotton wife-beater and faded blue jeans, air guitar-ing his mike stand before a massive crowd of people?"

"Of course," said Mustafa. "We are the champions!"

"Well that was Live Aid. Imagine you're up there singing 'We Are the Champions' in front of millions of Somalians. That's what I'm talking about. Rock City Puntland! Yeah!"

Mustafa turned to Faraad and asked, "Has the *farenji* convinced you?"

"Beats doing nothing," laughed Faraad. "First tell us your plan, Max."

"We're going to need four flotillas of eight pirate skiffs each, two out of Bosaso and two out of the Hafun Peninsula, towed by four mother ships. That's around thirty vessels, and no less than two hundred pirates. Can you help me organise it?"

"Wait a second," said Mustafa. "Who the hell's going to pay for all this?"

Derek and Abdulmajid both looked at Maxamid, who replied, "My sister Khadija is putting up half the money. We're still trying to raise the rest."

"Your sister? What's her interest in this ship? Is she the one getting paid?"

"Nobody's getting paid," said Abdulmajid calmly, "and it was Khadija's idea."

Not long ago that information would have been enough for Mustafa and Faraad to run a mile from the venture. But lately Khadija had become a local celebrity, a Somali politician in the making. She inspired Majeerteen pride and found respect even among the country's assorted misogynists. The two pirates looked at each other momentarily with raised eyebrows. Then, shrugging their shoulders in unison, they turned back to Maxamid and with a firm nod said, "We're in!"

Omar Abu Hamza stood in the madrasa behind a pillar under the arch of an ante-room, and watched a row of young scholars read from the Quran, their *kufi* caps teetering like unpicked cotton in the wind. Nadif was among them, but when he looked up from his scriptures, Omar ducked away into the shadows. At the end of the ante-room he opened a door and went through to a room where the imam, an elderly Arab man, was seated behind a desk. The office was spartan, with only three chairs and a desk. Scattered across rows of empty bookshelves was a handful of books: Qurans and the teachings of the salafi. "Wa salaam alaikum," said Omar, as he carefully closed the door.

"*Walaikum a-salaam*," said the imam, smiling warmly as he rose unsteadily to his feet. He was dressed in a grey cardigan over white robes and crowned by a tall white kufi cap. Peering sagely over a pair of round rimless spectacles and stroking a magnificent grey beard that turned black at its extremities, he asked, "Have you come about the boy, Nadif?"

"Yes. Is he ready?" asked Omar.

"He is ready," replied the imam.

"What have you told him?"

"Only that we require him to make the ultimate sacrifice."

"And he has agreed?"

"Yes, he has agreed."

"Good," smiled Omar. "Rubaysh will be pleased to hear this."

Rubaysh turned down a blind alley off Osman Street, checked that no one was following him, then stepped through a doorway and walked down a long entrance hall to another door that led to a staircase. As he climbed slowly and steadily up the two flights of stairs in the dark, he whistled the theme song from the American children's television programme "Sesame Street". It had been drummed into his mind during torture sessions in Guantanamo, and the tune would sometimes pop into his head while he was distracted by other things.

On the second-storey landing he knocked on a nondescript door and waited. A voice on the other side asked who was there in Arabic. Rubaysh replied. The door creaked open to reveal a windowless, one-room apartment with a blood-stained mattress on a rusted iron bed frame and a wooden chair in the corner. This was a safe house no one else knew about. Then, from behind the door stepped the Majeerteen elder Abdu Takar.

"Thank you for agreeing to meet me," said Rubaysh, shaking his hand. "I hope you can appreciate the risk I am taking lifting my cover like this. Not even Omar knows I'm here."

"It is a far greater risk for me to meet you, my old friend," said

Abdu Takar. "I would be torn from limb to limb if any of the other elders learned of my affiliation to al-Qaeda."

"You were supposed to deliver me Mehemet Abdul Rahman, but instead you delivered him to safety. Why?"

"He got the jump on me. I had to make it look like I had come to warn him."

"At least if you'd given me Khadija, that would have been enough."

"I can still deliver her."

"That is precisely why I called you here."

Abdu Takar eyed the Yemeni. "I need your confirmation first that when the revolution happens in Puntland, I will be given power."

Rubaysh removed his glasses, popped his neck then scratched his tussocky facial hair. "We have discussed this many times, Abdu Takar. As you know my first answer is always that Wahabism shuns political life, and there will be no rulers in our caliphates. Still, you needn't worry. You'll be rewarded for your bravery."

"Let me know when and I will make the arrangements."

"You can expect my call any day now."

"I must go," said Abdu Takar, heading for the door. "There's a meeting of the elders in thirty minutes. Maxamid, that hotheaded brother of hers, has something important he wants to tell us."

"Uh, one more thing before you go. Did you ever hear any of the Abdul Rahmans discussing lost treasure?"

Abdu Takar furrowed his brow and thought for a moment. "No. Not that I can recollect."

"OK," said Rubaysh. "God be with you."

Khadija craned her neck to see if she could spot Nadif among the crowd of worshippers coming out of the mosque after prayers. It was difficult to distinguish him from the others, as everyone was dressed so similarly. "Nadif," she called, smiling and waving after seeing him among a group of boys coming down the stairs. He glanced over to where her car was parked then looked away again and frowned. Then she saw the imam walk up to her son, accompanied by a Somali man, and take him by the shoulder. She leapt out of her Land Cruiser and dashed towards them. "Nadif!" The three of them stopped and looked back at her.

"Can I help you?" asked the imam when she arrived breathlessly at the spot where they were standing.

"I've come to collect my son," said Khadija.

The imam looked her up and down, making no effort to disguise his disgust with her attire, her "Terrorism Has No Religion" T-shirt, tight-fitting jeans and black leather ankle boots. "We're just on our way to the madrasa," he said bluntly. "You can come back later."

"No, he's coming with me now," insisted Khadija, grabbing Nadif's hand.

"Mother, why are you embarrassing me like this?"

"It's better if you come back in the evening," said the Somali man, squeezing the boy's shoulder. "The imam has taken time out from his busy schedule to tutor your son personally this afternoon."

"Who the hell are you?" asked Khadija.

"I am a friend of the imam's," said the man, "and a friend of Nadif's."

"I demand to know what right you have to be in my son's madrasa?"

"I could ask you the same question," said the man, stepping closer to her. She stared at them both with her lips parted. Without saying another word she yanked her son away from them and marched him back to her car.

In the final hour of daylight, with the sun's rays reflected off its crumbling, disused pilings, the abandoned Italian salt factory appeared on fire. Beyond it, off the coast of the Hafun Peninsula, the ocean turned indigo, darkening the depths of Davy Jones's locker. Khadija stood atop a rocky prominence on a hill above the factory, leaning on her brother's M1918 Browning Automatic Rifle as she addressed a crowd of around three hundred pirates seated cross-legged on the ground. Derek and Abdulmajid stood off to one side, next to one of a dozen blazing torches demarcating the gathering of people, listening to her every word. Beyond them, held at gunpoint, was a group of around thirty hostages, mostly Filipino, who were remnants of previous hijackings at sea, awaiting their ransoms to get paid. They were to act as human shields during the taking of the Turkish food ship.

"We're not murderers!" declared Khadija, loudly enough for her voice to echo off the factory walls. "We don't behead people, cut off their limbs, whip them in public. They call us *burcad badeed*, 'ocean robbers', but we're not the ones who came with giant nets and swept everything from the sea. We are the *badaadintu badah*, 'survivors of the sea'." The crowd roared.

"The outside world talks only about how we have taken hundreds of millions of dollars in ransom and sent a multi-billion dollar shipping industry into panic." Huge cheer. "But how many times have you run out of rations far from the coast and feared you would die hungry and in the cold, with nothing to show for it? When was the last time you brought home a decent catch for your family? We all have mouths to feed.

"There's an armada of maritime police out there, the biggest the world has ever known, yet they do nothing to stop the looting of Somali resources. They're only here to protect their own interests. How many honest Majeerteen fishermen have they arrested or even killed, while our coasts continue to be plundered and our livelihoods destroyed?

"The struggle for survival has become quite desperate for some of you. It used to be that *badaadintu badah* would only go after ships hapless enough to wander into these waters. Now some of us are prepared to kidnap on land, farther afield in Kenya, Ethiopia and even Uganda, and sell our captives to Islamists who then behead them like goats. We've come to regard Western hostages simply as valuable commodities, whether or not they come with a ship." She looked over at the hostages huddled together under the watchful eye of their guards. "But can we really continue to call ourselves survivors of the sea?

"Now the Islamists are at our doorstep, those self-hating Somalis. They see that we are weak. Consequently they are conspiring with al-Qaeda in the Arab Peninsula to turn our disadvantages into their advantage. Shabaab mujahideen are massacring Majeerteen for the sake of jihad. No one cares that this is happening, not even our own politicians.

"Where is the love in Somalia? I'll tell you where. It is among the Majeerteen. There are no conflicts between us. We depend on each other. Everything we do is done for clan, family, friends, community. We are the smartest, most resilient clan in Somalia, and Puntland is this country's most thriving enclave." Massive cheer.

"On this very spot where we are tonight, long before the birth of Jesus Christ, the Port of Opun, a city state known throughout the world, thrived for a thousand years. We were among the first globalisers. Our merchants led the global commerce between Asia, Africa, and Europe. We even carried incense, giraffes, and zebras to the Ming Empire of China. We were the champions of the world." Another massive cheer.

"But what are we today? A people whose only asset is hostages? What is Puntland but a chaotic haven for gangsters, where even the president is on the take? Whatever happened to the proud Majeerteen?"

Derek turned to face the sea beyond the crowd. Twilight was melting into darkness, blackening the water like an angry cephalopod. In contrast to every other Indian Ocean coast he knew, there were no lights on the horizon, no night fishermen out trolling the blackness for broadbills. Under those waves, lodged in a watery vault was Johnny Oceans's treasure. He knew its exact location. "All in good time," he thought. Then something strange caught his eye, where the ocean met the sky, a thin strip of swirling light stretching across the water from north to south; it might have been a horizontal moonbeam but there was no moon out. He'd never seen anything like it, a submerged aurora borealis. He turned back to Khadija, who was engrossed in oratory, raised his eyebrows and pointed to the horizon, which caused the Somalian to stop mid-sentence.

"There, you see!" she cried. The crowd responded by rotating their heads. "Behold a milky sea! This is surely a sign that our venture will be a success. Let us take courage from this good omen. This is our chance to demonstrate to the world that we're not just a bunch of lawless sea brigands, that there is purpose to what we do. The ocean is our domain! Let's take back what's ours!" Uproarious applause and cheering lasting a full minute followed Khadija's speech.

One by one, the pirates began to disperse and wander down the hill to their boats. The armada was about to set sail. Four mother ships would lead a flotilla of eight skiffs each, travelling through the night to different positions hundreds of kilometres apart: a cove east of Qandala, in the middle of the Gulf of Aden, on the far side of Abdul al Kuri, and in the shadow of the high cliffs north of the Hafun Peninsula. It was an ambitious undertaking, but they had the means and the numbers to pull it off. It was now down to the small team of specialists already on the island of Socotra to retrieve the *Mikanos* from its hiding place and set it on fire. Black smoke rising from the stricken oil tanker was the pirates' signal to launch their attack on the *Tristola*.

CHAPTER NINETEEN

As day broke over the Gulf of Aden the TSC *Tristola* followed an undeviating course towards the rising sun. The sea was calm and the sky unclouded. Covering the length and beam of the ship's vast deck were row upon row of containers neatly stacked to varying heights in a multicoloured medley that looked like a giant assortment of Lego blocks. With four large cranes secured equidistant from each other on the deck, the ultra-large container ship had its own onboard unloading gear, and resembled a travelling port. Two Indian naval frigates kept pace, both about a ship's length off her port and starboard sides.

Before entering pirate waters the *Tristola*'s crew had taken precautions, rigging coils of electrified barbed wire all around the ship, with extra fencing at the gangway openings. All accommodations were shut and locked and no one but essential crew had access to the engine room and the steering room. A back-up generator was in operation, and the heavy-duty anti-piracy gear was positioned: two long-range acoustic devices, one on each side of the ship, a laser dome at the bow, and an active denial system at the stern. An automatic identification system indicated the ship's location at all times. If ever it got switched off, naval and air assets would be alerted instantly and scramble to intercept.

Bathed in orange sunlight, the captain was lounging in his swivel chair on the bridge, assisted by his two most responsible officers, the communications officer, a.k.a. the COMMO, and the helmsman. All three were dressed casually in shorts and sneakers. Maddy Jones stood beside the captain, dressed in jeans and her well-worn navy hooded fleece. All of them were wearing sunglasses.

With its low ceiling, fluorescent lighting, and green laminate flooring, the bridge had the look of a hospital corridor, except that in this case every wall was replaced by large windowpanes that tilted outward, offering sweeping views of the ship's bow and stern.

The instruments indicated the ship was moving at a speed of twenty knots but, from where Maddy was standing forty metres above the deck, except for a faint vibration in her plimsolls she couldn't detect any motion at all.

She had quickly become friends with the Turkish officers who made up a quarter of the crew of thirty-two. The rest were Filipino. "How close will we get to the Horn of Africa?" she asked the captain, who was a lean man in his mid-forties with closely cropped grey hair.

"Cape Guardafui," said the captain. "In Somali, Ras Asir."

"If that what it's called when it's at home," laughed Maddy.

"We won't be passing close enough to see it. Our course will take us between the islands of Abdul al Kuri and Socotra before bearing south." He spoke softly, calmly, and in a singsong voice that seemed at odds with the fear in everyone's hearts as they plied through pirate-affected waters.

"I trust you know your way around, mate."

"We Turks have been sailing these waters for over five hundred years. There was even a time when we took part in the piracy here."

"Struth, that's reassuring."

"Mir Ali Bey, a 16th century Turkish corsair, joined forces with Somali pirates to torment non-Muslim ships sailing around the Horn, all for Ottoman glory of course. And with the help of local chiefs, he wreaked havoc down the Kenyan coast, unsettling Portuguese control from Mogadishu to Mombasa and sending its Navy packing. Only Malindi remained loyal, and only Malindi was spared when the Portuguese returned with an armada from Goa to repay the coastal people for their treachery. On the island of Pate, they killed the traitorous chief, removed his head, and then had it preserved so it could be carried on a pole in triumph back to Lisbon."

Maddy folded her arms and gritted her teeth. "That's not really what I want to hear right now, mate."

The captain chuckled, swivelled his chair back and forth, and said, "I'm only telling you because you asked about navigating these waters."

"So what happened to the Turkish pirate?" asked Maddy, her eyes fixed on the placid silvery ocean before them.

"Some say Ali Bey fell during the battle for Mombasa in 1587, others that for fear of being eaten by cannibals he gave himself up to his enemy, moved to Portugal and converted to Christianity. I like to think his *jinn* still lives here and helps guide Turkish ships through Ras Asir's perilous waters."

"Let's just hope Ali Bey's *jinn* is on our side, then," said Maddy, shuddering.

"Captain, ten o'clock," said the COMMO, pointing to a distant column of black smoke rising from a blaze beyond the edge of the horizon. An "action stations" alarm – short repeated blasts – on the Indian frigate off the *Tristola*'s starboard bow indicated they had also seen it. The port-side frigate followed suit then sped away at thirty knots in the direction of the smoke.

"What's happening?" asked Maddy, looking nervously at the others. "Shouldn't we be calling in the Air Force?"

"They're telling us to stay our course," said the COMMO, holding his forefinger to the headset. "Just one ship's going to check it out."

Unruffled by the alarms, the captain crossed his legs, sat back and said calmly, "We don't need to concern ourselves with an over-the-horizon event. If and when they need support, the Indian Navy will call for it." He raised a pair of binoculars to his compassionate eyes then added, "Anyway, I don't see pirates anywhere, do you?"

Maddy stood frozen to the spot while the others carried out their duties. The COMMO kept in touch with the frigates, the helmsman maintained course, and the captain spoke coolly to his crew over the horn, while stroking the grey stubble on his chin. "I want red team to go to the secure room, seal it and then operate the anti-piracy weapons. All other teams remain locked in your quarters." He turned to Maddy and smiled. "Don't worry, Supercargo, it's just a precautionary measure, we're not under attack."

"Yet!"

A towering wall of sandstone rock dropped to the spot where Maxamid's pirate flotilla lay in wait, a hundred and thirty kilometres north of Hafun. It was mid-morning and Derek was standing next to the towering Somali at the stern of the mother ship, a derelict French fishing trawler confiscated in the early days of piracy. Its antique engines were idling loudly beneath their feet and sending up puffs of putrid black smoke. Eight skiffs surrounded them, six heavily armed pirates in each, a hostile welcoming party, floating, waiting, ready for action. Staying so close to the east-facing cliffs the temperature was unbearable and the ocean more violent.

"Are you certain this will work?" asked Derek, trying to remain steady on the heaving deck.

"There's always a degree of uncertainty," said Maxamid. "Bringing you two along for instance. Still, as long as you and the Jereer remain on this mother ship until I give the order, everything should go to plan."

"What if the naval convoy doesn't fall for the decoy?" asked Derek, feeling a sudden wave of nausea.

"I'm certain at least one frigate will remain with the container ship. That's when the flanking manoeuvre comes into play."

"What's to stop the *Tristola* sailing out farther into the Indian Ocean?"

"The ambush at Abdul al Kuri will take care of that."

"You've thought of everything. What about the hostages?"

"That's where you come in. They will feel more comfortable in the hands of a *farenji* than the *badaadintu badah*. Once ashore you will take them to the hotel in Bosaso and put them on the next flight home."

"They'll be terrified."

"You'll have to keep them calm and controlled, otherwise one of them might turn on you."

"More easily said than done," laughed Derek.

"I always tell them, 'If you're strong, and you have a good heart, you will hug your children, kiss your wife, and see your house again before long. You will return to your country and live again among your people.'"

"Quite poetic," said Derek.

"'The Tale of the Shipwrecked Traveller'. It's what the serpent prince of the Land of Punt tells the shipwrecked Egyptian." Their conversation was interrupted by a savage retching sound coming from the bow. Abdulmajid was leaning over the gunwale, vomiting his breakfast into the deep blue sea, immediately alerting a flock of seagulls from the cliffs above." Maxamid reached into a duffel bag and pulled out two large cellophane packages. "Here, take this, and give the other one to Abdulmajid."

"What is it?"

"It's anti-piracy protection gear," said Maxamid, removing the contents one by one and handing them to Derek. "An aluminium poncho to protect you from the heat ray, beeswax for your ears to block out the screech of the acoustic cannons, and a welder's helmet to protect you from laser beams."

Derek put on the helmet and poncho. "Do I look like a Mexican astro-mechanic?"

"You'll also need this," said Maxamid, handing him a loaded Kalashnikov rifle.

"What? You said I wouldn't be in the line of fire."

"The key to a successful hijack is scaring the hell out of the crew as you gain access to their ship while at the same time making sure no one gets hurt. The only way to achieve that is with one of these. If you insist on joining us, you will have to carry one."

"But I don't know how to use an AK."

"You just release the charging handle like this, and then pull the trigger. But only if you have to."

"I think *I'm going to be sick...*"

"*Captain, pirates off the port stern! Pirates off the starboard bow!*" cried the COMMO. The captain was standing behind him, watching the radar screen which showed two clusters of green dots closing in on their position – one from the northwest and the other from the southeast.

"They're attempting a flanking manoeuvre," said the captain. "Full speed ahead!"

The helmsman relayed the order to the engine room and pushed the throttle forward. Before them the smoke continued to rise on the horizon, its source still unknown. The first Indian naval vessel had not yet returned nor reported back on the phenomenon. Meanwhile the green dots on the radar inched ever closer to the centre of the screen. Maddy was standing hugging her shoulders, watching them. "How fast can this ship go?" she asked. "Can we outrun them?"

"Maximum twenty-five knots," replied the captain, "which is no match for these damn pirate skiffs. Our best hope is the Indian Navy, who will do everything within their rules of engagement to prevent anyone from boarding this vessel."

"The commander of the second naval vessel is telling us to stay our course, Captain."

"Stay our course! *Stay our course!* Why the hell haven't they engaged them yet?"

"Looks like they are going after them now, Captain," said the COMMS. The Indian vessel fired her bow thrusters and set off on a turbulently tight turn that put her aft of the *Tristola* in seconds. Maddy and the captain spun around to the rear windows to watch its progress until their own ship's exhaust obscured it from view. They turned back to the radar screen. A larger dot moved away from the centre of the screen and the little ones began to follow.

"Looks like she's luring them away," said Maddy.

"Maybe they're the ones trying to lure her away from us," said the helmsman.

"Have faith in Ali Bey," said the captain, slapping both officers on the shoulder.

"However capable the Indian Navy, mate," said Maddy, "don't

you think you should call in air support?"

"Already done," said the captain. "An Australian surveillance plane is on its way."

"Surveillance plane?" cried Maddy. "Why not a bloody bomber?"

"I think you'll be impressed by the anti-piracy capabilities of the Lockheed P-3 Orion...Actually, Miss Jones, it's time you got down to the secure room."

Maddy opened the door of the bridge and was about to make her way to the gangway when a large aircraft suddenly flew past the port side of the ship, low over the ocean. With its uniformly slate coating, rotund fuselage and four fat propellers, it resembled a Second World War bomber. Behind the wings, painted a slightly darker shade of grey than the plane, was the Royal Australian Air Force roundel: a leaping kangaroo. She straightened her posture and sighed, "There go the blues."

The plane began turning over the water. "Captain,' said the COMMS, 'I'm receiving a radio message from the Orion."

"Put them on the speaker."

"*G'day! This Jake Laronzo, commander of the* Orion. *Is Madeline Jones on board?*"

"Right here, mate!" said Maddy, stepping back on to the bridge.

"*Kooroo! You OK, Maddy?*"

"No. Bloody terrified."

"*Don't worry, love. You can rely on this onion. A few smoke bombs ought to do the trick. We'll send the bastards back in a hurry. Sit tight.*"

"Please keep the frequency open, Jake," said Maddy, grinning. "It's reassuring to hear your voice." Against the captain's orders, Maddy remained on the bridge, listening to the radio as the Orion neared its target. The sounds from the cockpit crackled in and out.

"*Bloody hell...What's this, the Somali seventh fleet? We're seeing two flotillas. I count sixteen skiffs. I've never seen so many bloody pirates...It looks like the Indians have things under control, though. Yup, she's got them on the run. The muppets are fleeing.*" The officers let out a cheer and Maddy hugged the captain. "*Yemeni Coast Guard say they're on their way. We're going to turn around and check out the black smoke ahead of you,* Tiscola."

"That's where our other escort went," said the captain, "about an hour ago."

"*Roger, we're in radio contact with her now. Struth…Will you look at that.*"

"*What is it?*" asked Maddy.

"*We're looking at a massive fire on an oil tanker floating off the island of Socotra. Looks like it's been set ablaze on purpose. Wait a minute…Just spotted another flotilla of skiffs and a couple of whalers on the north side of Abdul al Kuri. This looks like a bloody ambush, people. How quickly can you execute a ninety-degree turn, Captain?*"

"I'll do my best, Commander," said the captain, "but a big ship takes a long time to come about."

"*You haven't got time.*"

"Emergency reverse!" said the captain.

"But we're moving too fast, Captain," cried the helmsman.

"I said emergency reverse!"

"Emergency reverse!" yelled the helmsman, relaying the order to the engine room.

After a moment there was a jolt, the first discernible motion since leaving the Bosporus, and the vibrations beneath Maddy's shoes began to intensify.

"*You have to execute your turn before you reach the island,*" said the Orion's commander, "*roughly ten kilometres ahead. It's the only way to evade their ambush. We'll slow them down with a blanket of smoke bombs.*"

"Starboard turn, reverse screws!"

"Starboard turn, reverse screws!"

"C'mon, damn you," said Maddy, gripping the edge of the counter in front of her. While the ship began making its slow turn southward the rest of the action was going on over the horizon. All anyone on the bridge could still see was the same column of black smoke that had been there since early morning.

"Helmsman, is the starboard screw reversing at full power?" asked the captain.

"Yes, Captain. But we need more crew in the engine room to manage the workload."

"Well, get on it!"

The radio crackled to life. *"How's that turn coming, Tristola?"* asked Commander Laronzo. This time he was shouting into his handset to be heard over the increased noise of his aircraft. *"Bombs away!...Bullseye, ya bastards. Buy you a tinny of Foster's for that one, mate. Let's make another flypast...Keep it up...Hang on, we've got company, coming in from the west...Ah, don't be alarmed, Tristola, but there's a squadron of MQ-9s coming up behind you..."* As he spoke three unmanned US Air Force Reaper drones buzzed the bridge of the ship. They were laden with weaponry. *"Fair dinkum. Those muppets don't stand a chance now."*

"Look!" said the captain, his eyes widening as he watched the squadron of drones fly ahead in formation. "See how they wobble in the thermals, like hunting pterodactyls lurching out across the open water. Fascinating..."

"There's the island," said Maddy, grabbing the captain's binoculars. A range of sandstone hills rose up from the water, like the knuckles of a giant fist lurking below the ocean. "That must be the smoke from their bombs I can see on the other side of it. I can also see the Orion circling above in the sky."

"How's that turn coming, helmsman?"

"The ship's heading straight for the island, Captain."

"Put more power into it!"

"Aye aye, Captain!"

"We're going to fly this onion a little closer this time," said the Orion's commander, *"to get a good look before those drones arrive...Lots of bloody pirate skiffs. They must have chewed a fair bit of khat before thinking up this operation. Struth...Oh, bloody hell...They've got hostages. Better tell the Yanks."*

"What does he mean?" asked Maddy.

"He means they must warn the Americans not to open fire on the pirates, or else there may be casualties among the hostages." At that moment there was a massive explosion on the other side of the island, and a burning plume of black smoke rose from behind the hills. This was followed by another and then another. "*Oh my God!*"

Meantime the *Tristola* was moving too quickly and not turning fast enough to avoid missing the rocks at the tip of the island. The sea around them grew paler, changing from indigo, to emerald, to turquoise. Grabbing the handset from the helmsman, the captain yelled, "*More power, damn it!*" The ship's hull started to moan and the thousands of containers on deck began to jiggle. "She's running aground! We'll be a sitting duck!" Nevertheless the ship kept moving, ripping a path through the reef, listing on the starboard side, as it rubbed shoulders with the island. Eventually the *Tristola* broke free of its obstruction and sailed safely past the island.

Maddy put her hand on her breast and gasped. "Bloody hell, that was close!" A soft breeze blew through the bridge.

"Too close," said the captain, scratching his stubble and biting his lip as he slowly lifted the radio handset to his mouth. "This is the captain. All hands report to your stations. I want a complete damage report, on the double!" He dropped the handset and breathed a heavy sigh of relief. "At least we're back on course for Mogadishu."

"No you're not," said a menacing voice. They hadn't seen the tall Somali man sneak on to the bridge but now he was standing behind them, pointing a massive rifle at the captain's head. "You're going where I tell you to go."

CHAPTER TWENTY

Derek and Abdulmajid stood on a wide beach, ten kilometres south of the distant headland known as Ras Asir, the apex of the Horn of Africa, where they could just see the ancient lighthouse of Guardafui, and six kilometres north of the cove where they had lain in wait, all night and all morning. An archaic pebble road snaked westward from their position through the hills towards the setting sun and Puntland's capital, Bosaso, two hundred and fifty kilometres away. Everything else was sandstone, sky and ocean.

Derek's enthusiasm for joining Maxamid's raiding party had quickly dwindled after he had given him the gun. Instead, he decided to wait on shore with Abdulmajid until the ship arrived. They weren't alone. On the promise of a sack of food each, about a hundred people, mostly women, had come from nearby villages to help unload the *Tristola*. No two hijabs were alike and each woman wore one, her round, brown, face beaming like a polished ebony mask.

"Here it comes now!" cried Derek, so delighted by the sight of the Tristola on the horizon that it might have been his figurative ship coming in. The women began to ululate.

"*Allah!* But where are they going to put it?" asked Abdulmajid.

"I expect they'll anchor her a couple of hundred metres off shore," said Derek.

"How will they get the containers on to land?"

"Good question. But Maxamid's a pretty smart guy. I'm sure he's thought of an ingenious solution."

The ship was coming up fast from the south, according to plan. Since being hijacked, it had completed a three-hundred-degree turn, on an annular course between Abdul al Kuri and Ras Asir that had taken five hours at maximum speed to execute. Above them circled three Reaper drones, which had been constantly monitoring the ship since its capture by the pirates, relaying live data back to the Americans operating them.

"Straighten the rudder!" barked Maxamid.

The helmsman struggled to straighten the ship's course. His palms were sweating, which made it difficult to handle the controls. Maddy was sitting in the captain's chair, her knees tucked up under her chin and her arms wrapped tightly around her legs. With her hood over her head her face looked pale by comparison. "The World Food Programme doesn't pay ransoms," she mumbled.

"But the Turkish Shipping Company does," chuckled the captain, who stood at the door with the barrel of an AK-47 in his back. "She's the supercargo," he said to Maxamid.

"We're not interested in ransom," said Maxamid. He was standing behind the helmsman, flanked by heavily armed Somali pirates of varying heights and builds.

"What are you going to do with us, then?" asked the captain.

"If you're strong," said Maxamid, "and you have a good heart, you will hug your children, kiss your wife, and see your house again before long. You will return to your country and live again among your people."

"Bullshit," whispered Maddy.

"I never talk bullshit," snapped Maxamid.

"Why did you hijack the ship if it wasn't for ransom?"

"We want your cargo," smiled Maxamid.

"Well, you can't have it," said Maddy, rising to her feet. "I'm responsible for this food, and I refuse to allow you to take any of it."

"And I'm a fucking pirate. You should be grateful for such a kindly outcome."

They were sailing parallel to the Somalian coast, in the shadow of a colossal bluff eroded by sandstorms and wind that loomed over the port side of the ship. Sheer cliffs, some as high as five hundred metres, rose from the pounding surf. Northward, towards the tip of the Horn of Africa, the hills tapered off into a broad beachhead that jutted out from the coast, directly ahead of them.

"Shouldn't we start to slow down?" asked the captain.

"Full speed ahead," said Maxamid. All at once the drones overhead flew forward of the ship.

"But we'll hit that beachhead," insisted the captain. "The ship's already run aground once today. Her hull won't take another. I say it's time to reverse the engines."

"I'm the one giving the orders, motherfucker. You'll do as I say."

"It's not slowing down," cried Abdulmajid, watching in horror while the Tristola continued a beeline course towards shore from the south, its massive hulk growing larger by the minute.

"Headed straight for us," added Derek. "Shit...*Everybody off the beach!*" Abdulmajid repeated the order in Somali, and ululation quickly turned to cries of anguish as the people began dashing for the hills. After climbing fifty metres to the top of a sand dune, Derek and Abdulmajid stopped and turned to face the sea again.

"Isn't anyone controlling the ship?" cried Abdulmajid. The vessel just kept on coming, barging through the surf and hurtling towards land like a colossal stranding whale. There was no way its draught could take the shallow water. But nothing could stop its headlong momentum. The hull began to bellyache as it struck the reef, screeching like scores of marine mammals in the throes of death.

When the *Tristola*'s bow struck the beachhead the mammoth vessel rose out of the water and quickly grew taller as it ploughed into the sand. Her three onboard cranes swayed violently back and forth, and the awful din of hull against shore continued to get louder as the ship hurtled past, forcing the onlookers to cover their ears.

In the shuddering vibration containers became dislodged from the ship's deck. Some tumbled off the ship into the sea, others on to land, buckling and breaking open as they struck the sand. One bounced off the deck and soared over the heads of the people on shore, barely missing a group of women when it crashed to the ground, spilling sacks of sorghum wheat.

Only after the ship was half way out of the water did it finally come to a standstill. The silence was deafening. Seagulls flew wildly over the bridge fifty metres up. Meanwhile three unmanned drones also hovered overhead, like vultures over a fresh kill.

One of the Reapers was less interested in the ship than it was in Derek and Abdulmajid, flying just twenty metres above their heads. In full view of the camera under its fuselage, for the benefit of its American operator, Derek showed them his middle finger. All three Reapers then retreated to watch the stricken ship from a distance.

A person stepped out of the *Tristola*'s bridge. It was Maxamid, brandishing his Browning with both hands high above his head. "WE ARE THE CHAMPIONS!" The crowd cheered and rushed to the shore, causing a melee as people scrambled for sacks of grain scattered across the beach.

"It's actually not a bad bit of parallel parking," said Derek, sizing up the mighty sideways-facing container ship. Waves lapped against the half of the hull still in the water. "It should be a doddle offloading the rest of the containers from that position."

The Somalis lowered a rope ladder from the deck that didn't quite reach the ground, leaving a gap of about three metres. And after relaying an order along a chain of pirates standing on her deck, the crew of the *Tristola* stepped out of their quarters, one by one, with their hands above their heads.

"They'll need some help bringing those people ashore," said Derek, starting down the dune. Then he spotted a beautiful young woman, walking towards the ladder with her hands on her head. He gasped and fell back into the sand. "Maddy!"

"How could *she* be on the ship?" asked Abdulmajid.

She then saw them. "Derek?" she yelled. "Abdulmajid? Oh, thank God you're here!"

"Don't worry," hollered Derek, staggering along the sandy ridge,

"I'm coming to help you, baby." With unsteady legs Maddy began a slow downward climb. The forty-metre-long ladder made for a precarious descent and when she finally reached the bottom she froze. Derek and Abdulmajid waited below, their wrists clasped in a firefighter's hold to break her fall. "It's OK. We got you. Go ahead and jump."

After a moment's hesitation she let go and fell bottom first into their arms. Derek took hold of her and swung her around and around in a passionate embrace, then put her down. "I'm so glad to see you two," she said, her eyes wide with excitement. "I've just been through the most horrible ordeal. But what are you doing here?"

"I could ask you the same," said Derek. "We had no idea you would be on board. You're supposed to be in Kakuma."

"You mean, you're not here to rescue me? Wait a minute!" said Maddy, narrowing her eyes at the two them then putting her hand on her hip. "Don't tell me you're involved in this hijack?" Derek cringed and smiled sheepishly. She slapped him hard across his grinning face. "You bastard!"

"Ow! That fucking hurt."

"To think I trusted you." She began wandering between the women who were eagerly collecting sacks and carrying them inland. Derek and Abdulmajid followed her. "I'm the supercargo for this bloody mess you see scattered all over the Somali Coast." She stopped, crouched down and brushed the sand from a sack of wheat. "See what that says there? 'World Food Programme' and 'Turkish Aid', not Derek bloody Strangely and the Pirates of Puntland."

"We plan to take it directly to the needy," said Derek, brushing his hair from his eyes.

She stood up. "That's my job. And if you'd let me do my job that's exactly where this shipment would have ended up, with the needy."

"Not all of it. You yourself said al-Shabaab was diverting much of the food aid."

"Oh, and you think you can do a better job of it than the World Food Programme, do you?"

"Perhaps."

"Well, you're fucking dreaming!"

"It wasn't his idea." Maddy looked over her shoulder to find a tall, slender Somali woman standing behind them. She smiled at Maddy, then added with an air of authority, "It was my idea."

"And who are you?" asked Maddy.

"Ah!" said Derek. "Meet Khadija Abdul Rahman, Johnny Oceans's widow."

"Do you mind explaining to me why you are stealing my cargo?" asked Maddy.

"All in good time, my dear," said Khadija. She smiled at Derek and asked, "Is this the girlfriend you were telling me about?"

"We only just met last week at Kakuma Refugee Camp," said Derek, gathering his windswept hair into a tidy ponytail. "She helped me and Abdulmajid escape."

"I see." It was obvious from his body language that there was more between them. Khadija turned to admire her captured ocean vessel. "Isn't this something," she sighed, thrusting out her arms out in wonder at the scale of the thing.

"Your brother certainly knows how to hook 'em," said Derek.

"Truly a great day for Somalia. C'mon, it's getting dark. I must get back to town and update my video blog."

Derek put an arm around each woman. "I can't imagine a more delightful way to journey back to Bosaso than in the company of such beautiful women."

But Maddy wouldn't budge. "I'm not leaving the ship." So Khadija and Abdulmajid continued on ahead.

"We really should let the pirates take care of all this, babe," said Derek, trying to coax her along. "It's in their hands now."

"I can't believe you would do this to me," she cried, pulling herself away from him and turning back towards the *Tristola*. "This cargo is my responsibility." She saw Maxamid coming up from the shore and felt sand crabs scurrying across her back.

"Get in the car," he growled, showing her the barrel of his BAR, and she quickly followed the others.

Maddy's participation in Khadija's video conference required dogged persuasion all the way back to Bosaso, but eventually she gave in and appeared alongside Derek. In Khadija's video, which had already been seen by thirty million viewers on YouTube, she made clear what had happened and why. "We are breadwinners, not warlords," she tweeted. As a consequence, she now had more than a million followers on Twitter.

Over the next three days the salvage operation proceeded in an orderly fashion, and thousands of twenty-five-kilogram bags were distributed to the needy across Puntland. Thanks to her compelling tweets, Khadija was able to organise convoys of pickup trucks and flotillas of fishing skiffs to arrive daily and help with the distribution of the food. Ultimately the *Tristola*'s crew also pitched in and Maddy took charge of logistics.

World opinion was mixed but so far no one had taken any action against them, except to divert the international shipping lane farther out to sea.

"There's no mistaking the nobility of the act, mate," said Maddy, sitting up in bed at the Hotel Huruuse with a sheet pulled up over her breasts. Derek was lying next to her tracing the outline of her shoulders and neck with his fingertip, while she spoke to her boss Frank Paterson on the phone in Australia.

"Since when did stealing WFP's food become noble?" asked Frank.

"This isn't about the World Food Programme," continued Maddy. "It's much bigger than that. They've taken ownership of the whole damn issue, Frank. The hijacking of the *Tristola* for her cargo of food is simply a means to an end. It's a huge sensation in Somalia, mate. This sort of thing has never happened here before, certainly not across clan lines."

"How the hell did you succumb to Stockholm Syndrome so bloody quickly?"

"I didn't. I saw what they were trying to do and came to my own conclusions." Derek gaped at her, shook his head then laughed, for which she beat his face repeatedly with her pillow.

"Sounds like bloody Stockholm Syndrome to me."

"On the contrary. It's down to one incredible woman, Khadija Abdul Rahman."

"Yeah, I see her face on the news every night. Look, whatever your sympathies, Mad, I want you on that flight home tomorrow afternoon. Do you understand?"

"All the hostages are flying home tomorrow, Frank. They want to prove to the world that ransom has nothing to do with the taking of this ship. We would have left earlier if there had been a flight available."

"Yeah, yeah, I heard all that. Just be on the bloody plane."

She hung up and turned to Derek. "He's pissed off."

"I don't blame him. He wants his girl back. Now, where were we...?"

Like a divine gesture, the last beams of sunlight streamed into the ravine in the Karkaar Mountains where the al-Shabaab base was located, and shone through the only window of the house built into the rocks, striking Mehemet Abdul Rahman's M-60 machine gun, which was propped against the wall and surrounded by a nest of ammunition. Omar Abu Hamza, Dahir, Ahmed and five other mujahideen were inside, some seated on wooden chairs, others on the floor, trying to listen to a Radio Shabelle broadcast of an interview with Khadija Abdul Rahman, over the din of menacing buzzing outside. "This woman is brave," said Omar, "I'll give her that."

"She's an apostate," said Ahmed. "What she's saying is profane. She must be stopped."

"She's a Somali star," laughed Omar. "We would be hated by everyone."

"That didn't stop us shooting that playwright in Mogadishu last week. He was also a star, spreading anti-Shabaab rubbish just like her."

"Ahmed's right," said Dahir. "She should be executed."

"Let's do it now!" cried Ahmed. "She only lives over the mountain."

"It's at least a hundred kilometres over rough road," said Omar, rising to his feet, "and I don't see the point of killing her." He walked over and picked it up the M-60 machine gun. "She's not renounced Islam. That's something, at least."

"There are only two guards posted at her gate," said Ahmed.

"Are you deaf?" asked Omar, examining the American weapon in his hands. He had not taken the time to inspect it before now. "Listen to them out there, like gigantic mosquitoes. They're everywhere now, keeping track of the stolen food aid and, it would seem, watching over Mrs Abdul Rahman. Drones are her bodyguards." Omar released the M-60's swinging lever latch, and its barrel fell to the floor with a loud clatter. "So, that's what that does."

"Omar's right," said Dahir. "Since yesterday, when the pirates arrived with food for Galaga, there have been drones constantly circling over the Karkaar Mountains. It might not be wise to go off all half-cocked."

"Are you saying we just let the *sharmouta* keep her head?" asked Ahmed, now also on his feet. "With all the filth that's pouring from her mouth?"

"No," said Omar, "I'm merely saying we should not be too hasty. We must plan." He crouched down to pick up the barrel of the M-60. "It might be appropriate that she died by her own dead husband's gun, or it might be appropriate that we concentrate on taking that ship away from her. They're only half way through unloading its cargo. We should take it from them and feed our own people. There are many among the Wahabi who are also starving."

"It is Kafir food," said Ahmed. "We don't need Kafir food in Somalia, nor foreign aid. Certainly not from outside the Islamic world."

"Speaking of food," said Dahir, "why don't I go get us something to eat in Galaga?"

"I'll go," said Omar. "Fresh air would be nice, even though it's full of black, stinking drone exhaust."

"At least in the mountains the fumes quickly disperse," said Dahir, throwing him the vehicle keys. He was only too pleased to defer the assignment to his commander.

Omar stepped out into a narrow, shadowy ravine. In the late afternoon doldrums, the large black jihad flag hanging above the door was limp. Just one drone remained in the sky, and it was circling high over the hills. Nevertheless, he was wary of attack, and skulked cautiously along the sheer walls of sandstone, down the path that led to the car park. The Land Cruiser was bathed in sunshine.

Searching through the dozens of keys attacked to Dahir's keychain, it took him a moment to finally find the right one. He opened the driver's door, climbed in behind the wheel, then put the key into the ignition. Before starting the engine he first engaged the battery, turning the ignition counterclockwise only slightly, then waited for the sound of the cooling system to kick in. A screeching raven landed atop a dead tree opposite the car, and the wind blew a ball of tumbleweed across the car park.

Satisfied that he'd waited long enough, Omar started the engines and put the vehicle into reverse. He was about to accelerate when all at once he heard a tell-tale sound that caused him to swiftly dive for cover: a solid fuel rocket, hurtling through the air at four hundred and twenty-five metres per second. In an instant the missile struck, exploding in a tremendous fireball that completely obliterated the al-Shabaab base. Omar was the only survivor.

The television crew had already packed up and were waiting in the car outside the house in Bender Siyaada. "Thank you for being so obliging with us this afternoon," said the Arab woman journalist from al-Jazeera, raising her hand in farewell.

Khadija smiled. "I look forward to watching it tonight. *Masha Allah*, my message will bring hope to Somalians." She was standing next to the polished ship's bell that her late second husband had fastened to the ornate door frame to act as a doorbell. With a blast of loose gravel the crew sped away. Khadija went back inside and shut the heavy Zanzibari front door behind her.

She kicked off her heels and collapsed on to her sofa. Solitude was a rare pleasure these days. A soothing offshore breeze and the surf's irregular tempo helped her gather her thoughts. It pleased her that she had managed to restore so much of her home's former glory. With painstaking care and countless tubes of superglue she had made it her nightly duty, after posting on the Internet, to put all the pieces back together. Now if she could only do the same for her country.

From the side table she retrieved her hardback copy of Hirsi Ali's book *Nomad: From Islam to America*, opened it where she had left off and began reading. Could such a woman ever be elected in Somalia? Until recently she would have said, never in a thousand years. But the image of Somalia was changing. The country had its first female foreign minister and Somali women could now join the police force. There was certainly no shortage of female talent.

The doorbell rang – an unwelcome interruption. She put down her book and got up from the couch. Searching the house as she walked back towards the front door she wondered if the al-Jazeera crew might have left something behind. Through the peephole she saw a familiar trollish face. "Khadija, it's me, Abdu Takar," he said, beaming from ear to ear. "Please open the door."

She opened the door only wide enough to poke her face through and asked, "What is it? I'm trying to rest."

"I have some good news. It's about the madrasa in Bosaso that Nadif attends. The elders have decided to shut it down."

"You drove all the way out here just to tell me that?"

"I thought you'd be pleased to hear it."

"I am, but…" Khadija froze. Someone was creeping up behind her. She spun round to find a large man, his head covered by a blue *keffiyeh*. The man grabbed her in a bear hug. She struggled to break free. "Allah be my witness," she whispered, "I want no conflict with you." Abdu Takar pushed open the door, then pulled a hypodermic needle from his robes and stabbed it firmly into her shoulder. Khadija's tussle for freedom quickly subsided, and she fell limp to the floor.

CHAPTER TWENTY-ONE

In a secure briefing room at Camp Lemonnier in Djibouti, a fifty-four-year-old man, dressed in faded jeans and a loud, burnt orange Rayon shirt, sat cross-legged with his fingertips pressed together, his face obscured by shadow. He was the United State's most important intelligence asset on the Horn of Africa, a tier-one operator known simply as "Marlin". Seated opposite him in desert fatigues were the men who ambushed him in northern Kenya, and Robert, the "Karamajong guide", all of whom were in fact Navy SEALS sent on a mission to bring their man in from the cold.

At the head of the rosewood conference table, wearing desert fatigues bearing four stars, and leaning back in a swivel chair smoking a fat cigar, was the commander of the United States Africa Command (AFRICOM), General Kirkpatrick. Middle-aged, red-headed and Southern, the general spoke with a calming lilt that belied her warrior face. "Don't forget we lost twelve good sailors in those attacks, Marlin," she said. "And we took care of those rogue cutters too. But hijacking the *Tristola* has changed everything. This situation is now fixed in our disposition matrix."

"What the hell's a disposition matrix?" asked Marlin.

"I wish you'd get with the damn programme," said the general, sitting up. "The disposition matrix is a resources grid. It tells us not only who's on the kill list, but what needs to be done to achieve the broader outcomes of stability and prosperity in the region. We've got so many goddamn divisions cross-pollinating with each other these days, it's impossible to tell who's screwing whom any more. The United States government is sick to death of turf wars between the CIA, DIA, FBI and NSA. The disposition matrix is an effort to codify our counter-terrorism policy for a sustained conflict. This drone campaign is set to continue for at least another decade, Marlin."

"Maybe I didn't make myself clear," said Marlin. "I do not dispute the success of drones in finding, tracking and taking out militant jihadists. But against the pirates you're dealing with a whole different ball game. Indiscriminate drone attacks on these guys risk escalating the presence of radical Islamism in Puntland, and alienating the one group of people who can help us keep it at bay."

"Up until now the Majeerteen have resisted jihad," said the Turkana warrior who had pretended to slit his throat outside Kakuma.

"That's because they're businessmen. But if we keep sending in Reapers to take out rogue fisherman, we risk driving these people towards insurgency. And I don't need to tell you what would happen if the *badaadintu badah* joined forces with Shabaab."

"I understand your concerns about the pirates, Marlin," said the general. "But these people need to understand that there are consequences to taking hostages. The cost of diverting shipping away from Cape Gardafui alone runs into the millions."

"Look, I know the Majeerteen, OK. They're hurting right now. And there's only so far they can be pushed. All these attacks in recent days have sent them into a desperate spin. They need our help."

"Be that as it may, Marlin, the president's going nuts watching the news every night. Homeboy wants to retaliate."

"At the risk of everything I worked to create in Puntland?"

"Hasn't your wife already ballsed it up?"

"My wife's only doing what she believes is right, and she has widespread popular support among Somalians. They see her as some sort of heroic outlaw. I can't say I approve of what she did but I think it would be wrong to persecute her for it."

The general stubbed out her cigar then leaned forward in her chair. "If there's one thing this administration has learned in the past couple of years it's to get behind popular movements in the Muslim world. But piracy is illegal, and hijacking that ship to steal her cargo is a major international crime."

"I know what it is, ma'am. Nevertheless, putting aside all concerns about my wife, I still think it would be loco to launch a drone attack against the *Tristola*. Besides, these are my people. I don't want any of them getting hurt."

"What about that goddamn gorilla guide friend of yours?" asked the general, sitting back and shaking her red head with dismay. "When I think of what we had to do just to get him and his pal to Puntland. It took fewer military resources getting Dorothy and Toto back to Kansas. Only to have them participate in a pirate attack the moment they arrived? Jesus Christ! I mean, who the hell do they think they are?"

"Strangely was a convenient beard, just like in '98. But the guy's a maverick. You know that. As for Abdulmajid, well, we all know where he came from."

"They gave them the details of the goddamn ship. *They took part in the hijacking.*"

Marlin tugged at his collar then moved into the light. "*Forgedaboudit.* No one got hurt in the process. And the hostages are flying out of Bosaso tomorrow. Without any outside intervention the whole thing has gone off totally peacefully. What real harm's been done, when compared to the feel-good factor that's been created among Somalis? Hell, you and I know the World Food Programme has got insurance for this sort of thing, so does the Turkish Shipping Company. With this one act of piracy the Majeerteen may have effectively foiled the Islamists' plans for jihad in the north."

"I very much doubt that, Marlin. And frankly, I'm surprised by your naïvety. Al-Shabaab is by no means defeated in Somalia. Why, only yesterday we intercepted a dhow on its way to Puntland that was loaded with weapons from Al-Qaeda in the Arab Peninsula. AQAP grows stronger by the day. With those two groups now coordinating their efforts across the Gulf of Aden, hell, we have a force to contend with."

"Exactly what I'm talking about, General! And there's no way we should risk pushing the pirates into that mix."

At Camp Lemonnier's eastern perimeter, near the shores of the Gulf of Aden, the landscape was devoid of everything – structures, vegetation, shadows. General Kirkpatrick strolled along a concertina-wired fence with her hands clasped behind her back. Marlin walked next to her, wearing sunglasses, his mouth screwed up like he was sucking on a lemon. The temperature was forty-five degrees Celsius and the humidity eighty per cent. A formation of Marines in desert fatigues, wearing black gas masks and heavy flak jackets, jogged past, unperturbed by the midday heat. One of them, carrying a black and white skull-and-crossbones standard, saluted the general, yelling, "Reporting for duty in Djibouti, ma'am!" then marched on with the others.

"You know how I feel about Khadija, John," said the general. No one was within earshot so she thought it would be OK to use real names. "She's a brave woman, and she has my greatest admiration. But she's put us in an awkward position."

"I can straighten things out, Kitty," said Marlin, "if you let me go back. I'm not much good here. No one else knows Puntland and its politics better than I do."

"Can't argue with that, but it's not like it was back there, John. There's a price on your head. Al-Rubaysh is still at large. Last spotted, he was in Aden, about a week ago, but we're getting snippets of intel that say he's now in Bosaso."

"Let me handle Rubaysh," said Marlin, wiping the sweat from his forehead. "I can take the *motoscafo*. Anything to get away from this goddamn inferno."

"I wouldn't put your chances very high," sighed Kitty Kirkpatrick, "even with the speedboat." She surveyed her unfinished base, spread out like the detritus of ground zero across the flat, open scrubland, The avian life picking away at the ground around the end of the runway didn't flinch as a squadron of Predator drones took off over their heads, one after the other. "So you don't like it here, huh, John?"

"Why the fuck did they have to put Africa command in the hottest place on earth? Jesus, your air-conditioning bill must be half of the United States defence budget."

General Kirkpatrick laughed, removed her cap and shook the dust from her hair. "Not for long. A pair of geologists from the Navy Geothermal Program are out here right now to see if they can't power the base on hellfire."

"Geothermal electricity? Makes damn good sense."

"Of course it makes sense. We're smack in the middle of a tectonic triple junction, where three continental plates diverge. Everywhere you look there's fire and brimstone. Some days we have to wear gas masks just to deal with the acrid odour of volcanic activity. Forget terrorists, we're under chemical attack by the forces of nature."

"*Fiery the Angels rose, and as they rose deep thunder roll'd. Around their shores: indignant burning with the fires of Orc.*"

"Is that Blake or 'Blade Runner' you're quoting there, John?"

"It's just something to throw into your disposition matrix, General. I mean, what in the hell are we trying to do here?" He watched a fleet of bulldozers busily moving earth at the northern perimeter of the base. Black and white sacred ibis stood nearby, transfixed by the activity, waiting for unearthed provender. "Running out of space to park your drones, General?"

"We're running out of space for everything, John. There are more US troops in Djibouti than there are in Iraq. Three thousand two hundred soldiers, civilians and contractors are assigned to this camp, including three hundred and fifty special forces and a detachment of the Japanese Maritime Self-Defence Force to help fight the pirates." Marlin frowned. He'd lost an uncle in the Pacific War. The thought of Tojo coming after the Majeerteen did not sit well with him. "Congress just approved a one-and-a-half-billion-dollar upgrade. We're planning to extend the runway, build new hangars and billets, and construct a huge new compound, right here where we're standing, to accommodate a threefold increase in special forces. And, yes, we need more room for drones. Lemonnier's quickly becoming a permanent base for drone warfare. "

"The weapon of choice for the Obama administration," said Marlin, smiling contemptuously.

"Homeboy loves his drones," said the general. "Loves Lemonnier too. Never visited as far as I know, but he thinks he's doing good for his grandmother-land with this base, you know, for his ancestors on the Dark Continent. Truth is we're here to turn the lights *on*."

"Still think Africa's a hellhole, huh, Kitty, after all I've taught you?"

"Hell, no! I love this godforsaken place just as much as you do, John. So does the United States. We're here to strengthen democratic principles and foster conditions that lead to a peaceful, stable, and economically strong Africa."

"Give me a break..."

"If we don't care about this shit, who will? The Chinese? They don't give a rat's ass about Africa, just what's underneath it."

"When the Marines took over this base, what was then an old French legionnaire outpost, it was only meant to be an expeditionary encampment. Now suddenly Camp Lemonnier has become America's beachhead for freedom and prosperity on the continent. Don't you think we might have bitten off more than we can chew here, General? I mean, how's the disposition matrix going to pan out for ordinary Africans?"

"Hell, Africans are all over this shit. We're training a dozen of their national forces right here at Lemonnier, teaching them to be mighty fine soldiers too."

"Really? Is that what we're doing? Or are we just footing the military training bills for a bunch of corrupt governments whose leaders concur with our anti-Islamist outlook (for the time being) but can't feed their damn people, let alone their forces, because they're too fucking busy stuffing their own pockets with money from the national treasury?"

"Holy crap, you sound like that damn journalist from the *Washington Post* who's been snooping around, trying to get the scoop on what it is we really do at this base."

"*Forgedaboudit*," laughed Marlin. "I don't even know."

General Kirkpatrick ceased walking, straightened up and turned to Marlin. "One of the things we *do* do here is tackle piracy."

"Right. And I know that. All I'm saying is that the pirate situation is trickier."

"I've seen your file, John. I know all about your smuggling days in Florida. How the Company coerced you into joining, then arranged with the DEA to have your slate wiped clean. How you used your family's casino racket to front intelligence gathering in East Africa during the 1990s. The fact that you trained pirates in paramilitary activities in those early days in Puntland. I know all about you, Johnny Oceans. Being a good agent has its consequences. I'm worried the lines of conflict may have become blurred in your mind..."

Johnny raised his sunglasses and peered back at her, with dark, one-way baby blues that siphoned everything but gave nothing back. No one could fathom the conflicts within his soul, between right and wrong, truth and lies, loyalty and betrayal, cruelty and mercy. He lowered the sunglasses, but before he could say anything, they were interrupted by a serviceman bearing a note for the general. She read it, then looked back at Johnny with a funereal gaze and swallowed hard. "John," she said, gently resting her hand on his shoulder, "your wife's been kidnapped."

CHAPTER TWENTY-TWO

"We must continue with the food distribution," insisted Abdulmajid. He was standing next to Derek against a wall in Khadija's living room with his hands behind his back.

"Shut the fuck up, Jereer!" yelled Maxamid Malik, standing before them with his BAR in one hand and a bundle of *khat* in the other.

"But it's what Khadija would have wanted," protested Abdulmajid.

Maxamid aimed the barrel of his rifle at the Bantu Somali's head. "Speak again! I dare you to open those fat lips of yours one more time."

"Lay off him, Max!" cried Derek. "You're not the only person upset by your sister's abduction."

The two-metre-tall pirate lord swaggered to within centimetres of the safari guide's face, his hennaed goatee at Derek's eye level. He smiled broadly, bearing half a dozen gold teeth, then said, "I like you. But I would not hesitate to kill you. Do you understand? Now, I'm in charge here. You will both do as I say."

He walked into the living room, sat down on the couch, propped up his rifle, and opened the packet of khat. After stuffing a fist full of leaves into his capacious jaw, he looked back at the other two and gestured for them to join him.

Abdulmajid needed no encouragement. He nipped forward, grabbed a handful of leaves then retreated back to the wall. "I'd love to," said Derek, "but I have to take Maddy and the others to the airport."

"The hostages are going nowhere," snapped Maxamid, searching the bundle for the juiciest leaves. "I've already sent my boys to the hotel to make sure they stay where they are."

"C'mon, Max. We had an agreement."

"That was before my sister got kidnapped."

"How's holding on to these people going to help her?"

"It's how I operate! Hostages are bargaining chips."

"But we don't even know who kidnapped her, man. What if it's terrorists?"

"No matter who it was, those hostages are my only leverage. They could prove useful in the negotiations for Khadija's release, as part of an exchange..."

"What?" cried Derek.

"Yes, that's right, I will gladly trade your girlfriend's life for my sister's."

"That's not how they work," said Abdulmajid, through a mouthful of leaves.

"Who asked you?" snapped Maxamid.

"Let him speak, for Chrissakes!" Derek turned to Abdulmajid. "How do you know how they work?"

"Because I used to be one of them."

"One of who?" frowned Maxamid.

"Before I fled to Kakuma I was a mujahideen for al-Shabaab in Kismayo." Both Derek and Maxamid gaped at him. It was a startling revelation. "OK, so now you know my whole story. The fact remains, I understand how these people work." He took a deep breath, then looked solemnly at the floor. "Unless they issue demands, it's very unlikely Khadija will be spared execution."

"Why, you..." Maxamid was on his feet, about to lunge at Abdulmajid, but Derek intercepted. "Get out of my way! I've heard enough shit from this Jereer!"

"What the fuck, Max," pleaded Derek. "Why are you so determined to go at this half-cocked?" The doorbell rang. Maxamid pushed past him and went to answer it. A moment later he returned with Abdu Takar and two Bosaso police officers. "What's the news?" asked Derek, eyes fixed on the new arrivals in anticipation.

"No news, I'm afraid," said Abdu Takar, bearing an expression that suggested he had exhausted every avenue.

"And your damn bodyguards?" asked Maxamid. "Where the fuck were they yesterday afternoon?"

One of the police officers spoke: "We found their bodies washed up on the beach about a kilometre from here."

"Both had been shot in the head," said the other policeman, "at close range."

Abdu Takar shook his head solemnly and wrung his hands. "It's a terrible thing that has happened, Maxamid. The whole clan is praying for Khadija. I know we'll hear something soon."

Maxamid lowered his head, tilted it slightly then rolled his eyeballs upward so he could continue to regard the Majeerteen elder through the blurred follicles of his bushy eyebrows. "We need all the help we can get," he said quietly, then smiled.

"Right. So let me accompany these officers back to Bosaso, and get on with the search. C'mon, you two."

"You do that," mumbled Maxamid, squeezing the barrel of his gun. "May Allah guide you." Then, as soon as he heard the front door shut, he hissed, "Abdu Takar's the bastard behind this!"

"How do you know?" asked Derek.

"Those bodyguards could not have been shot at point-blank range by someone they didn't know. These were highly trained men, his men. It's him! I know it's him! And I will kill the betraying motherfucker, slowly. But only after he tells me where my sister is."

Derek found Maddy on the third-storey balcony of her hotel room. She was wearing a white silk chiffon skirt and a pale blue, long-sleeved cotton top, with a neckline that revealed her cleavage. As she gazed out to sea amber beams and sea breezes played alluringly with her hair. Beyond her, spread out along the shore between sandstone mountains to the east and west, lay the port of Bosaso. Except for a handful of telecom towers and minarets, the city was mostly bungalows arranged in a tidy grid. There seemed to be a deliberate effort on the part of its residents to beautify their single-storey skyline with an array of pastel-coloured rooftops that matched the sky at twilight.

"Hey, Maddy," said Derek, stepping on to the balcony.

She turned around. "Derek, what the hell's going on? They won't let me leave my hotel room."

Derek embraced her and ran his fingers through her hair. "It's Maxamid. He's lost the plot."

"Yeah, well, I've missed my bloody flight now," cried Maddy, pulling away from him.

"Don't worry, babes. It's just a temporary setback. We'll soon get you back to Brisbane." He looked at her and smiled. "Although, if I'm honest," he crooned, "I can't say I'm disappointed you're still here. You are truly stunning..."

"Any news about Khadija?" asked Maddy, gripping her shoulders against the cold.

"Nothing," replied Derek. "Everyone fears the worst." Again he sought to comfort her with an embrace but she was not in the mood. Instead she gripped the railing with both hands and stared at the ocean.

With the setting sun glinting off the face of it, Derek's Kobold Phantom Tactical was beaming like a lighthouse.

"I've been meaning to ask you," said Maddy, "how far you got with your treasure hunt?"

"Haven't had time. All I know is it's near the spot where we beached your ship."

"Any idea *what* it is?"

"Not a clue."

Maddy sighed, and whispered, "I wonder." They said nothing for a spell as the sun set on the Gulf of Aden.

"How many vessels has this narrow sea devoured?" asked

Derek. "Hungry ships sailing east past a lifeless desert in search of the Orient, skippered by explorers, merchants, warlords, their curiosities ablaze under an unrelenting sky? Obsessed seamen are no match for mermaids, you know. Sirens who wait on the rocks, sea cows sent to torment, to lure those long away from home to their deaths."

Maddy turned to him, touched his forehead seductively then smiled. "Are you my sea cow?" she asked, batting her eyelids.

"I love you," said Derek. They kissed passionately until the phone rang. "I'll get it," said Derek, walking back into the room. "Hello?"

"Mr Strangely?"

"Yes."

"This is hotel reception. There are two gentlemen here to see you."

"I'll be right down," said Derek. He replaced the receiver then stepped back out on to the balcony to give Maddy another kiss. "I won't be a minute, babes."

As Derek turned the corner at the bottom of the stairs he spotted two thickset Somali men slouched in the hotel lobby's blue vinyl armchairs, wearing sunglasses, black suits and ties. They stood up as he approached them. "Derek Strangely?" asked one, producing his identification card from his breast pocket.

"Yes."

"Puntland Intelligence Agency. Please come with us."

"What's this about?"

"Just come with us." They said nothing more as they escorted him out of the hotel and into an unmarked car, then drove him four blocks away to an office building where he was hustled up two flights of stairs to an empty office and told to wait.

Alone in a locked room, Derek began to sweat. He could only imagine what might be in store for him. After entering the country illegally he had wantonly participated in the hijacking of a ship passing through Somali waters. If the authorities also had hold of his rap sheets from Kenya and Ethiopia, he was truly up shit's creek.

The office window was ajar and he considered escaping. But the sight of a *farenji* climbing out on to a ledge would not go unnoticed. They might even try to shoot him down. No, there was no point in running. It was time to face the music. He heard someone turn the key in the lock behind him and froze as the door swung open. "YOU!" cried Derek.

"I'll explain everything later," said Johnny Oceans. "Right now I need your help. So far, we've been unable to detect any intel about where they're holding my wife. There's been no electronic chatter whatsoever, and nobody knows anything. Is there anything you can tell me?"

"I don't believe this..." said Derek, gaping at his resurrected friend and shaking his head with utter astonishment. "How many goddamn lives do you have?"

"Derek! I need you to focus," said Johnny. Derek blinked a couple of times. "Do you have any clues about where Khadija's being held?"

"Max thinks Abdu Takar's behind her kidnapping."

"*Forgedaboudit.* Abdu gave her and the kids refuge when I escaped Puntland."

"Well, you'd better get to him before Max does because he's screaming for blood."

"Out of the question! You're the only one outside the PIA I've dropped cover for. It's crucial I stay dead. *Capisce?*" He glared sombrely at Derek until he was certain the gravity of his words had hit home. "Let's just wait here until we hear what Max has to say."

CHAPTER TWENTY-THREE

Yusuf Ali al-Rubaysh gripped the back of the wooden chair, while Khadija sat stoically on the edge of the blood-stained mattress with her hands tied behind her back. They were the only two people in the windowless one-room apartment. A naked bulb hung between them from the middle of the ceiling, bathing the room in a garish light. "You're a beautiful woman," cooed Rubaysh, whose face remained covered by a black *keffiyeh*. "It would be a shame to change all that."

"Torture me if you must," whispered Khadija. "I told you everything I know."

"You know, it's quite unusual for al-Qaeda to use torture," laughed Rubaysh. "We're pretty adept at inflicting a torturous death, but our victims are typically executed before demands for secrets are made. But then, you see, I went to 'water-boarding' school. I am what they call a Gitmo alumni; I learned the art of torture from the Americans. And I don't often get the opportunity to show off my talents."

All the power was in the hands of Rubaysh, and Khadija knew this. She took care not to enrage him. He wanted information which she had, but the only way she believed she would survive was if she held out for as long as possible. She drew courage from her new-found prominence in Somalia, believing that if she was killed it would only serve her country.

"I hear you are the new Arawello, and that you'll soon be snipping off men's penises in Somalia. Do you believe in God?" Khadija stared blankly at him. "You refuse to wear even a hijab. Always in tight jeans and form-fitting T-shirts." She straightened her posture. "Don't worry. I won't rape you. I'll leave that to the men outside. They can't wait. How did you meet?"

"What?"

"Johnny Oceans. How did you two meet?"

"My brother Maxamid introduced us."

"Were you curious?"

"About what?" asked Khadija, keeping her gaze on the floor.

"About the size and nature of a *farenji* penis?" Khadija shook her head. "Yes you were. Yet you did not see the obvious contradiction, having sexual relations with a Kafir? Was he even circumcised?" Khadija tried to maintain her composure. "Tell me about your trips to the Hafun Peninsula together."

"I already told you...Yes, I went with him to Hafun, but he told me nothing about why he was there, and spent the whole time scuba-diving. I don't swim."

"You lying *sharmouta*!" screamed Rubaysh, shoving the chair across the room, which caused her to jump. He moved closer to the Somali woman, glowering at her with cold-blooded eyes, trying to instil the fear of death in her. He knew he couldn't kill her until she gave him the information he needed, and even then he planned to hand the task over to somebody else. But it was not in his plan to physically harm her in the meantime. Rather, he would use psychological torture. He whistled a cheery tune. "Do you know what that is?"

"'Sesame Street'?" asked Khadija, looking up at him.

"It was played endlessly for days on end, blasting in my ears. Now I can't get it out of my head. Funny, eh?"

"I'm sorry about what happened to you in Guantanamo."

"Why? It made me strong. Much stronger than you will ever be."

"Torture is a terrible weapon," whispered Khadija.

"But I'm only getting started," laughed Rubaysh.

Maxamid Malik appeared possessed as he approached Abdu Takar's house on the outskirts of Bosaso. He was flanked by five of his most merciless *badaadintu badah*, some armed with AK-47s, some with RPGs, and had his own M1918 Browning Automatic Rifle slung over his shoulder at hip level, with his finger on the trigger.

When he reached the front door, rather than knock, he blew a hole through it with his BAR. People began screaming. So as not to break his stride, he fired again and again then glided through the gap. Inside he found Abdu Takar in the living room, cowering behind five of his young children. A pirate fished him out by his turban and dragged him to the dining-room table.

Before the Majeerteen elder could say a word, Maxamid plunged a knife through his hand, binding him to the wooden table. The old man screamed in agony. "Where's my sister, Khadija? WHERE HAVE YOU TAKEN HER?"

The minutes passed like hours while Derek and Johnny waited for news, sitting on the floor of the abandoned office with their backs against the wall. Derek had just completed rolling a joint with some weed and papers he'd managed to score in the port, and was admiring the workmanship. Johnny, who insisted on checking Derek's phone every few minutes for messages, was growing ever more frustrated by the lack of what he called 'humint', apparently short for human intelligence. From personal experience, Derek could certainly relate to the concept of non-human intelligence, but he doubted military commanders had gorillas and chimpanzees in mind when they came up with the term.

"So, how do you like Puntland so far?" asked Johnny.

"Wild," said Derek, lighting his joint. "You'll never believe how I fucking got here."

"Riding on a Reaper drone, handcuffed to a Somali refugee?"

Derek stared at his old friend, dumbfounded. "How the hell did you know that?"

"Just a stab in the dark," laughed Johnny.

"You were tracking me, weren't you?" asked Derek.

"I followed your every move after you left Kakuma. Made sure you stayed the course."

"How?" asked Derek. He looked at the heavy watch on his wrist and then began to chuckle. "Right. I should have known."

"Why are you still wearing it?" asked Johnny, grabbing Derek's arm. "That's a five-thousand-dollar timepiece you're flashing around there."

"It was your dying gift to me," said Derek, pulling his hand away. "No way would I ever take it off."

"That's stupid. When you get back to your hotel, ask them to put it in their safe, all right. Otherwise, they'll mug you." Johnny stood up and went to the window. "Do you know how many cutthroats there are in Bosaso? Believe me, you're a very lucky man to still have your hand...Nothing is what it seems here."

"So I was just a pawn in your game?"

"A somewhat reluctant pawn, I might add. The number of times we had to intervene to make sure you got to where you were supposed to go. Remember Gabriel?"

"He was one of yours?" Derek began to see his friend in a whole new light, or rather a whole new gloom. Notwithstanding the passing years, the black-hearted intelligencer peering out of the office window at the busy street below, with a thousand-metre stare, was not the same cool dude he used to get baked with in Malindi, who boasted he could "put everything on thirty-three as a last resort, and then thirty-three would come up". Derek noticed he'd replaced the white puka-shell choker around his neck with a black stone pendant depicting a leaping fish, and asked, "What's the significance of that?"

"It's from my smuggling days."

"Oh, that figures, you were a smuggler too...Just who the hell are you, Johnny Oceans?"

"It's complicated," said Johnny, pacing the floor of the empty office, "but I *will* explain, Gorilla Man."

"You work for the CIA, right?"

"Wrong. I work for the DIA, the Defense Intelligence Agency."

"A war hero!" laughed Derek, taking another hit of his joint. He offered it to Johnny, but he declined.

"Civilian," said Johnny. "Back in the mid Eighties I got hauled up in Dade County on smuggling charges. The DEA wanted to throw the book at me, but the Defense Department had other ideas. They saw a skill in me they liked: inconspicuous import-export. It takes all kinds of talents to execute black ops, some that go beyond military training. They co-opted me into their intelligence service, and sent me to the Kenyan Coast to start gathering intel on Islamists in the Horn of Africa."

"They sent you straight from Miami? Just like that? No training? Damn, you must have been one hell of a smuggler."

"There were no bozos in my game. But no, like everyone else, I had to first go to the Farm, in Virginia, followed by months of psychological training, and then I did a two-year apprenticeship under Billy Waugh in Khartoum."

"Billy Waugh?" asked Derek.

"Sergeant Major William Waugh. Only the greatest American agent this world has ever known. He had Osama bin Laden in his sights in '95. We could have stopped him in Khartoum. What a different world we'd live in today if Billy had been allowed to pull the trigger, but Clinton wouldn't do it...We should have never let him get away."

"Who, Bill Clinton?"

"No, Bin Laden."

"Right...in Khartoum. Instead you woke up in the morning with blood on your hands, and the head of Khartoum in your bed, just like that movie producer in *The Godfather*...What's his name?"

"Wolz."

"Right, Wolz."

"You really should cut down smoking that *bangi*, my friend."

"Oh, that fucking does it, man," cried Derek, throwing his spliff across the floor, and rising to his feet. "You used to be the goddamn poster boy for the legalise pot campaign, attend every Cannabis Cup in Amsterdam, *never* take your goddamn DNA GENETICS T-shirt off. Now...Jesus, Johnny, what the hell happened?"

"I had to stay focused. I had an important job to do."

"Which was? I'd really like to know what inspired all this."

"Sure," said Johnny, picking the joint up, "just as soon as I get a little brain food."

"Johnny boy!" cried Derek, high-fiving his friend.

He took a few tokes then handed it to Derek. They both sat back down on the floor with their backs against the wall, then Johnny continued. "After Puntland declared independence from Somalia in 1998, my instructions were to go deep under cover in the north, watch developments closely and recommend contacts. The DIA wanted me to recruit and train a standing army. Meantime I became involved with the pirates who were an unknown quantity back then, and pretty soon I was in trouble with Bolling."

"Bolling?"

"It's the air-force base where the DIA has its headquarters."

"Right. Why were they pissed off?"

"I crossed the line."

"Really? How so?"

"Cut off from the casino business and with no money from the family, I had to find an income. The DIA provided me with a couple of thousand dollars a month, but I was meant to use that for micro-loans to fishermen, which was our recruiting platform."

"God, you must have been destitute."

"That's what got me in trouble. Now and again I would let the pirates know about the location of one or two offshore tuna factories, *badda bing badda boom*, and then take a cut of the ransom." Derek looked at him, mouth agape. "I was only trying to maintain cover."

"I bet that put a weed up command's ass," laughed Derek, holding in a toke.

"*Forgedaboudit!* They dragged me across the coals when they found out. A lot of painstaking work went into creating my false identity, and I wasn't protected by diplomatic immunity."

"Baptism by fire..." said Derek, blazing his joint.

"There was more to come. The real shit hit the fan when the mob came looking for me. Remember them?"

"Who, Bobby, Jimmy, Petey and Tony? How could I fucking forget?"

"Well, those paisans weren't as concerned about my welfare as they let on to you."

"Now that you mention it, they never really had anything nice to say about you. Why was that?"

"Lots of reasons, which I won't go into now. Suffice to say I hadn't entirely tied up all my loose ends before leaving Uncle Bobby's casino. Anyway, it didn't take them long to find me, but after sending half a dozen hit men after me, and never hearing from any of them again, they decided I must have some kind of fucking force field around me. So, they devised a different way to carry out their vendetta…" Johnny straightened up and blinked several times. "You see, they knew how much I loved fishing and diving. Consequently, they arranged to have tens of thousands of tons of toxic waste dumped right off the coast in front of my house in Bender Siyaada."

"Fuck! That must have hurt."

"Profoundly," gasped Johnny. He paused to gaze at Derek with fathomless ultramarine eyes. He was sounding the depths of a friend to whom he had just divulged more than he had ever divulged to anyone else before. "I was so fucking angry, I nearly blew my cover," he whispered, "but that's what they wanted, those fucking paisans…Luckily for everyone concerned, I didn't give them what they wanted. I learned a hard lesson that year, the first of many."

As Derek listened to Johnny's backstory, he began to understand why his friend had become so tormented. And with so many divided loyalties, it was easy to see why honesty was such an abstract concept to Johnny. Why should he believe him now? The look on Johnny's face said he was finally telling the truth. Still, he would probably never reveal the full story to anyone, except God.

"You sound like the good guy's Keyser Söze," laughed Derek. "'*That most beautiful trick of the devil…*'"

"Uh, no, *rafiki*, I'm sure the actual quote is…" Derek's phone began to buzz and he quickly fetched it from his pocket. "It's a message from Maxamid," he cried. "They've found Khadija!"

Johnny leapt to his feet. "Where?"

"In an apartment off Osman Street."

"Right. Get back to the hotel. I'm going in."

"Let me come with you!"

"No fucking way. I operate alone. And remember, I'm still dead. Don't let nothing slip about the ghost of Johnny Oceans. *Capisce?*"

"*Capisce.*"

Rubaysh was growing tired of Khadija's resistance. His attempts at psychological torture weren't working. He tried to break her with sensory deprivation, denying her sleep and forcing her to wear blacked-out goggles, earmuffs and a surgical face mask while making her stand for hours on end. She was proving much more resilient than he expected. His threats only strengthened her resolve to reveal nothing. He was beginning to doubt she knew anything about the treasure. Either that, or she was holding out, believing it was the only thing keeping her alive.

He decided to try a different tactic. "Your son, Nadif, just turned sixteen, am I right?" Disturbed by this new line of questioning, Khadija sat up abruptly and nodded. "You must be so proud, to have raised such a firm disciple of salafi."

"What – what are you talking about?" she asked.

"Oh, didn't they tell you? It would seem Nadif has already joined our holy war."

"No, please, I beg of you, not my son!"

"He will make a splendid martyr, don't you think? I personally will see to it he has a heroic role in the jihad, and does honour to his mother and clan in martyrdom."

"All right! I'll tell you what you want to know."

"That's better," smiled Rubaysh.

"But you must promise to let Nadif be."

"I promise."

"OK. The location of the treasure is engraved on the back of Mehemet's watch."

"A fat lot of good that does me now," cried Rubaysh. "He's dead. You'll have to do better than that if you want to save your son."

"Wait! Before my husband died, he gave the watch to his friend, Derek Strangely, who's here in Bosaso, at this very moment, staying at the Hotel Huruuse."

"How convenient!" Rubaysh smiled, turned, and rapped on the door. Two mujahideen brandishing swords stepped into the room. "Take care of her," said Rubaysh, brushing past them. "Make it slow and painful."

With no time to spare Maxamid and his pirates stormed the building off Osman Street in a pandemonium of gunfire and shouting that sent panic through the neighbourhood. During the ensuing battle, her captors were killed and Khadija was freed unharmed. Rubaysh had already fled the scene. Maxamid bundled his sister into a car and sped away before the Puntland Intelligence Agency arrived.

Marlin was already there, lurking in the shadows. He knew he couldn't yet blow his cover, not even to his distraught wife. Once he learned she was in safe hands, he and a handful of PIA agents began searching the area. There was nothing in the apartment that offered any clues. But, after a tip-off, they discovered an al-Shabaab safe house two blocks away.

They went over it with a fine-tooth comb but uncovered nothing. As a final measure, Marlin decided to recheck the kitchen appliances. While examining the sink he spotted the end of a copper wire peeking up through the drain. He got under the sink, a dank and filthy cockroach ecosystem that stank to high heaven, and started dismantling the plumbing. It was a communication line of some sort. He followed it through the down pipe and out into the Bosaso sewer system. Ultimately, he found it led out to sea.

Khadija went directly to her son's madrasa, causing an uproar as she stormed through the holy learning halls, violating places reserved for men. When she reached the imam's office, she threw open the door. The elderly Arab rose to his feet in disgust. "What have you done to my boy?" she screamed. She began pulling the books from his bookshelves and throwing them at him one after the other, to punctuate her questions. "Where in these damn books does it say you can turn innocent children into murderers?" She quickly ran out of books.

"Get out of here at once," thundered the imam. Seeing his Qurans and the teachings of the salafs scattered across his office floor made him purple with anger. By now a crowd of students had burst through the door after her and thrown Khadija to the floor. Then a thunderous gun blast made everyone freeze.

"Take your fucking hands *off* her!" roared Maxamid, single-handedly removing each enraged Islamist from the scrum atop his sister. He then wielded his weapon at them, like a burning flame to a pack of wild dogs, which held them at bay while he helped her to her feet. "Imam! Where is Nadif?" he asked, swaggering over to the old man.

"We haven't seen him for days," laughed the imam.

"Is that so," smiled Maxamid. "I bet you know where he is, though, don't you."

"Sadly I don't. You see the mujahideen are very tight-lipped about their plans for my students. I only provide them with boys who have the piety and mettle to make the ultimate sacrifice for Islam. The rest is in Allah's hands."

"Which is where you're going to be in a second," said Maxamid, aiming his BAR at the imam's head. He was about to pull the trigger but Khadija stopped him.

"C'mon, Max," she said, grabbing his arm. "These hyenas aren't worth a minute more of our time."

CHAPTER TWENTY-FOUR

Rubaysh's cover was blown and his presence in Puntland had become known to the intelligence services. Yet rather than consolidate his gains and retreat to Aden, the Yemeni al-Qaeda commander had decided to call a meeting of the mujahideen officers of the northern faction of al-Shabaab, at midnight in a mud hall on the edge of the ancient dhow port of Qandala, half way between Bosaso and Ras Asir. Once the three-dozen attendees had been thoroughly screened for tracking devices and bugs, the meeting commenced.

Rubaysh was dressed in a thick black turban, white robes, and a green camouflage flak jacket. He stood next to a small table with a glass of water, lit by an array of candles around the edge of the room, while the others sat cross-legged on the floor. Omar Abu Hamza sat at the very back of the hall, obscured by the gloom. This was the first he'd seen of the Yemeni commander in days.

"Ahmed and Dahir are dead," said Rubaysh, with feigned solemnity, "along with five other brave mujahideen. We ask Allah to grant them the upper paradise and the company of the Prophet Muhammad. May Allah, the Almighty, give success, in this world and in the world to come, to all mujahideen who are sacrificing their lives."

"*Allahu Akbar!*" said the officers, punctually and in unison.

Rubaysh moved in closer to the crowd, candlelight casting a

dozen entangled shadows of his form across the ceiling. "The mujahideen have taken the initiative. We've forced the enemy to adopt a defensive position everywhere they go. Even they have admitted that they've been forced to retreat from many of their military centres.

"We have infiltrated their ranks in ways and means which remain unknown to them...unknown unknowns." A murmur of laughter spread across the room. It was an inside joke. "Many in the enemy's own ranks have also shown willingness to help the mujahideen. As a result, the foreign invaders and their allies, in their military bases and barricaded garrisons across the Islamic world, are coming under more attacks, more crushing blows in the name of global jihad. We've seen it in Afghanistan, Iraq, Libya, even Fort Hood, Texas, brave mujahideen carrying out decisive and coordinated attacks, inflicting heavy losses, both human and hardware, on the enemy."

"*Allahu Akbar!*"

He walked slowly across the room then back again, casting a cold gaze on the faces of the assembled officers. While his words rang true, so did the opposite: the enemy had infiltrated the ranks of the mujahideen. A gut feeling told him there was a traitor among them.

"Camp Lemonnier is only seven hundred kilometres west of here," he continued, calmly and deliberately, "in the Gulf of Tadjoura. The Americans claim it's their only base in Africa, but that is a lie. At least it's the most visible and heavily defended. No less than four thousand troops are stationed there," he said, deliberately exaggerating. "Did you know, Camp Lemonnier is run on hellfire? Yes, it's true! Satan's centurions are feeding off the fires of hell. And so we must send them back down to hell, from whence they came."

"Death to the Kafir!"

"AFRICOM and CTF 150 believe they're here to help poor Africans. Bleeding-heart sentimentalists! Any warrior will tell you, don't mix warfare with humanity. But these people are brought up on 'Sesame Street': Big Bird, Grover, Elmo and Ernie, and the Cookie Monster. Do you know what that does to their brains?" Rubaysh's eyes grew wider and his face became flushed with anguish. He grabbed his neck and popped it aggressively, glaring all the while at the gathered mujahideen, then quickly realised he'd gone off on a tangent and completely lost them. "At any rate, it's all lies. Their sole purpose in Djibouti is to launch attacks against Yemenis, Somalis, Malians, Africans, to send unmanned bombers they call Grim Reapers to murder your people, innocent men, women and children, while they lie sleeping in their beds at night. They *are* the spawn of Satan..."

"Death to the Kafir!"

"Indeed...death to the Kafir. We will drive them from Africa, just as we did in 1994, when we brought down their Blackhawks and dragged their servicemen through the streets of Mogadishu, we will make the Americans weep over the day they ever came to the Dark Continent."

Searching the room with his palms pressed compassionately to his heart, he gazed into the face of each and every one of them. "My dear Somali mujahideen, the fellowship I feel with you transcends even history. My ambition has always been to extend a hand across the Gulf to my fellow jihadists in Africa. The telegraph line was just the beginning. We will part the sea as Musa did with his mighty staff, for the glory of Allah, reestablish the bond between our great continents in the name of global jihad."

He gazed at the mud floor at his feet and he pondered how best to deliver this next bit of information. He took a gulp of water, a deep breath, brushed off his robes, then stood up tall. "Tomorrow, eight brave mujahideen will launch a terror attack that far exceeds September 11th 2001. May Allah, the Almighty, give success, in this world and in the world to come, to the brave mujahideen."

A murmur of astonishment rippled across the hall. "Tell us about the attack," said Omar. "We also want to participate."

"And so you will, in your own way. But it would be a grave mistake to divulge the details at this time, my friend. The walls have ears...No, the global jihad must be allowed to work its mysterious ways without interference of any kind. Suffice to say, by evening

prayers, you will have heard all about the glorious suicide mission."
He stepped back so his back was against the wall, then lowered his
voice. "In spite of that, the global jihad does require the service of the
brave al-Shabaab mujahideen tomorrow, which is why I called you
here tonight. By way of a distraction, while AQAP's much bigger
offensive gets underway, you will take that ship from the pirates and
destroy its cargo."

"The ship at Ras Asir?" asked a mujahideen.

Rubaysh stepped forward a little farther with every sentence.
"This is a call to battle, my fellow Wahabi. The time has come to
crush the satanic pirates. Puntland is in flux. Brave mujahideen have
taken initiatives of the war into their own hands. Your jihadic attacks
on sea and land on the servants of Satan have been successful in
creating turmoil in the region, making it ripe for jihad." He stopped.
"But now the Majeerteen seek to redeem their criminal ways by
making false promises about feeding the hungry, and cross-clan
cooperation. We must break their swagger and smother their boasts.
Only the Wahabi can help Somalis solve their problems and fulfil
their demands. We are the only ones who can spread justice."

"*Allahu Akbar!*" cheered the crowd and continued chanting.
Rubaysh smiled and nodded his head and smiled again. He'd
obviously pressed the right button. Then he raised his hands to signal
they should stop their rabble-rousing.

"When do we attack?" asked Omar.

"You must organise a detachment of your best mujahideen
tonight. Before morning you will travel in two battalions to King
Osman's palace in Bargaal. There's an oasis nearby, in a box canyon,
which you can use for cover against drones. I have preprogrammed
two GPS units to guide you directly to the most strategic battle
positions – both at high vantage points on the coastal mountains –
and to synchronise your separate operations in the hours before
sunrise. You will use a flanking manoeuvre to take the ship, and begin
your assault at first light."

"Wouldn't it be better," asked Omar, stepping into the light,
"after we take the ship, to distribute the food to the needy instead of

burning it? There are many among the Wahabi who are also starving."

Rubaysh glared at the Somali, straightened his posture, took a deep breath and let the aura of power around him flicker back to full brilliance. "It is the will of Allah...The cargo must be destroyed." He took another sip of water. It was time for the finale. "I know, like me, many of you were disgusted when you heard about Khadija Abdul Rahman's behaviour in the madrasa this afternoon?"

"Death to the apostate *sharmouta*!"

"I agree she should suffer, but death would be too immediate. I have something far more painful to inflict on her." Omar watched Rubaysh closely. The kidnapping of Khadija had caught everyone off guard. If, as al-Jazeera claimed, she was abducted by al-Qaeda, then why hadn't Omar been informed? He suspected al-Rubaysh was somehow involved. But what was his motivation?

"Nothing will devastate that woman more than the loss of her son Nadif to the cause of jihad," continued the Yemeni. "Call him in!" After a moment Nadif stepped in from a side door, dressed in religious garb, beaming proudly for the audience of mujahideen, who cheered him on. Rubaysh took his hand and pulled him into the light. "That's why I arranged for the boy to join tomorrow's suicide mission. Have you recorded your final message?" he asked, squeezing the boy's shoulder.

"Yes, Father."

"Good. Then you must go. May Allah, the Almighty, give you success, in this world and in the world to come."

"*Allahu Akbar!*" cried the crowd.

As Nadif departed, a wind blew through the room, extinguishing all but one candle. For a moment the only visible thing was Rubaysh's aquiline physiognomy, quivering menacingly in the feeble light, like a living mask. In due course, the rest of the candles were re-lit and they heard the sound of a boat speeding away from shore. "The global jihad will be served well by that brave boy," said Rubaysh. "*Inshe Allah*, Nadif will succeed in his jihadic mission."

"*Allahu Akbar!*"

"Right. It is time for *each* of us to do our jihadic duty," said Rubaysh, clapping his hands and smiling. He gestured for the assembled mujahideen to disperse and they began to leave the room.

"Where exactly will you be, when these two heroic attacks take place?" asked Omar. Everyone stopped and turned, expectant of the answer.

"That's the most glorious thing of all, my friend, but far too important to reveal at this time. Trust, however, that it is in preparation for the triumphant day, soon to come, when our two great nations unite, when we rejoin the continents of Africa and Asia and spread our caliphates like wildfire in one victorious holy war across the entire world, from the Horn of Africa over the Arabian Peninsula into Europe and Asia, and finally America, where we will rid the planet of Satan's followers. Trust me, my mujahideen friend, we will not spare a single Kafir on that day!"

"What day?" asked Omar.

"The day after tomorrow," replied Rubaysh.

"*Allahu Akbar!*" cried the remaining mujahideen, who then left and headed for their vehicles in the car park.

Once outside, in the dark, Rubaysh dragged Omar off to one side. "Bastard!" he snapped. "What was the purpose of all those questions?"

"Let go of me," protested Omar.

"You're working for the Americans, aren't you?"

"You're insane."

"That's how you survived the attack in the Karkaar Mountains that killed Ahmed and Dahir. It was *you* who called in the drone strike." A couple of other Shabaab officers began to gravitate towards them.

"And where were you at the time?" asked Omar. "Taking Mrs Abdul Rahman hostage?"

"I should kill you right now," said Rubaysh, pulling a 9-mm from inside his camouflage jacket and aiming it at the Somali.

"Why, so I don't tell them about the treasure, is that it? Yes, I know all about your Land of Punt treasure..."

Rubaysh looked daggers at Omar, and had a good mind to assassinate him right then and there, but Somali mujahideen were all around now, glaring at him. Blood was thicker than water. Apart from that, an important mission needed to be carried out at dawn. Killing Omar would do nothing for morale. Rubaysh replaced his pistol.

"Get out of my way, *baaayir*!" spat Omar. "You are no more Wahabi than that American gun you just put away." He pushed past the histrionic, bellicose Yemeni, then added, "Shabaab has genuine jihad to wage."

Khadija awoke suddenly from a nightmare and sat bolt upright in bed. She was bathed in sweat. In her dream, she had been hostage to a Yemeni tribal warlord in pre-Islamic Arabia who was set on revenge for the murder of his people against the perpetrator's entire tribe, men, women and children, but not before raping her and killing Nadif. She rose from her bed and stood by the window. The garden was lit up, which suggested her brother was still awake, so she slipped into her robe and went downstairs to join him.

Maxamid was seated on a stool in the kitchen watching al-Jazeera on a small TV on the kitchen counter, while picking at a bowl of fruit. "Go back to bed." he growled, as Khadija sauntered in.

"I had a bad dream," she said, wiping the sleep from her eyes.

"Try and go back to sleep," insisted Maxamid. "It's three o'clock in the morning."

"Is that coffee?" she asked.

"You want a cup?"

"Please," sighed Khadija.

Maxamid stood up, unfolding all two metres of his lanky form – his afro nearly touched the ceiling – then fetched a mug from a cupboard above the stove and filled it with the dregs of the jug of black Arabica he'd been drinking.

"We've been through so much, you and I," she said, taking the cup and warming her hands on the heat of it. "After Daddy died, you were so vulnerable. Suddenly the man in your life was gone, and you were meant to cope somehow. My heart went out to you, little brother. The same thing happened to Nadif, and..." She put her hand to her lip in an attempt to choke back her tears.

"I'm sure he's safe," said Maxamid, touching his sister's hand. "He's a smart boy."

Khadija took a moment to regain her composure. "We must resume the food distribution first thing tomorrow morning," she said. "I'm putting Abdulmajid in charge."

"A Jereer, in charge?" laughed Maxamid.

She stared angrily at her brother. "*We'el!* During my entire three-day captivity, not a single bag of the ship's cargo was offloaded for the starving in Somalia. You knew what we were trying to do, yet you chose to act like a gangster. The guards you posted to keep watch over the cargo were letting bags go for a price. The whole scheme collapsed, and there's still tens of thousands of tonnes of food on board. Abdulmajid is the only person who gives a damn."

"There's no fucking way I want an adoon in charge of this operation!" said Maxamid, as he selected a Granny Smith apple from the fruit bowl.

"*Masha Allah*, you saved my life, Max, and I love you, but you're such a hothead, and you really don't get this. It's a peaceful operation. All you want is war."

"Fine," said Maxamid, biting into the apple. "But you're not going near that ship."

"It's my operation. I need something to keep me busy, otherwise I'll go insane worrying about Nadif...Oh, Max. I have such a bad feeling about him."

"Allah will protect him," whispered Maxamid.

"What, now suddenly you're an imam?" she laughed, then she began to cry. Maxamid pulled her into a gangly embrace. They *had* been through a lot together. He squeezed her shoulders and said, "I am so proud of you."

"And I'm proud of you," she said, resting her head on his shoulder. "I wish Mehemet was still alive. He'd be so proud of us too."

Maxamid smiled. "I guess I'm going to have to find you a new husband."

She laughed and pushed him away. "Why do I need another husband when I've got you?"

Unbeknownst to them, concealed in the darkness of the twisted juniper, palm and aloes draped across the garden, stood Johnny, watching through the kitchen window. All he could hear were the waves against the shore and the crickets chirping, but he could still read the pair's lips. Khadija had always been closer to her brother. At times the cultural divide between him and his wife was vaster than the ocean. He so desperately longed to hold her. She had such tender lips, so beautiful.

Suddenly Khadija glanced outside, and Johnny ducked back. She searched the garden for a moment, then turned back to her brother to continue her tête-à-tête.

Johnny sighed, dropped his head to his chest, and wondered, "What will she think of me when she finally learns the truth?" He was scared of losing her. If only he could find Nadif. He pulled a small portable sat phone from his pocket and checked it for messages. Intel said the boy had definitely been recruited by Shabaab, but after that all humint had vanished. There was nothing, nor was there much he could do to intensify the search in the meantime, except keep a keen ear out and stay in touch with PIA. He knew he stood a better chance of protecting his family if he remained in the shadows, at least for now.

Without an air of malice about them, eight teenage boys sat meekly in silence, racing through the night. Nadif was among them. The boat transporting them across the Gulf of Aden looked very much like his uncle's skiff, long and narrow and with two powerful outboard engines at the back. Its helmsman refused any eye contact with the passengers. Nadif watched the ocean hurtle past, and prayed the massive blue marlin was still down there, bowed but not beaten. His uncle was wrong to pursue such a great fish. In the end, with no lawful reason for its torment, they could not even mention Allah's name, as they had made mischief in the earth.

With every thrust of a wave, his heart jumped between fear and joy. Fear about his family, his mother. Joy in knowing the benefits of his sacrifice would vastly outweigh the cost. He was no more militant than the average Somali. Like most of the other boys in the skiff, this was his first act of terrorism. The promise in the afterlife was reward enough for him. For the sake of a greater cause, however, this one heroic deed would be known throughout the centuries.

Few of them had been given much training, and they were armed only with Kalashnikovs, one grenade launcher between them, and a piece of paper on which al-Rubaysh had scribbled some rudimentary instructions about steering an ocean vessel. There was one, Ali, who was much older than the others, in his early twenties. He'd fought in Afghanistan. Rubaysh had appointed him commander of the suicide crew.

"Will it be painful?" wondered Nadif. "How long will I take to die?" He tried to disassociate himself from disturbing thoughts, and remembered a song he'd once heard by a female Syrian pop singer. It was about a mother who mourned her son's death until she realised that he had died for a good cause and he would be glorified for what he did.

CHAPTER TWENTY-FIVE

Against the advice of her brother, in the wee hours of morning Khadija had departed Bender Siyaada in her Land Cruiser and headed to the *Tristola*. The journey would take her at least four hours. Maxamid had insisted she use the coast road, despite it being a longer route, as it was safer than the interior road plus it allowed him to follow in his skiff. He was shadowing her, a couple of hundred metres off shore, tracking the Land Cruiser's headlights along the mostly abandoned road and easily keeping pace.

She had just passed through Qandala, and was driving northeast over the flats along the Gulf of Aden coastline. As the thin band of light on the horizon turned from blue to turquoise to gold, the terrain grew brighter and more striking. The nearer to the tip of the Horn she got, the higher the land rose. Isolated bays and towering cliffs made it ideal country for clandestine activities, and the coast was littered with as many seaworthy vessels as wrecks.

While travelling parallel to each other on land and sea, the siblings passed a multitude of pirate landmarks they both knew well: the cove where the Canadian yacht *Di Mi Manera* was hidden, the fishing village that played host to the captured crew of the *Sandra*, and the spot where the Indian Navy, believing it was pursuing a pirate mother ship, fired on the Thai trawler *Pra Sawat,* killing all but one of her crew, who bore witness to their blunder.

As she turned a hairpin corner on her ascent up Mount Felix, Khadija's phone began buzzing, and she quickly pulled over. Only her immediate family had this number. Her heart sank when she discovered it was only a message from Maxamid, warning that after Bereeda she'd have to turn inland. "I'll see you on the other side of Ras Asir."

The Hercules chartered by the World Food Programme to fly the hostages out of Puntland was waiting on the seaside runway, glittering in the first rays of dawn like a run-ashore monster grouper, its four huge propellers static but ready to spin. Bosaso's newly refurbished Bender Qassim International Airport was the busiest in Somalia, but that morning the terminal building was empty. Apart from a handful of airport staff milling about and the officers and crew of the TSC *Tristola,* there were only Derek and Maddy.

Maddy was wearing pumps, sweat pants and her navy fleece, and Derek, new clothes he'd bought in Bosaso: flipflops, blue khanga shorts, and a yellow sleeveless shirt. They had been locked in an embrace for a full five minutes.

"Where's your watch?" asked Maddy.

"I put it in the safe at the hotel."

"Why?"

"Because…Well, because you just can't be too sure."

"Are you still going after the treasure?"

"That depends. I don't expect I'll hang around here too much longer. Now that Khadija's back, we should be able to get the rest of the food off to where it's most needed in the next couple of days."

"She's certainly a brave woman. I wish I had an ounce of what she's got. Be sure to let me know if there's anything I can do from my end when I get home."

"Represent, girlfrien'!" laughed Derek, making a "one love" sign with his fist. "When you get back to Brisbane, tell them what you've seen here. Tell the world!"

"Where will you go next?" she asked, tilting her head sympathetically while running her hands through his long grey hair.

"Back to Kampala, though I don't expect I'll be there for long. You know me, I like to keep surfing the continental plates in search of the next big thing."

"On that note, mate." She gave him a parting kiss then turned to leave.

Once they had all passed through immigration Maddy turned to bid him farewell one last time through the glass partition. It had been a feature of Derek's life to wave goodbye to his loved ones at airports. Watching her pass through the gate, he worried their separation would be permanent. She certainly was one hell of a woman.

As he turned to go, he suddenly came face to face with a man standing behind him in sunglasses and traditional Arab robes, grinning. It was Johnny Oceans. "Not bad, huh?" he said, showing off his garb.

"A regular Larry of Arabia," laughed Derek.

"C'mon," said Johnny, hustling the Canadian away, "we're going scuba-diving."

They exited the terminal building through the airport's restricted area, whereby Derek got one last glimpse of Maddy as she boarded the Hercules up the stairway. Upon seeing him being led away by a man in robes, she stopped half way and gestured, "What's going on?" Derek gave her a thumbs-up and blew her a kiss.

Johnny led Derek past the army barracks behind the airport and down a fifty-metre path to the beach. Seagulls hovered and squawked above the shore, and a gentle breeze, warmed by daybreak, blew against their faces. When Johnny reached the beach, he began removing his robes and sandals. Beneath his disguise he wore a turquoise Grateful Dead T-shirt and a pair of tattered navy Bermuda shorts. His footwear and robes stacked upon his head, he then began wading into the water. Hearing the melancholic sound of the plane carrying his lover flying away, Derek looked up to watch it disappear from view, then turned and waded in after his friend.

He hadn't noticed it before now, but anchored off shore in the placid surf, silhouetted against a path of golden rays shimmering across the Gulf of Aden, was a speedboat with lines so sensual it made the hair at the back of Derek's neck stand on end. Except for the words "Midnight Express" written in white italics just below the gunwale, the entire vessel was jet black, with a glossy flow coat. "That's quite a craft you got there," laughed Derek, then added in his best Sean Connery impersonation, "engineered for a deadly purpose, no doubt."

"Pure performance," said Johnny, as he vaulted over the gunwale of his singular boat. "A high-speed rum runner."

"Is it yours?"

"It belongs to the Company," said Johnny, helping him aboard.

"Why does it have four engines at the back?" asked Derek.

"Because we couldn't fit five. *Forgedaboudit!*" After weighing anchor Johnny started the engines and let them idle for a bit while he stood in the cockpit and pointed out some of the unique features of his *motoscafo*. "Her cabin and cockpit are fully armoured. You could be in the head having a dump and you wouldn't get touched by a strafe of .50 calibre bullets."

Derek sat back on a vinyl bench and admired the array of advanced technologies in the cockpit. "What does that do?" he asked, pointing to what looked like a cinema projector secured to the side.

"This mother," said Johnny, patting the large black metal device, "is a long-range precision weapon, a forty-kilowatt high-energy laser. It can burn a hole through forty millimetres of steel in just a few seconds. Most of our weapons on board are non-lethal. There's an arsenal of laser rifles and dazzle weapons in the hold. Should things turn nasty, however, we do have very lethal weapons to play with, including a drone launcher."

"What? You're saying this thing's also an aircraft carrier?"

"I'm talking about little radio-controlled BattleHawks that weigh only five pounds," said Johnny.

"I get the picture," laughed Derek. "Half-pint drones."

Johnny pushed the throttle gently forward to power the row of four 250-horsepower Mercury Verado engines astern, then selected the appropriate soundtrack: Steppenwolf, "Born To Be Wild". Gradually the boat began to pull away from shore. "You wanna know the most incredible thing about this baby?" asked Johnny over his shoulder, loud enough to be heard above the din of engines and rock and roll. Derek nodded. "Her twin-step monocoque hull. Watch," he said as he increased the throttle, "when I accelerate, it displaces a huge amount of water at the back. The rising, displaced water then creates an upward kinetic force that adequately lifts the boat above the surface so as to seriously reduce drag and boost her speed and fuel efficiency. On calm seas she can top sixty knots, that's seventy miles an hour, or a hundred and ten kilometres an hour..." Behind them, the coast retreated like a kicked blanket on a balmy night.

Derek could no longer hear what his friend was saying. Still, although the sound of the engines was thunderous, the ride was smooth, much smoother than he expected it to be. Feeling only sun rays and wind resistance against his face, he had the sensation of being flipped from the vertical to the horizontal plane and falling down the side of an infinitely proportioned, ripple-glass skyscraper. He had never travelled so fast over open water before, and never felt so alive.

In accordance with the International Regulations for Preventing Collisions at Sea, the chemical container ship *Galbraith* had her navigational lights arranged in patterns of red, green and white, at her aft, forward and stern, indicating she was constrained by her draught. In the hour before dawn the vessel was heading south-southeast through the Red Sea at fifteen knots, three-quarters of the way along her fifteen-thousand-kilometre sea voyage from Montréal to Mundra.

In six hours she would sail into the Gulf of Aden, pirate waters. A team of armed guards had come aboard in the Yemeni port of al-Hudaydah, to maintain a twenty-four-hour anti-piracy watch until they reached Indian territorial waters. Nevertheless, the ship's crew was on high alert. Barely a week had passed since the *Tristola* was hijacked. Everyone aboard feared being taken hostage by Somalis. Everyone except the captain.

Captain Douglas was standing at the bridge smoking a pipe, his round bewhiskered face weirdly lit up by the plethora of meters, dials and displays on his dashboard. He objected to having Hart Security on board, in particular their weapons, given the number of times, during his long career in the Canadian Merchant Navy, that he'd passed this way without incident.

The door to the bridge swung open, letting in a blast of hot air along with a tall, fearsome-looking man carrying a walking stick. He was Hector Pardon, the white Kenyan and former mercenary commanding the security team. "Good morning," he said, smiling. "You're up early, Captain."

"Please leave your weapon outside the door," said the captain, stony-faced.

The grin on Hector's rugged features quickly disappeared. "Sorry...?"

"Just do it," insisted the captain.

Hector placed the gun outside the door, then asked, "Are you the only person on board ship unconcerned with pirates?"

"What troubles me more, Mr Hector," said the captain, removing his pipe, "is having weapons on board my ship." He picked up his binoculars and checked the sea ahead. Atop a high cliff on Quonin Island lay Abu Ali Lighthouse, its lamp still stabbing the morning mist. It indicated they were presently less than a hundred nautical miles from Bab-el-Mandeb, the gateway to the Gulf. "We're taking a risk carrying arms through foreign waters."

"Your shipping company seemed to think it necessary."

"That's because they're prepared to offset the fifty-thousand-dollar cost against their insurance. I say it's a waste of money."

"A waste of money, really? If the crew of the USS *Cole* had not been constrained by maritime weapon laws, they might have been able to defend their ship. That al-Qaeda attack killed seventeen American servicemen."

"That was a terror attack. We're talking pirates here."

"No ship carrying armed guards has ever been hijacked."

"Neither has one carrying chemicals."

"Do you actually believe pirates avoid chemical container ships intentionally?"

"I *know* they do," snapped the captain. "It might have something to do with all the toxic waste that's already been dumped in Somali waters."

The bridge offered a commanding view of the ship's decks, the detail of which was beginning to emerge from the gloom. The combination of desert dust and morning dew had covered everything in a layer of brown grime. Hector watched his men patrolling its decks over sealed cargo compartments. "What exactly is your ship's cargo?" he asked. "All I've been told is that it shouldn't get wet."

"The *Galbraith*'s carrying one hundred and sixty thousand tonnes of sodium amide, which is highly reactive to water."

"Seems a bit harebrained transporting it by sea," laughed Hector.

"It's the safest way to transport sodium amide crystals between continents. If disturbed, or if the seals to its compartments are broken, the compound quickly becomes explosive. I reckon it would be far more harebrained taking it by plane, train or automobile, don't you?"

"What happens when you hit rough seas?"

"You can rest assured, there's not much that can rattle the *Galbraith*. Like me, she's a most phlegmatic seafarer."

"What about the deep draught on this vessel? Aren't you worried about hitting the rocks?"

"At the moment, I'm far more concerned about having your men and your weapons on board my ship. This cargo's explosive enough."

"At any rate, by the time we hit the Gulf it will be high noon and much easier to spot mother ships and skiffs. If we do come under attack, I'll make sure my men use every non-lethal weapon available, and concentrate on apprehending the blighters, rather than killing any of them."

"With all the paperwork that goes with it? No, sir! You can kill as many as you like. Just keep them and their guns off my damn ship!"

The day was clear and bright, with not a cloud in the sky. Heading west, away from the rising sun, the ship cast one long shadow across the sea. Nadif and the rest of the suicide crew had gathered on the bridge, high above the decks at the back of the vessel. It felt as if they were flying.

As instructed, they had boarded the MSC *Chitra* in the middle of the night. By the time they came aboard every one of the Indian crew had been asphyxiated by hydrogen sulphide gas, and their corpses lay strewn about the decks gaping skyward through bloated faces. Their executioner, a Yemeni man, left via the skiff on which the suicide crew arrived, ordering them to dump the bodies overboard, which they did.

Meanwhile the ship sailed blithely on, following a westerly course across the Gulf of Aden, showing no signs that it had been hijacked. Being a gas cargo vessel, it had four massive semi-spheres protruding from its decks. Locked away in those bulbous compartments was the ship's deadly cargo. The only thing the boys had been told was that it would explode once it came into contact with the other ship. Their instructions were to make sure they stayed on course and arrived no later than midday at Bab-el-Mandeb, the Gate of Tears, where if everything went to plan, they would collide with the *Galbraith*.

Ali, the commander of the suicide crew, was at the helm, steering the ship westward, with the RPG propped up beside the control panel. Hanging from the ceiling above his head were two gas masks, part of the standard safety equipment on board this peculiar cargo ship. Below it was a mini-automatic radar plotting aid, a MARPA. He would not be needing that device. A battle-hardened mujahideen, he took the task more seriously than the others on board, who were just kids. He wished that like him they had been better trained.

One of the boys paced up and down the quarterdeck in front of the bridge, his Kalashnikov slung nonchalantly over his shoulder, whistling an uplifting tune. Like the other boys, he was completely detached from the task at hand. Not that they had been brainwashed, or anything, they simply understood that the best way to stay focused on the job was to not think about it at all.

He stopped and smiled at Ali through the window. Then, all of a sudden, an object fell from the sky and struck the boy on his head, and he collapsed. Ali and the others rushed outside to see what had happened. The boy was dead, but beside him lay a tortoise that was still very much alive.

They all looked up. There, circling above the ship, was a immense bird. When they realised what had occurred the boys began to fall about with laughter. Nadif quickly identified it as a lammergeier. But what was it doing so far from shore? It was enough to knock him out of his trance and he decided he had better write a farewell text to his mother.

Floating in the dazzling morning sunshine, the *Midnight Express* looked like expensive Italian footwear that had been tossed into the Trevi Fountain after an all-night soiree. Derek stared blankly at his phone then replaced it in his pocket. "There's no reception out here, Gorilla Man," said Johnny. "We're midpoint in the Gulf of Aden. But don't worry. There's a sat phone on the boat's control panel that's tapped directly into the Company. If anyone important needs to reach me, they know how."

"What is it," asked Derek, "three days now you've been back in Puntland and you still haven't let your wife know you're alive?"

"Not until I find out what Rubaysh is up to."

"Is that why we're out here? All you said was 'we're going scuba-diving', but you still haven't told me why. To begin with I assumed it had something to do with the Land of Punt treasure." Johnny smiled at Derek. "That's quite a riddle you left me back there, after you pulled your stunt in Kakuma. I eventually worked it out. But you never told me what the treasure was..."

"I can't say for sure. All my research points to it being the Staff of Musa."

"Musa?"

"Moses. The Muslims call him Musa, and the Jews, Moshe. Same guy, different names."

"Didn't you check inside the box?"

"Nope. Right after I found it in the desert, I reburied it at sea."

"That's bullshit, and you know it. There's no way you wouldn't have looked inside."

"I'm telling you God's honest truth, I did not look inside the box."

"Why?"

"Out of fear."

"Fear of what?"

"Fear of what's inside! You never know with these ancient holy relics. I mean, you've seen the climax to 'Indiana Jones', when the Nazis open the Lost Ark of the Covenant…Yeesh!"

"So you're honestly telling me you never looked inside?"

"Look, Gorilla Man, you either believe me or you don't. *Capisce?* Now let's get a descent line down. There's something far more important at the bottom of the Tadjoura Trough we need to destroy."

"Oh yeah? What?"

"An antique telegraph line. I think al-Qaeda's using it to communicate with al-Shabaab."

By the time Khadija turned away from the coast the sun was up and beaming directly into her eyes. She flipped down the sun visors and donned her Police aviator sunglasses. The surrounding landscape was breathtaking. Despite hundreds of millions of years of weathering from wind and sea, the enormous tectonic forces which tore the Arabian Peninsula from the Horn of Africa were still very much imprinted on the place. This was one of Africa's most rugged, inhospitable, and remotest regions.

Her phone buzzed again. "What is it now, Max?" she cried, pulling over for a second time. But on closer inspection she saw it was a message from Nadif: *"I'm not afraid of storms, for I'm learning to sail my ship."* In a fit of anxiety she tried desperately to call him, but the signal was too weak. She was in the middle of a steep box canyon. "At least he's still alive," she gasped, holding her phone to her breast.

She was barely ten kilometres from her destination. The two distinctive bluffs that marked the entrance to the Indian Ocean beachhead were within view. Network coverage was sure to be stronger there. Accordingly, she put the pedal to the metal and sped on down the road.

A sign up ahead read, "Guardafui Lighthouse". With split-second precision she took a sharp left turn, screeching her tyres across the tarmac as she drove. Undoubtedly there would be reception at the lighthouse. It was less a road than a dried-up riverbed but she followed the tracks of the last vehicle. The barren river soon led to a washboard of dunes, but she wasn't daunted by the rough terrain, and drove her Land Cruiser across it like a speedboat over high seas.

The higher she drove, the more she began to catch glimpses out of her righthand window of the Indian Ocean shoreline. Oddly, there was smoke rising from the *Tristola*. What could be burning? The distraction made her drive her Land Cruiser into the side of a dune. After that, the car would not budge. It was stuck in a sand trap. She leapt out and continued on foot. Her view of the burning *Tristola* grew with every metre she climbed. It was clear a skirmish of some kind was underway. "One thing at a time, girl," she thought, trying to call her son. Still no signal. She would need to climb to the top of the ancient lighthouse.

Cape Guardafui lighthouse blended in well with its surroundings as it had been built out of sandstone hewn from the nearby mountains. To make it more easily recognisable during daylight, "daymarks" had been incorporated into its design, using layers of stone larger in circumference than the rest of the tower, and grouped in bands of three, like navy stripes. The tower rose four storeys to a cupola-roofed lantern room that was surrounded by an iron gallery platform. Completed at the start of the 20th century, the lighthouse had long since been abandoned. A brass plaque beside the door told of Italian shipwrecks and a brave general.

She tried the door. It was open, so she quickly scrambled up the wooden spiral staircase. The rickety stairs were insubstantial and first one collapsed under her weight, then another. Eventually she reached the floor below the lantern room and stepped outside on to the gallery platform. At last, her call went through to Nadif.

"I wasn't going to call you at all, Mother," he said. "But then a lammergeier dropped a tortoise from the sky on the head of one of the boys on the ship, just like that story you told me when I was a child, about Aeschylus."

"What are you talking about?" asked Khadija, frantically looking around. Waves crashed against the rocks of the promontory below her and beyond, to the south, her ship was on fire. "What ship? The *Tristola*?"

"The *Chitra*, an Indian ship. We're on our way to Bab-el-Mandeb. I'm never coming back, Mother. But..."

"No!"

"Please don't mourn me, Mother. Understand that what I'm doing is in the name of Islamic jihad, and God's will."

"No, please, Nadif, no! It is not God's will that you do this! It's God's will that you come *home*!"

"I want you to know that I died for a good cause, for the glory of Islam, Somalia, and Africa. This day will be remembered until the end of time, for the magnificent and wondrous attack, more infamous than 9/11 – more shock and awe than Baghdad. The final blow which drove the Kafir from Africa. Goodbye, Mother, I love you." He hung up.

"Nadif! *Nadif!*" She tried calling back, but he had switched off his phone.

CHAPTER TWENTY-SIX

The *Tristola*'s decks were ablaze with petrol fires. An essential guard of two-dozen badaadintu badah was bravely defending her against a two-pronged attack by mujahideen, who were amassing below in her shadow, preparing to board. "*We'el!*" cried Maxamid, steering his skiff headlong towards the stricken vessel. He decided to use the ship as cover and approach unseen on its starboard side. Waves were crashing against the hull. When close enough he cut the engines, slung his BAR over his shoulder, then made his way to the bow of his skiff. The swells made it difficult to grab hold of the ship, but this was his specific skill and in no time he had shimmied up the side.

Once aboard he began issuing orders to his fellow pirates. "Use the bilge pump to put out those fires. We need more units bow and stern. Get on the anti-piracy weapons! Use the ADS, the LRAD! We'el! Use your goddamn pirate skills! C'mon!" He swaggered through the flames, knelt down beneath the port-side gunwale and aimed his Browning Automatic Rifle through a mooring hole as wide as a lifesaver. Abdulmajid joined him with a Kalashnikov and they began picking off attacking mujahideen one by one. "Nice shooting," laughed Maxamid. "I wonder if those bastards know one of their own mujahideen is up here bravely fighting alongside badaadintu badah?"

"How many do you think are down there?" asked Abdulmajid.

"Two hundred," said Maxamid, "but we have the advantage of defending a very large metal ship that's almost insurmountable under fire."

"Not when we're running out of ammunition," cried Abdulmajid. "We've lost half our men, leaving us outnumbered ten to one. And I think I just spotted many more jihadists coming down from the mountains."

"Don't worry, our own pirate reinforcements are on their way."

"Regardless," insisted Abdulmajid. "We must organise ourselves if we're to continue to stave off the attack."

The mujahideen ceased firing. Accordingly, so did the pirates. Someone on the beach yelled, "Give up the ship. We only want your cargo. Throw down your weapons, and we'll let you live!"

"I've got an idea," whispered Maxamid, smiling mischievously and holding his index finger across his goatee. Crouching down beneath the line of sight, he crept along the gunwale to where a metre-wide black disc was attached on a swivel mount: the ship's Long Range Acoustic Device. It was a combat loudspeaker, with a unidirectional metre-wide bearing. He switched it on, carefully aimed it at the commander, picked up the microphone and said, "GO TO HELL, *MUJAHID*!" He then let rip with an unrelenting blast of ear-piercing cacophony that sounded like Armageddon's seven trumpets.

Only those mujahideen in the line of fire received the full excruciating volume, which forced them to let go of their weapons and cover their ears. That's when the pirates opened fire. As Maxamid swept the beam of the LRAD across the battlefield in a metachronal rhythm, it was like watching a Mexican wave. He turned to Abdulmajid. "Check this out." He switched the selector to "ghost battalions" and the sound of warfare suddenly increased a thousandfold. For added measure, he spoke two shrill, pain-inducing words of his own into the microphone: "BADAADINTU BADAH!"

Derek was the first to surface from the dive. As he swam towards the boat he heard his ringtone chiming. He climbed aboard and quickly answered the phone. "Khadija?" he said. "Now wait a minute, slow down...Who? Nadif? On board what ship?" By now Johnny was standing next to him in a dripping wetsuit. After Derek mouthed it was his wife on the phone, he snatched the handset from him.

"Khadija, sweetheart...it's me. Yes, I'm still alive...Baby, please stop crying. I'll explain everything later. Right now I need you to speak clearly and tell me what's happening...OK...When was this...? I'm on it!" Johnny leapt into the helm chair and the *Midnight Express* took off at full throttle.

"All faraxs are stupid," screamed Khadija, kicking the side of her paralysed vehicle. She opened the door with "No Weapons" written across it, climbed in, then started the engine. Shifting into reverse, she slowly eased the car out of its sand trap. "Which way do I turn?" Knowing her husband was alive and on his way to rescue Nadif had certainly emboldened her, but she was not about to run headlong into battle.

"*GO TO HELL, MUJAHID!*" said her brother, his voice as clear as if he was sitting next to her, even though he was ten kilometres away. Should she go to his aid? She could see maybe two hundred mujahideen on the beach, pinned down by a handful of the pirates on board the ship. Two flotillas of pirate skiffs were approaching from north and south of the beachhead. Reinforcements of mujahideen were also on their way, approaching from the south and west. It had all the hallmarks of another long war between the Somali clans.

A squadron of drones hovered over the western mountains like a swarm of robot wasps. "Whose side are they on?" she wondered. "No doubt the Americans will gather terabytes of data from a safe distance then take out the wrong side. But which side is the right side?" She no longer supported either.

"*BADAADINTU BADAH!*" cried Maxamid from the decks of the *Tristola*.

She checked her iPhone. It had a full set of bars. "Wait a minute," she thought, swiping the screen to launch her Twitter account. She tapped out a message: *MAYDAY MAYDAY MAYDAY*

All ships in Somali waters. Tristola under attack by Shabaab. Present position, 10km south of Ras Asir. 25 souls aboard. It was unlikely that crews would be reading their tweets as they navigated their ships around the Horn of Africa. Still, with more than two million followers, there was a chance that before long, someone in the right place at the right time might see Queen Arawello's distress signal.

"General Kirkpatrick," said the communications officer, "I've got the asset on the line now."

"Put him on speakerphone...Marlin?"

"General?" yelled Oceans, so he could be heard over the din of outboard engines.

"We got a war going on between Shabaab and the pirates over here in the Indian Ocean. Why the hell are you headed for the Red Sea?"

"Al-Qaeda terror plot, ma'am. There's a suicide crew on board an Indian ship called the *Chitra* intent on crashing into another ship at Bab-el-Mandeb. My guess is the attack on the pirates is meant to act as a distraction."

After she was handed a memo, the general replied, "OK, we've got the *Chitra*'s coordinates."

"Patch them directly into my Garmin."

"That suicide ship's less than a hundred miles north of here, Marlin, and the combined naval task force is already in the area. I think we can take care of it."

"Leave the *Chitra* to me, General! Please, before you go launching anything, give me a chance to board the ship and overpower the suicide crew."

"We have to disable that ship by any means, Marlin. Hell, I can't see no good reason why I shouldn't green-light an attack right now."

"My son is one of the suicide crew!"

There was a brief pause, during which Kitty Kirkpatrick rubbed her chin. "OK. We'll hold back. But I am sending in a unit of SEALs to help you take that ship."

"Thank you, General, but I think we can manage."

"Who, you and that goddamn safari guide? Team Six is on its way."

Hanging up from the asset, General Kirkpatrick immediately turned to the others and demanded a list of all the ships sailing south through the Red Sea and their cargoes. Rows of consoles and officers suddenly came alive with frantic activity. The general relit her cigar, shook her head in disbelief, then added, "Is it me, or does the asset's kinfolk know how to make a goddamn nuisance of themselves?"

A Marine chief warrant officer dashed in, clutching a sheet of paper. "I think I've hit on al-Qaeda's plot," he said, breathlessly.

"Well, let's have it," said General Kirkpatrick.

"The *Chitra*'s cargo is nitrous oxide. Now, there's a Canadian chemical container ship called the *Galbraith* on its way through the straits as we speak, carrying a cargo of sodium amide."

"And? I'm not a goddamn chemist. Explain!"

"According to CTC," said the chief warrant officer, "when you mix those two compounds together you get sodium azide, which is acutely toxic." He was young for his rank, and the look of terror on his face as he spoke suggested he had not seen much combat. "Inhaling the dust can induce a variety of symptoms, including blindness, bleeding from the ears, and rupturing of internal organs, followed within minutes by death..."

The general let out a big sigh, smiled disparagingly, then said, "Somebody get me the president."

General Kirkpatrick immediately put Camp Lemonnier on high alert and called the most senior officers in Africa Command to a situation room on the base. It was a soundproof rectangular room with a large monitor covering the wall at the far end behind the general, who was seated at the head of a rosewood conference table. She greeted the assembled brass: an Air Force major general, a Navy rear admiral, a Marine lieutenant colonel, and the Japanese vice admiral in charge of the Marine Self-Defence detachment. The Marine who'd discovered the terror plot was also in attendance, seated at the opposite end of the table with his laptop. In front of each person was a pad, pencil and pair of three-dimensional glasses. Everyone was dressed in grey camouflage battle fatigues.

"Officer," said the general, solemnly, "could you please give us the facts?" The Marine tapped his keyboard and a large high-definition image appeared on the monitor. It was an upside-down map of the region. He had purposely oriented it this way, to shake everyone out of their mindsets. Delineated by contrasting desert coastlines, the waters of the Gulf of Aden and Red Sea stood out in brilliant ultramarine. The place where they met was Bab-el-Mandeb, the Gate of Tears, the epicentre of the impending disaster.

"The point of collision will be a little over a hundred and ten kilometres north of here," said the chief warrant officer, pointing his cursor to the location of the base, "and the prevailing southwesterly winds through the straits are certainly strong enough to spread the toxin across the coasts of Eritrea, Djibouti, and throughout the Gulf of Tadjoura." He tapped his trackpad and a purple overlay descended on the affected area.

"Jesus Christ," said the Air Force general, sitting up.

"I've spoken to the commander in chief," said General Kirkpatrick. "He advocates the use of UAVs. Now, we all know homeboy's got a jones for drones, but in this case what other options do we have?"

"I recommend we launch an immediate F-15 airstrike against the *Chitra*," said the Air Force general, "get this job done good and proper, and prevent the damn thing colliding with the *Galbraith*."

"But then we run the risk of making our own dirty bomb," said the admiral.

"Well, we sure as hell can't just let these two ships collide," said the Air Force general. "Apart from the human toll, there's the environmental damage. A chemical spill will take decades to clean up, and at a price we can't afford."

"What about the damage this will do to international shipping?" asked the Marine lieutenant colonel. "The price of oil will sky-rocket. This sort of thing can knock the world economy right back on its ass."

"I understand what's at stake, Lieutenant," said General Kirkpatrick. "But it sounds like things might get even messier if we try using ordnance against this toxic cocktail. Officer," she said, turning to the chief warrant officer, "bring up the disposition matrix."

"Yes, ma'am." He tapped his keyboard and the map on the large monitor began to rotate towards its proper orientation, while at the same time zooming out from the Middle East until it was a spinning globe in space. A scintillating green grid appeared above the image then shrink-wrapped itself around the globe. By now all the brass around the table had each put on their 3-D glasses.

Suddenly tiny nodes began to emanate from the grid and expand into spherical moons that orbited the earth. Each represented an intelligence asset, military resource or social-political issue relevant to the crisis, with a size that corresponded to its capacity to solve the problem. Intelligence assets were in geosynchronous orbit above their locations in the world, issues appeared as burning suns beyond the assets, and military resources were all in low orbit, flitting back and forth in real time according to the demands being made on them by the combined forces and intelligence units of the United States government.

The image rotated every eight seconds, allowing the generals and admirals to see the full picture, in 3-D. Camp Lemonnier was flashing red, hovering steadily above itself with a bundle of military resources wrapped around it, while the future prosperity and safety of Africa burned as big and bright as the equatorial sun under which the continent lay. Clearly Marlin was the most important intelligence asset, spinning in geostationary orbit directly over the Gulf of Aden, and bright blue from the plethora of aquatic multimedia intel within. General Kirkpatrick turned off the monitor and addressed the assembled brass as they removed their glasses. "I say before we start blowing shit up we give Marlin a chance to foil the attack from the inside."

The *Midnight Express* was planing over calm seas at sixty knots. As much as time was of the essence, velocity was the essence of this singular craft. Derek sat aft, near the engines, watching the distant mountains of the Hadramaut Coast of Yemen whiz past.

He was unable to catch any of what his friend was saying on his sat phone, but it was gratifying to watch him in action, applying his assortment of specialised skills all at once. The whole time he'd been friends with an intelligence agent, and had absolutely no idea. "I guess that's what makes him a special agent," thought Derek. "For all I know, Aturu, my *askari*, is a tier-one operator."

Johnny checked the fuel gauge. At full throttle the boat was burning a litre every six seconds. He reduced his speed to fifty knots. The *Chitra* was still about fifteen nautical miles away. It would hence take them twenty minutes to reach it, but he had to conserve fuel. He turned to Derek.

"What's your strategy?" asked Derek.

"We need an eye in the sky. Grab one of those BattleHawks."

Derek searched through the arsenal of future weapons in the hold then held up what looked like a miniature drone. "Is this it?"

"That's the one," said Johnny.

"What do you want me to do with it?" asked Derek, examining the thing. It reminded him of one of those styrofoam planes with an elastic-band propeller he used to play with when he was a kid, except this one was bulky, dark and lustreless.

"Take it to the bow. There's a launcher bolted to the deck. *Careful how you carry the damn thing! Jesus!* That's a carbon-fibre, reinforced polymer bomb you got there, with a forty-four-millimetre charge."

"Now he tells me," muttered Derek, as he made his way unsteadily to the bow. "*Maybe if you slow the fuck down, this a highly explosive weapon in my hands won't blow the fuck up in my face!*"

"*Forgedaboudit!* Gotta keep pace. Besides, you haven't had this smooth a ride since high school."

As the *Chitra* neared the straights of Bab-el-Mandeb, the Yemeni and Djiboutian coastlines began closing in on either side of the ship. The sun was at its highest point in the sky, casting no shadows and indicating it was time for Dhuhr prayers. Accordingly, while the ship remained on its collision course, less than fifteen minutes away from its intended target, the suicide crew gathered on the quarterdeck and laid out prayer mats facing Mecca. Birds spiralled overhead with haunting rhythm. The boys feared another might drop something on their heads, and conducted their prayers with one eye looking skyward.

Ali remained at the helm, maintaining the ship's bearing to remain on course for disaster. He spotted a blip on his radar screen, a small craft approaching rapidly from the rear. It was the onset of a counter-attack. "This is it," he shouted. The boys abandoned their prayers and rushed to his side. "CTF 150 is on our ass. Get out on the decks and prevent anyone from boarding."

Just then what looked like a bird swooped down low over the ship's decks, and Nadif noticed it wasn't a bird at all but a drone. He grabbed the RPG, and ran back outside. Taking aim, he fired at it, but the drone took automatic evasive action and dodged the projectile, which exploded on the surface of the ocean. The drone then circled around the vessel and began a flightpath that would take it directly into the side of the bridge. "It will kill us all!" cried Ali.

"Shouldn't have done that, son," cried Johnny, as he twiddled furiously with the knobs. The video feed on his instrument panel zoomed in with crosshairs on the face of his stepson standing on the quarterdeck of the *Chitra*, then grew larger and larger by the second. "Jesus Christ!" he yelled. "The onboard target detection system has locked in on him and won't let me pull out." He looked up. The *Chitra* was within view, less than half a kilometre away, though with his naked eye he was unable to spot the drone. "Hold on!" he cried, thrusting the throttle forward as far as it would go. The engines whined with disapproval. "Here, take the helm!"

"But I don't know how to drive this thing!" cried Derek.

"Take the goddamn helm, and keep it full on!" Johnny dived into the hold and fetched his MK-15 rifle, a long-range sniper weapon

accurate to up to two kilometres. He rushed forward, laid himself flat across the bow, propped up the rifle on its bipod, pressed the cheekpiece against his face, then took aim through the gun's superior telescopic sight. He could see the drone and it was hurtling at twenty-five metres per second towards Nadif, his wife's firstborn.

Just then the *motoscafo* hit a wave, and he accidentally fired off a shot. The muzzle break reduced its recoil, and the gun hardly budged, but a second later the .50 calibre bullet that he fired missed. He had only four rounds left, and the drone was now less than fifty metres from its target, so he focused on aiming ahead of the thing then quickly squeezed off three more rounds. At a distance of twenty metres from the bridge, the drone exploded.

"Boo yakka!" cried Derek from the helm.

"*Masha Allah!*" sighed Johnny. "Next time keep it steadier. *Capisce?*"

The drone exploded near enough to kill one of the boys, injure three more and throw the other two on the *Chitra*'s quarterdeck on to their backs. An almighty hissing noise was now emanating from one of the rotund gas cargo compartments on the decks below.

Their commander, Ali, stepped calmly out from the bridge and told Nadif to take the helm. Stepping around to the rear quarterdeck, he now had visual contact with the speedboat closing in on the ship's stern. He steadied the RPG, stood firmly on the quarterdeck then took aim. Once the speedboat was close enough, he pulled the trigger, and planted a grenade directly on its bow. "You see," he yelled, "that's how it's done."

Nadif looked over his shoulder and saw that the speedboat was still coming. He was terrified. Undoubtedly there were commandos on board who would kill the suicide crew, who now numbered only six.

A Chinook helicopter was approaching from the south. "Navy SEALs," hissed Ali. "Don't worry, I know how to deal with those bastards. I saw this done in Afghanistan." Again he raised his weapon. All at once boys standing with him on the quarterdeck began to chuckle; even those who lay bleeding from the drone explosion started giggling. Soon everyone was laughing. Ali looked down at the decks where gas was issuing upward in a vertical stream and immediately dashed back into the bridge to grab one of the gas masks hanging above the helm. Nadif took the remaining mask. It was too late for the others, who were all in fits of laughter.

"What the fuck?" cried Derek, still at the controls, adrenaline pumping as he closed in on the *Chitra*. A grenade had just exploded forward of the speedboat's bombproof windshield and he was equally surprised by the lack of damage as he was by the blast. The *Midnight Express* just kept on running.

"Bring her up to mid-ship!" hollered Johnny, moving towards the bow of the boat with a harpoon in his hands, a laser rifle and M-60 machine gun slung over his shoulder, and half a dozen stun grenades and miscellaneous equipment fastened around his waist. He then saw an approaching Chinook and cursed it. "Fucking Team Six! They'll kill everyone on board."

Derek tried to stay out of the line of fire from the ship's bridge, keeping as close to the hull as he could manage, without bashing against it. Once the speedboat was within range, Johnny took aim at the *Chitra* decks with his harpoon and fired. A grappling hook hurtled through the air and landed on the deck with a loud clatter. After tugging on the wire a couple of times, he was confident the hook had acquired a secure fixture. Then, taking a firm hold of the harpoon grip, he pressed a button on its handle and was swiftly hoisted upward to the ship's gunwale.

With Johnny getting safely aboard, Derek pulled the *Midnight Express* away from the ship, but immediately came under fire, so he quickly tucked back in again. He had no choice but to stay within the shadow of its hull. "I didn't sign up for this hero bullshit!" he groaned. The Chinook was coming in fast towards the port side, and he could see a gunner hanging out of the open side pointing a .50-calibre at the ship's decks.

Johnny was on the deck of the *Chitra* crouched behind a ventilator shaft. Gas was hissing from the large semi-spherical container in front of him. A sign on the side read "Nitrous Oxide. Do Not Inhale" so he donned a gas mask. Up on the bridge he could see that only two of the suicide crew were wearing them; the rest were behaving like lunatics. One of those wearing a gas mask was aiming his RPG at the approaching Chinook, so Johnny took his laser rifle from his shoulder, got him in his sights and blasted him with blinding light. Startled and blinded the boy nonetheless fired his weapon but the grenade missed its target. "Stand down!" commanded Johnny into his mouthpiece. "Assets on board!" The Chinook pulled back and continued hovering over the ocean. Johnny began to move forward.

Ali was temporarily blinded and stumbling around on the quarterdeck, in danger of falling on to the decks below. Nadif was the only one of the suicide crew not presently impaired. He kept hold of the helm. A warm wind blew through the bridge. The target ship was only five hundred metres ahead, and trying to evade their attack, so he adjusted his bearing so as to remain on a collision course. The captain of the oncoming ship was screaming orders at him through the ship's radio so he shot it with his AK, screaming, "Die, kafirs!" Then he spotted man in a gas mask sneaking across the decks, so he let go of the helm and went outside to deal with him.

"*Pan-pan! Pan-pan! Pan-pan!*" cried Captain Douglas, broadcasting on all frequencies. "Chitra, *this is the* Galbraith, *on a collision course with your vessel. Pan-pan! Pan-pan! Pan-pan! Our heading is a hundred and seventy degrees...Adjust your course! Adjust your course!*"

Regardless of what his instruments warned, the captain knew his ship was on a collision course with the *Chitra*, because its position remained static, relative to the coastline of Djibouti.

"Why don't you just steer away from her?" asked Hector Pardon, who was standing next to him.

"I can't," said the captain, turning the wheel by a small measure. "My ship's constrained by her draught and there's hardly any room to manoeuvre in the straits... Any ideas would be very welcome right now!"

Hector Pardon picked up his walkie talkie and issued a deadly command to his men: "Open fire!"

"What the hell good will that do?" yelled the captain.

"By eliminating the crew," said Hector, "we'll stop them adjusting the ship's course." Hector's men scrambled into positions across the *Galbraith*'s decks and then began firing their high-powered weapons at the approaching ship.

Just then a Chinook helicopter flew above the decks, and through a loudspeaker commanded, "CEASE FIRE!"

The *Chitra* was bearing down on them, now only two hundred metres away. There was no way to avoid a collision. "Reverse engines," commanded the captain.

"Why?" asked Hector.

"It will lessen the impact."

Derek tried pulling away a second time from the hull of the *Chitra*. He needed to get a better view of what was going on on her decks. Luckily, this time the speedboat did not come under fire. He spotted Johnny scrambling up the metal stairs that led to the bridge. Then he noticed someone on the bridge above taking aim at his friend with an AK. Derek let go of the helm, snatched a dazzle gun from the hold and, without a moment to spare, blasted the culprit with a flash of blinding laser light. The boy dropped his weapon.

The *Midnight Express* began to decelerate, and Derek turned to the high-energy laser mounted on its side. "I wonder what I can do with this mother?" After brief examination, he found the on switch, and flipped it upward. There followed a high-pitched whine that steadily became even higher until it was eventually inaudible. Not sure how to operate the damn thing, Derek was nevertheless determined to use it to assist Johnny. He attempted to aim it at the suicide ship but it required considerable strength to manoeuvre.

At the back of the device was a scope and two buttons: a red one with "*auslöser*" written above it, and a green one with "*eingabe*". He pressed the red button. Nothing happened, so he tried the green one.

Still nothing. "Hmm," thought Derek, scratching his head. He pushed the red one again. Suddenly, a fat red beam burst from the other end and hit the wake of the ship, causing it to abruptly boil. "Wow," laughed Derek, working the heavy mounting so he could aim the weapon at the bridge. He looked through the scope and saw boys scattered around the quarterdeck. They all seemed to be suffering from some kind of affliction, expect one who was wearing a gas mask and crouching below the window, with a loaded RPG in his hands.

When Johnny reached the bridge, he found the suicide crew had all been incapacitated, either by laughing gas or blindness, and presented no challenge to him whatsoever. Nadif had his hands over his gas mask, disoriented by temporary blindness from a dazzle gun. Johnny snatched the mask off his face and threw it overboard before dashing on to the bridge.

Once inside he spun the wheel port-side as far as it would go. The *Chitra* began to change its bearing, but only slightly. It was still on a collision course with the *Galbraith*. He then pulled back on the reverse thrusters. Yet, with no one in the engine room, he got no response from the vessel. A familiar-looking panel above his head told him the ship was equipped with collision-avoidance electronics. He switched it on and, from the radar screen, quickly selected the ship he wanted to avoid. Loud warning alarms then began chiming, and the panel flashed: "COLLISION UNAVOIDABLE. COLLISION UNAVOIDABLE."

Ali was crouching below the window behind him. He took his last grenade and carefully loaded his RPG. At such close range he did not expect to survive the explosion but the al-Qaeda attack would not be foiled and jihad would be served with his martyrdom. He stood up slowly and aimed his weapon through the window at the back of Johnny Oceans's head. Suddenly it became too hot to handle and he was forced to throw it to the decks below.

Undeterred, he then picked up a Kalashnikov from the quarterdeck. As he stood up he found Johnny facing him with his .38 snub-nose drawn. Before Ali could release the charging handle, the

American shot him three times in the chest and once in the head. The mujahideen then staggered backward and tumbled off the quarterdeck into the ship's wake, where he spun face-down in an eddy, surrounded by a growing pool of blood, until eventually floating away.

The gap between the *Chitra* and *Galbraith* was now barely fifty metres and closing fast. It remained to be seen if Johnny's efforts were enough to avoid collision. The tip of their bows missed, narrowly swinging past each other, but then their hulls met and metal began grinding on metal, letting out a stentorian groan, as if a giant sea monster was surfacing from beneath. Both vessels then tilted outward, as the force of impact began to push them away from each other. As the two ships drifted apart, the groaning soon stopped. The collision had been avoided, but only just. From where he stood, Johnny could hear the cheers of the crew of the *Galbraith*.

Nadif stood blinking on the front quarterdeck, struggling to recognise the figure of his dead stepfather, now very much alive and driving the ship. At first he wondered if he too had died, but reality quickly sunk in. He opened the door to the bridge, stepped up to the man and threw his arms around him.

CHAPTER TWENTY-SEVEN

"We Are the Champions" blared from the *Tristola*'s decks, echoing like rolls of thunder from the mountains surrounding Ras Asir. It was mid-afternoon, and the battle was at a stalemate. After repelling wave after wave of attack, the pirates had all but lost their will to resist, and could proffer only songs about "fighting 'til the end".

The mujahideen had also had the fight knocked out of them. Consequently, they were now sheltering behind windswept sand dunes on the beachhead, with their *keffiyeh* wrapped tightly around their heads. It was the only way to get any respite from the unrelenting cacophony of the ship's LRAD. In just a few hours they had been forced to endure more Kafir music than they'd ever heard in their entire lives.

Omar walked between them, offering encouragement to the wounded and prayers for the dead, trying to determine their next move. After many unsuccessful attempts to storm the ship, they had suffered enormous losses yet were still no nearer to their prize. He was satisfied they had brought the fight to their enemy but couldn't help thinking it had all been for nothing. And where was Rubaysh? If it was so important they crush the pirates, then why wasn't he fighting alongside them?

Omar's ambition had only ever been the creation of a caliphate to govern Somalia. Global jihad didn't mean much to him. He just wanted peace and stability in Somalia and for it to be an independent Muslim state, as it had once been. He knew al-Shabaab was defeated in all but name. Only a few hundred of them remained – more on the sands of Ras Asir than anywhere else – and fighting a drawn-out guerrilla war was not the answer. He turned to the hills for inspiration.

With sand and sun in his eyes he could scarcely recognise the surrounding landscape. Still, there was something odd about the contour of the terrain. It seemed to be shifting but it was impossible to tell with the naked eye. He picked up a pair of binoculars from a dying mujahideen, unravelled his *keffiyeh*, and panned around. To his amazement he saw people, thousands of people, gathered on the distant hilltops.

The few remaining pirates were crouched below the gunwale of the ship. The mujahideen had retreated out of their line of fire, which was just as well since they had nearly exhausted their ammunition. At the conclusion of Queen's triumphant anthem, Maxamid and Abdulmajid stood up to survey the battlefield. Dozens of bodies were scattered across it, many of them the *badaadintu badah* who had landed on the beachhead as reinforcements. Maxamid could see the faces of several of his friends among the fallen. "We will honour our dead," he said, thumping his fist against his chest.

"Many mujahideen also lost their lives," sighed Abdulmajid.

"They brought the battle to us," snapped Maxamid. "They deserved to die."

"What's that?" asked Abdulmajid, pointing beyond the beachhead. "There, lining the hilltops. My God, there must be thousands of people."

"*We'el*," cried Maxamid. "And at sea!"

Abdulmajid looked back at the Indian Ocean then whispered, "Allah!" There, arranged in a semicircle, about a kilometre off shore, were thirty, maybe forty merchant ships of various shapes and sizes, floating side by side. "What do these people want?" he asked.

A skiff was sailing towards them from the middle of flotilla.

Standing tall in the centre of the boat was a woman dressed in a long white rippling *direh*.

"Khadija?" said Maxamid. "Quick, we need to help her on board." They ran to the side and lowered a rope ladder. After a moment Khadija climbed aboard and stepped up to her brother. They smiled at each other and embraced. Abdulmajid also got a hug from her. She then glided to the opposite gunwale where she could be seen by all, resplendent in the golden sunshine.

It was truly astonishing. Everywhere she looked she saw people, along the edges of the canyons, the hilltops, the shore, the sea, keeping a safe distance from the battlefield but nevertheless bearing witness. In response to her distress call, they had come by land and sea, not as a show of force, no one came armed, but as a demonstration of people power, to express solidarity for Queen Arawello's brave quest for peace and prosperity in Somalia. These were ordinary Majeerteen, who like her had had enough of war. They began to move in closer, a few dozen brave souls to begin with, but soon everyone was swarming down the hills to the coastline.

She turned to the combatants and yelled, "You can drop your weapons now. You're surrounded and outnumbered." There followed a loud clatter of weapons as both pirates and mujahideen complied. "Your women and children are suffering from all your clannish and religious hatred," she continued. "The time has come for Somalia to be liberated, from war, poverty, and humiliation."

The crowd of onlookers began to chant, "*Arawello! Arawello!*"

"The Islamist does not concede defeat," said Rubaysh, "but merely pulls back after a lost battle, and bides his time – the end justifies the means." He was sailing south along the Indian Ocean coast of Somalia aboard an old dhow, closing in on the exact spot off the Hafun Peninsula where the treasure was located. It had not taken him long, after a helpful receptionist handed over the Kobold watch locked in the safe of the Hotel Huruuse, to figure out Johnny Oceans's riddle. Now, no one could stop him from possessing its power.

"It's something of a treasure itself," he smiled, admiring the expensive timepiece on his wrist.

"What exactly is it you're looking for?" asked the old Majeerteen sailor at the helm, looking at the clutter of antique diving gear scattered across the hull of his dhow.

"The Staff of Musa," smiled Rubaysh. He saw no harm in telling this simple fisherman his plans. It was a relief to be able to confide in someone.

"Is that what lies at these coordinates you've given me?" asked the sailor, using his Kamal to check their position. "Don't you think after all this time at the bottom of the ocean, it might have disintegrated?"

"Rubbish," laughed Rubaysh. "The staff is impervious to the ravages of time. It was carved by Adam from the tree of knowledge as he was leaving the Garden of Eden, then passed down from patriarch to patriarch until it was placed in stone. Only the prophet Musa was able to remove the staff from where it had been entombed. And as you know, he used it to save the Israelites. A dreadful waste! When Musa died, they buried his body at Maqam El-Nabi in Jericho. But his staff was taken to Jerusalem and again entombed in stone."

"How then did it wind up here, in Puntland?"

"The staff remained in the possession of the Judean kings until the First Temple was looted and destroyed by Nebuchadnezzar II. The Persian king stole a great many things from Shlomo's Temple including the Ark of the Covenant, though curiously he was never able to remove the staff. Six hundred years later, at the hands of the Roman general Titus, Jerusalem was again sacked. Thereafter Titus returned to Rome with all the remaining sacred relics from the temple, including the Menorah and the Shulchan. Yet he too had to leave the staff behind. A further seven hundred years passed before Islamists became the rightful rulers of Jerusalem. There they found Musa's staff still entombed in stone. Why? Because neither the kings of Judeah, Persia nor Rome were righteous enough in God's eyes to shift it. From then on its power remained solely in the hands of Muslims. Moreover, to protect it from the invading infidels during the

Seventh Crusade, Sultan Baybars al-Bunduqdari, the Lion of Egypt, removed it from Jerusalem and took it to the Land of Punt. Nearly a thousand years have since passed during which the power of the staff has remained dormant..."

"What do you plan to do with it?" asked the sailor. "Sell it to a museum?"

"Fool! It's not an artifact to be admired. It has no material value whatsoever. It is a simple stick to make plain Allah's purpose. Soon it will be in the hands of those Allah wishes to direct in his holy war: the right people at the right time in the right place."

"I see," said the sailor, scanning the coast with weatherbeaten eyes, looking for landmarks. He spotted something in the sky. "What's that, over there, above the cliffs on shore?"

The Yemeni looked up, shielding his eyes against the sun, then gasped in horror. It was a Reaper drone, heading straight for the dhow. Staring in disbelief at the Kobold on his wrist, he cried, "Oh no! How could I be so fucking stupid." He tried desperately to remove it, but no matter how much he struggled the watch refused to be unclasped. Then he heard the sound of a missile being fired, and knew that it was all over. Yusuf Ali al-Rubaysh's last mortal thought was of treasure and lost opportunity, but not paradise.

"*Arawello! Arawello!*" chanted the crowd carrying Khadija above their heads, as they marched up the beachhead. Maxamid, Abdulmajid and the rest of the pirates had all followed her down the rope ladder from the ship and were standing among the mujahideen. Those who'd fought against each other all day long were now side by side, a defenceless ragtag cluster of combatants, disarmed as much by weariness as the undeniable show of peaceful solidarity that surrounded them.

"Did any of the food survive?" asked Khadija, coming down from the crowd.

"I made sure of it," laughed Abdulmajid, "at least fifteen tons."

"Where haven't we delivered any?"

"Lower Shabelle," he replied.

"Shabaab-held territory," said Khadija. "We'll never get this food to those people."

"I'll take it," said Abdulmajid.

"But you will surely be killed," protested Khadija. "You said yourself, they're hunting you like an animal, wherever you go."

"So, let me go to them," said Abdulmajid, smiling. "I used to be a mujahideen myself. *Inshe Allah*, if I should succeed, it will be a great day for Somalia."

"I'll help you," said a voice from behind. Abdulmajid, Maxamid and Khadija looked up together and saw one of the mujahideen walking towards them and removing his *keffiyeh*. "My name is Omar Abu Hamza," he said. "And I also used to be a mujahideen."

EPILOGUE

The skirmish between the *badaadintu badah* and al-Shabaab ended with neither side claiming victory, though henceforth it would be known as a glorious battle by all who participated. Maxamid and his fellow pirates went back to guarding the Puntland coast, and keeping their tuna stocks up by whatever means they saw fit. They demanded the world crack down on the root causes of piracy in the Gulf of Aden, not just the pirates. There was talk of a new international maritime treaty recognising the integrity of Somali waters.

While Omar made clear his desire to defect to Somali government forces, there was still the question of his leadership role in various acts of mass murder. Amnesty was no longer automatic under the new rules of the new government. He would have to stand trial for terrorism, though it was likely the courts would be lenient, in light of his willingness to help distribute the last of the food into al-Shabaab-controlled territory.

At that moment when Abdulmajid's food caravan crossed the boundary into Lower Shabelle, an enduring flame of hope was lit for the future of this so-called failed nation state. Barely a drop in the ocean, the food was nonetheless symbolic of a rare show of unity in Somalia, which would be remembered for many years to come.

Nadif was allowed to return home, under the supervision of his stepfather. "I know I have a lot of explaining to do, Khadija," said

Johnny, as he sat down to supper with his wife and children in Bender Siyaada.

"Please, Mehemet, don't say anything," she said, putting one hand on his shoulder and the other on Nadif's. "I am just grateful to have my family back. This is God's will."

Derek returned to Kampala via Djibouti, Nairobi and Entebbe airports. Much to his surprise he found Maddy waiting for him in the arrivals lounge at Entebbe. "Don't flatter yourself, mate," she laughed, wrapping her arms around his neck. "They insisted I spend a couple of weeks on R and R before returning to my job at Kakuma. So, here I am. You can take me wherever you like, Gorilla Man…"